Korax would s░   n-
gineering first, he ░   ░w
Haines rising from ░░. ░░░░░░░ ░░ ░░░ sciences station,
Uhura from communications, and Lieutenant Leslie
from the primary engineering console, but Sulu and
Chekov still sat at their posts. "Now!" he yelled, and
the two men finally moved. Kirk waited for the young
ensign to pass him, then followed him up the steps to
the outer section of the bridge.

By the time Kirk arrived at the turbolift, the entire
bridge crew had entered before him. As he himself
stepped inside the car, he saw Sulu's eyes widen, the
lieutenant peering past him, back onto the bridge. Kirk
guessed in that moment that the Klingons had begun
to materialize behind him. He reached for the lift's activation wand, but Leslie already had his hand on it.
"Deck two," the lieutenant said. Kirk expected a disruptor bolt to blast him in two at any moment, but then
the doors squeaked closed behind him. As the turbolift started to descend, he realized that they'd actually
made it.

And then an explosion rocked the lift, knocking it
sideways. Kirk hurtled forward, raising his arms to protect not just himself, but his crewmates. His head struck
the side of the lift, and then—

Everything went dark.

Also by David R. George III

Novels

The 34th Rule (with Armin Shimerman)

Twilight (Mission: Gamma, Book One)

Serpents Among the Ruins (The Lost Era: 2311)

Olympus Descending (in *Worlds of Deep Space Nine, Volume Three*)

Provenance of Shadows (Crucible: McCoy)

The Fire and the Rose (Crucible: Spock)

Novellas

Iron and Sacrifice (in *Tales from the Captain's Table*)

STAR TREK®

CRUCIBLE: KIRK

THE STAR TO EVERY WANDERING

David R. George III

Based upon STAR TREK®
created by Gene Roddenberry

POCKET BOOKS

New York   London   Toronto   Sydney   Lost River

An *Original* Publication of POCKET BOOKS

 POCKET BOOKS, a division of Simon & Schuster, Inc.
1230 Avenue of the Americas, New York, NY 10020

This book is a work of fiction. Names, characters, places, and incidents are products of the author's imagination or are used fictitiously. Any resemblance to actual events or locales or persons, living or dead, is entirely coincidental.

This book is published by Pocket Books, a division of Simon & Schuster, Inc., under exclusive license from CBS Studios Inc.

ISBN-13: 978-0-7434-9170-9
ISBN-10: 0-7434-9170-X

This Pocket Books paperback edition March 2007

10 9 8 7 6 5 4 3 2 1

POCKET and colophon are registered trademarks of Simon & Schuster, Inc.

Cover design by John Vairo Jr., art by John Picacio

Manufactured in the United States of America

For information regarding special discounts for bulk purchases, please contact Simon & Schuster Special Sales at 1-800-456-6798 or business@simonandschuster.com.

To dear, sweet Karen,
My bright, constant star,
The light in my life,
The beat of my heart.

Love lies not beyond unapproachable frontiers,
Or else I did not write, and have loved never.
Love alters not with time's hours and days and years,
But bears out even to the edge of forever.

FOREWORD

Every Wandering Thought

So finally, after penning the outlines for the McCoy and Spock novels of the *Crucible* trilogy, I arrive at the Kirk tale. And this one event, this crucible, that I had envisioned impacting all three of the main *Star Trek* characters, had affected the good captain in a very clear and obvious way. I readily see the story that surely must flow from the events in one of *Trek*'s most popular episodes, and I know just how it will tie in with the overall themes of the other two books.

I know at once that I can't write such a novel.

Here's the thing. For good or ill, I like to defy reader expectations. I strive in my writing not only to deliver a satisfying story, but also to surprise. When it works, that can be a very good thing. But there's a risk involved there too, in that a reader who has strong expectations going into a novel might be disinclined to enjoy it if those expectations aren't met. I know this, of course, and yet I nevertheless like the challenge of attempting to deliver something new and unanticipated to readers that they will still end up appreciating.

In this case, after writing the McCoy and Spock novels of the *Crucible* trilogy—*Provenance of Shadows* and *The Fire and the Rose,* respectively—I realized that I had myself established reader expectations for the third volume. I couldn't have that. If I take readers from Point A and then to Point B, you can rest assured that I'm going to do my best to avoid following that up with a tale that brings them to Point C. Too obvious. *Way* too obvious.

So I began again. I examined Jim Kirk's life, knowing which of his characteristics and experiences I wanted to illuminate, and I searched for a different lens through which to do it. I found it in a place I hadn't expected, and I ended up putting together a tight little tale that actually surprised even me—partly for its relative brevity (I tend to write long, as many of you might have noticed), partly for its linear nature (well, *mostly* linear), and partly because of its content. I hope that means that I'll end up surprising readers too. I guess you'll find out.

Let me not to the marriage of true minds
Admit impediments. Love is not love
Which alters when it alteration finds,
Or bends with the remover to remove.
O, no, it is an ever-fixèd mark
That looks on tempests and is never shaken;
It is the star to every wand'ring barque,
Love's not Time's fool, though rosy lips and
    cheeks
Within his bending sickle's compass come;
Love alters not with his brief hours and
    weeks,
But bears it out even to the edge of doom.
    If this be error, and upon me prov'd,
    I never writ, nor no man ever lov'd.

—William Shakespeare,
Sonnet CXVI

Kirk: Spock . . . I believe . . . I'm in love with
        Edith Keeler.
Spock: Jim, Edith Keeler must die.

—"The City on the Edge
of Forever"

CRUCIBLE: KIRK

THE STAR TO EVERY WANDERING

OVERTURE

Chasms

He had all the time in the world. All the time in the *universe,* really.

The twisting, writhing ribbon of energy that had torn apart two *Whorfin*-class transports and taken three hundred sixty-eight lives, that had trapped the new *Excelsior*-class *Enterprise* and then sent a jagged tendril blasting through the starship's hull as it escaped, had deposited Captain James T. Kirk in a place where time—where reality itself—held no meaning. He could go anywhere, do anything. He could relive his past, revise it, even envision a future for himself that had never been. . . .

Edith, *he thought, as he so often did, but this time, he watched as she gazed skyward, at the constellation of Orion to which he had just pointed. After a few seconds, she turned to him. Standing together on a sidewalk in New York City, in the year 1930, they moved closer to each other. Their lips met for the first time, the touch of her flesh warm and soft and loving.*

Kirk stopped, slamming his eyes shut, knowing that

he could not do this. Although the memories had always stayed with him—had always *haunted* him—he had never allowed himself to remember for very long. Even more than a quarter of a century later—or more than three hundred years later, depending on the method of reckoning—the loss remained too great for him to bear.

And so he started again, sending himself back to the moment of his entry into this impossible, timeless place. He could go anywhere, do anything. He could relive his past, even revise it. . . .

Gary, he thought as he peered at his old friend standing in the makeshift brig at the lithium cracking station on Delta Vega. Kirk would make certain to get the ship and crew away quickly, stranding the mutated helmsman here with enough provisions to survive until Starfleet and the Federation Council could determine how best to deal with him. Kirk didn't want to do it, but he had no choice given the circumstances, and at least Gary would live.

And he started again. . . .

Sam, he thought as he looked from the sedated form of Aurelan and across the room to the motionless body lying on the floor of the office. Kirk recognized his brother, even dressed in the orange lab coveralls and with his face turned away. Surely the Enterprise *had arrived at Deneva in time, though, and Bones would be able to treat Sam, to restore him to full health.*

And started again . . .

David, he thought as he walked toward Carol and away from the towheaded young man. In the tunnels deep beneath the surface of the Regula planetoid, Kirk realized that he had all these years later come face-to-face with his grown son. Now, at last, he could have a relationship with David, and the disconnection of the years past would give way to a long future of kinship.

And again . . .

Spock, *he thought as he watched his closest friend slide down the transparent bulkhead, his body decimated by the radiation within the containment chamber. Kirk followed him down on the other side of the partition separating them. Spock had saved the* Enterprise *and its crew of trainees from being destroyed by the Genesis Wave, and now the medical staff would find a way to save Spock.*

And again, and again, and again . . .

. . . until he stood out in the crisp daylight air of the Canadian Rockies, amid the majestic snow-covered mountains, in front of his isolated and rustic vacation home. With a swing of the axe in his hands, he chopped wood for the fireplace, alive in the simplicity of the effort, in the physicality of the exertion. The day ahead, which had once been filled with ugly complications, would now be filled with joys only—he would see to that. But all of that would come later. For now, he let it all go and reveled in the fresh air and the silence surrounding him.

And then, unexpectedly, a man stood there staring at him. He wore a uniform Kirk didn't recognize, although the skewed chevron of the Starfleet emblem stood out clearly on the left side of his chest. It didn't matter. Kirk wouldn't let it matter.

"Beautiful day," he told the stranger, then swung the axe once more, splitting another piece of wood.

"Yes, it certainly is," the man said, walking slowly over. He cut a striking figure, with his bald pate and ramrod-straight posture. Kirk did not ignore the man, but he did continue chopping wood, even getting the stranger to set a log section in place for him. *"Captain,"* the man said, suggesting that he might know Kirk's identity, although it might simply have been a function of recognizing Kirk's own uniform, though he'd removed his crimson jacket. *"I'm wondering, do you realize—"*

"Hold on a minute," Kirk said, not wanting to have a conversation that caused him to realize anything. *"Do you smell something burning?"* He really did detect the hint of smoke coming from the house, but he utilized it as an effective distraction. Leaving the axe buried in the stump on which he'd been hewing wood, he descended the curved stone staircase to the open front door, then hurried through the living room to the kitchen at the back of the house. There, in the middle of the long island, he saw smoke rising from a frying pan sitting atop the heating surface. *"Looks like somebody was trying to cook some eggs,"* he called back to the stranger, not wanting to be rude. As he rounded the island and carried the pan across to the sink, he said, *"Come on in."* He turned on the faucet and washed the burning eggs down the drain, adding, *"It's all right. It's my house."*

But *it's not,* Kirk told himself, discerning something not quite right about the situation. *"At least it used to* be," he said, remembering as he brought the cleaned pan back to the cooking surface. "I sold it years ago."

The uniformed man had entered the house and now stood just a couple of meters in front of Kirk, on the other side of the island. "I'm Captain Jean-Luc Picard of the starship . . ." He hesitated, and Kirk knew the name that he would say next. ". . . Enterprise."

From out past the captain, Kirk heard the gentle tolling of chimes. "The clock," he said, moving from the kitchen and into the living room, recollecting more. He reached the wooden shelf that extended from the fireplace mantel, atop which sat an elegant, hand-crafted timepiece he remembered well. "I gave this clock to Bones."

"I'm from what you would consider the future," Picard said. "The twenty-fourth century."

A dog barked, a deep, throaty exclamation. Kirk turned to the still-open front door, to where a Great Dane now sat, peering inside. "Butler!" Kirk said, thrilled to see his old companion. He walked toward the dog, who got up and came into the house. Kirk dropped to his knees as he reached the canine, but while that action felt right, the sense of there being something wrong increased. "Butler," he said. "How can you be here?" He looked to Picard in the hope that the captain might be able to provide some answers. Of Butler, Kirk said, "He's been dead seven years."

And then, from above, came a woman's voice, instantly recognizable. "Come on, Jim, I'm starving," she said. "How long are you going to be rattling around in that kitchen?"

Kirk turned away from the dog, who then ambled off. "Antonia," Kirk said, understanding that this had all happened before. "What are you talking about?" he asked Picard. "The future? This is the past." He rose back to his feet. "This is nine years ago." He remembered it so well.

Just in front of him in the living room, on a small table, sat a wooden box, the antique piece decorated and held together with ornate metal fleurs-de-lis. Kirk stepped forward and opened it, knowing what he would find within. He pulled out a small, black velvet bag and extracted from it a golden horseshoe, a miniature red rose attached to the arch. My going-away present to Antonia, Kirk thought, recalling once more the events to come, recalling this very time. "The day I told her I was going back to Starfleet," he said, and he felt now what he had felt then: relief, shame, sadness. He had hurt Antonia, he knew, and maybe he had hurt himself too.

Slowly, he padded past Picard, around the island, and back into the kitchen. From atop the rear counter he picked up a pair of objects, speckled orange. "These are Ktarian eggs, her favorite," he said, holding them up for Picard to see. "I was preparing them to soften the blow."

"I know how real this must seem to you," Picard said. "But it's not."

Kirk didn't care. He didn't want to care. He set the horseshoe and one of the eggs down, then turned up the heat on the cooking surface.

"We are both of us caught up in some kind of temporal nexus," Picard continued.

Kirk tried hard to ignore the words and whatever they implied. After cracking the egg into the frying pan, he asked Picard to retrieve an herb for him from a kitchen cabinet. As the twenty-fourth-century captain did so, Kirk scrambled the egg with a whisk, holding the pan over the heating surface.

"How long have you been here?" Picard asked.

"I don't know," Kirk answered honestly, taking the herb and adding a dash to the pan. He remembered starting to chop the wood, but before that . . . he didn't know. Evanescent images flitted through his mind, elusive as a long-ago dream. "I was aboard the Enterprise-B in the deflector control room and—" He suddenly thought about seeing Antonia again, and he recalled the tray he had prepared . . . this morning, whenever that had actually been. He asked Picard to continue whisking the eggs, and then, as he went to retrieve the tray from the far counter, he resumed his story. "The bulkhead in front of me disappeared and then I found myself out there just now chopping wood, right before you walked up." Not entirely true, but close enough. Whatever had come between the Enterprise-B and now had emerged from within his mind and then faded away.

He thanked Picard and took the pan from him, dishing the egg out onto the plate on the tray. "Look," Picard said with some hesitation, "history records that you died saving the Enterprise-B from an energy ribbon eighty years ago."

"You say this is the twenty-fourth century?" Kirk asked.

"Uh huh."

"And I'm dead?" Kirk said.

"Not exactly," Picard told him. "As I said, this is some kind of—"

"Temporal nexus," Kirk said along with Picard. "Yes, I heard you." He'd heard, but he'd disregarded the information. He wanted to focus on this re-created day, on this last time—and maybe not the last time— with Antonia. He mentioned completing the preparation of her meal just before a toaster finished heating three pieces of bread. Kirk squeezed past Picard to get them, then set the toast on the plate.

"Captain, look, I need your help," Picard said, his voice suddenly forceful. "I want you to leave the nexus with me." Kirk tried to ignore him, picking up the tray and heading out of the kitchen and toward the stairs that led up to the second floor. Picard followed. "We have to go to a planet, Veridian Three," he insisted. "We have to stop a man called Soran from destroying a star. Millions of lives are at stake."

Millions of lives, *Kirk thought as he mounted the first steps, and then he pressed himself to let it go. Still, he stopped partway up the stairs. "You say history considers me dead," he said. "Who am I to argue with history?"*

"You're a Starfleet officer," Picard said sternly. "You have a duty."

"I don't need to be lectured by you," he snapped back, Picard's words uncomfortably close to the ones Kirk had repeated to himself all the long years of his life. "I was out saving the galaxy when your grandfa-

THE STAR TO EVERY WANDERING

*ther was in diapers." He paused for an instant, decid-
ing to change the tenor of his response. "Besides
which," he said lightly, "I think the galaxy owes me
one."*

*Picard regarded him for a moment, then turned
away. Before he did, though, Kirk took note of the expression on his face, one he had seen many times before—most often in a mirror. "Oh, yeah," he said
beneath his breath. He walked back down the steps and
over to stand beside Picard. "I was like you once," he
said. "So worried about duty and obligation I couldn't
see past my own uniform." Once, he had saved three
and a third centuries of human history, possibly Earth
itself, maybe even the Federation, and all it had cost
him had been the love of his life. "And what did it get
me?" he said. "An empty house." He had lived too
long with the pain.*

*Picard looked at him, and Kirk could see that the
future captain of the* Enterprise *actually understood.
"Not this time," Kirk told him, and he started back
over to the steps and then to ascend them. "This time,
I'm going to walk up these stairs and march into that
bedroom and tell Antonia I want to marry her." When
he reached the second floor, he balanced the tray
against the jamb, took hold of the knob, and threw the
bedroom door open wide. "This time," he said, determined, "it's going to be different."*

*Inside, Antonia looked up at him from where she
still lay in bed, her long hair spread out on the pillow
behind her head, the dark strands contrasting the
white fabric. She gave him a wide smile, and he re-*

turned it. He glanced back at the door for a moment
as he pushed it closed with his foot, then turned back
to see—

Not the master bedroom of his vacation home, but
a barn. For a moment, he felt disoriented. Horses
whickered and the dry, earthy scent of hay filled the
air. The tray now gone from his hands, Kirk peered behind him, but the doorway through which he'd just
come—through which he thought he'd just come—had
gone too. He didn't know what had happened, but as
he looked around, he recognized his location. Not only
that, he also thought he knew when he was. This time
it's going to be different, he'd said, and maybe now,
he could ensure that from the beginning. With his own
thoughts and hopes, he realized, he had chosen to
come to this place, to this time.

Kirk moved to his left, deeper into the barn. By
turns disconcerted and thrilled at this new setting, he
gazed all around. As he did, he saw that Picard had
again come after him.

"This is not your bedroom," the captain said.

"No, it's not," Kirk said. "It's better."

"Better?"

"This is my uncle's barn in Idaho," Kirk said. He
had always thought of the place in that way, even long
after his father's brother had died and passed the
property on to him. "I took this horse out for a ride
eleven years ago," he said, walking over to the already
saddled beast he had called Tom Telegraph. "On a
spring day," he said. He moved to the nearest door,
lifted its wooden latch, pushed it open, and gazed out

into the sunshine. "Like this one," he said. "If I'm right, this is the day I met Antonia." He looked back over at Picard. "This nexus of yours, very clever. I can start all over again and do things right from day one." This time, he thought, he would not be left with an empty house. Without another word, he crossed back to Tom Telegraph, mounted his saddle, and rode him outside.

He recalled where he'd met Antonia, up on the crest of a hill out past the ravine he'd so often jumped. Breaking the horse into a gallop, he headed across the open countryside in that direction. The rays of the midmorning sun warmed Kirk's face, the steady beat of Tom Telegraph's hooves accompanied by the whisper of the switchgrass through which they moved. It had been a long time—too long—since Kirk had ridden, and it felt good to be doing it again.

I know how real this must seem to you, *Picard had said,* but it's not. *And Kirk knew the truth of that. He hadn't gone back to the day he'd met Antonia, only to some remarkable simulacrum of it. But with a great sense of liberation, he also thought that might be enough for him. He remembered Christopher Pike, the man he'd succeeded to command of the* Enterprise. *A strong, vital man, Fleet Captain Pike had been horribly mutilated when during an inspection tour of an old cadet vessel, a baffle plate had ruptured. Pike had saved numerous lives, hauling one young officer after another from the delta rays inundating the affected area, but in the process had condemned himself to life in an automated wheelchair, unable to do anything but*

*move slowly about and signal "yes" and "no" in re-
sponse to questions. But then Spock had taken his old
captain back to the forbidden world of Talos IV, where
the powerful mental abilities of the small population
there had then allowed Pike to live an illusory life of
the mind, apparently happily. Why couldn't Kirk do the
same here in the nexus? Why shouldn't he?*

*Kirk directed Tom Telegraph into a moderately
wooded area. Amid trees and bushes, he pushed the
horse toward the hill, and before it, to the ravine. They
picked up speed as they approached the meters-wide
chasm. Kirk loosened the reins, leaned forward out of
the saddle, and grabbed hold of Tom Telegraph's
mane.*

*At the ravine, the horse leaped up and forward. He
crossed the gap in the earth and landed in stride. Up
ahead the hill rose to its crown—*

Something's wrong, *Kirk thought. He swung the
horse around and to a halt, peering back at the ravine.
Tom Telegraph had cleared the dangerous natural ob-
stacle with no trouble, with apparent ease, even. Kirk
hadn't been concerned for a second.*

But I should've been, *he thought.*

*Kirk spurred the horse on again, back toward the
ravine. Again he prepared for the jump, and again Tom
Telegraph soared into the air and across the open
space. They landed, and once more Kirk stopped the
horse and faced back in the direction of the chasm.*

*Behind him, he heard the approach of hoofbeats. He
waited as Picard rode up, coming to a halt a few meters to his left. Kirk looked over at him, then pointed*

toward the ravine. "I must've jumped that fifty times," he said. "Scared the hell out of me each time." And then he revealed the uncomfortable truth: "Except this time. Because it isn't real."

Kirk fell silent, the superficiality of this faux existence weighing heavily on him. In the distance, a horse whinnied, and he looked up to the hilltop for which he'd been headed. "Antonia," Picard said.

Antonia, Kirk thought as he saw her sitting tall astride her own horse. Romeo, Kirk recalled the beast's name, and then: Not Romeo. And not Antonia. "She isn't real either, is she?" he said. "Nothing here is. Nothing here matters."

Kirk walked Tom Telegraph toward Picard and his horse and started to circle around them. "You know, maybe this isn't about an empty house," he said, even as he knew that it was. But he couldn't do anything about that, could he? He had cleared out his house by choice, for the good of the many. He could not undo that. On the other hand, he could help Picard attempt to save millions of lives. "Maybe it's about that empty chair on the bridge of the Enterprise. Ever since I left Starfleet, I haven't made a difference." Kirk finished going around Picard, coming to a stop a couple of meters to his side.

He thought for a moment. He had left Starfleet for several reasons, but largely because of that empty house. If he couldn't fill it, if he couldn't change his life in the way that he wanted to change it—and his time away from the space service suggested that he couldn't—then didn't he have a responsibility, to himself as much as to others, to return to the duty and obligation of which he and Picard had spoken?

Slowly, he stepped Tom Telegraph to the side, until he stood next to Picard's horse. "Captain of the Enterprise?" Kirk asked.

"That's right," Picard said.

"Close to retirement?"

"I'm not planning on it," Picard said.

"Let me tell you something: don't," Kirk said, recollecting his own mistakes and seeing in Picard a kindred spirit. "Don't let them promote you. Don't let them transfer you. Don't let them do anything that takes you off the bridge of that ship, because while you're there, you can make a difference."

"Come back with me," Picard said. "Help me stop Soran. Make a difference again."

Kirk had already decided that he would. He could not stay here in this place, in this time, or in any place or any time that the nexus offered. He had already stayed far too long. No matter how many events he relived here, no matter how many mistakes he rectified, none of it would truly matter to his life.

He took Tom Telegraph in front of Picard's horse so that Kirk could face the captain directly. "Who am I to argue with the captain of the Enterprise," he said with a grin. "What's the name of that planet, Veridian Three?"

"Yes."

"I take it the odds are against us and the situation is grim," Kirk said, warming to the idea of taking on this challenge.

"*You could say that,*" Picard agreed.

How many times had Kirk rushed into a burning building? As many times as he had made it safely back out, save once: he had gone down to the primary deflector control center aboard the Excelsior-class *Enterprise, had apparently succeeded in saving the ship, but he hadn't returned. Now, finally, he would—and he would storm right back into another burning building. "You know, if Spock were here, he'd say that I was an irrational, illogical human being for taking on a mission like that," he said. "Sounds like fun."*

Picard smiled, then turned his horse and started back the way he'd come. Kirk peered up at the top of the hill one last time, at the imitation of Antonia, and he knew that he'd made the right choice. He went after Picard, having no idea how the captain intended to get them to Veridian Three.

As they trotted forward, though, Kirk saw a brilliant white light suddenly blossom, as though emerging from the fabric of existence around them. The gauzy blue of the sky, the green of the trees, the flaxen hue of the switchgrass, all bled and faded. The field of white grew to envelop Picard and his horse, then engulfed Kirk and Tom Telegraph as well. For a subjectively immeasurable span of time, he could see nothing, could hear nothing, could sense nothing. Even the feel of his own body vanished, as though he existed only as thought. He wanted to run but had no legs, wanted to scream but had no voice—

And then with dizzying swiftness, the force of gravity held Kirk. Light shades of brown formed before his eyes, and a hot, dry wind brushed the flesh of his face. He smelled the dust of the arid region, tasted the grit of the air. The rapid change of place unsettled him.

He took a moment to steady himself, no longer on horseback now but on foot, and then suddenly an explosion boomed not far behind him. He turned from the sandstone wall he had been facing to see a cloud of dust rising before a stone ridge twenty-five meters away. Debris showered down upon the rocky topography like rain. Kirk thought he saw motion at the base of the cloud, a quick flash of red and black, but it seemed to disappear behind an outcropping.

He stepped forward, thinking he knew the source of the movement, but then through the daylight shrieked two bright green pulses, the discharge of an energy weapon. Kirk threw himself backward as the shots pounded into the same stone ridge where the previous explosion had taken place. A huge force field blinked orange above the area as another cloud of dust went up and a huge slab of rock tumbled side-over-side to the ground.

As more rubble peppered the area, Kirk waited. The source of the blasts remained hidden from view around the rocky mountain by which he stood. Seconds passed, and then a minute. He surveyed the ragged terrain, strewn with rocks and boulders, cut with fissures and grooves. When he saw and heard nothing, he prepared to move, to try to find Picard or this Soran of whom the captain had spoken. But then a hand appeared on the edge of a crevice that ran across the landscape in front of Kirk. He stepped up to it and peered down to see Picard climbing upward. They made eye contact, and Kirk lowered himself to his knees and helped the captain up.

"I take it that was Soran firing at you," Kirk said.

"It was," Picard confirmed. "He's got that handheld weapon, but he's alone here. If we go at him from two sides, one of us should be able to stop him." As Picard gazed in the direction from which the energy fire had come, he explained that Soran had briefly experienced the nexus himself eighty years ago, aboard one of the very transports that the skeleton crew of the *Excelsior*-class *Enterprise* had endeavored to save. Prior to that, Soran had lost his entire family in an unprovoked attack by a brutal alien species, and apparently the nexus had allowed him to overcome the pain of that terrible loss, at least while he'd been within it. Having been swallowed up himself by the timeless other-space and subjected to its effects, Kirk found that eminently understandable.

According to Picard, after Soran had been beamed from the transport, and consequently from the nexus, he had then spent the ensuing decades searching for a safe means of reentering it. The energy ribbon, which made a circuit through the galaxy every thirty-nine years, functioned as a doorway into the nexus. Soran had developed a scheme to reroute the path of the ribbon so that it would intersect the surface of a world—this world, Veridian Three. In order to accomplish that, he had deployed a trilithium weapon of his own design to collapse a star, Amargosa, thereby affecting the gravity in this sector. Now, he intended to do the same thing to this system's star. After Soran had then made it back into the nexus, the shock wave resulting from the destruction of Veridian would tear apart each of its six planets, including the fourth, home to a preindustrial society numbering two hundred thirty million.

"Soran has covered these crags with a complex of platforms, bridges, and ladders," Picard said. "It appears that he'll launch his trilithium missile, then make his way to the highest platform to wait for the ribbon to sweep him up into the nexus."

"How much time have we got?" Kirk asked.

"Minutes only," Picard said.

"Then let's go."

Kirk threw his closed fist through the scaffolding, catching Soran on the side of his face. The white-haired man fell backward and off the top of the rocks, fifty meters or more above the ground. Kirk heard him grunt once, but Soran did not scream.

As quickly as he could, Kirk extricated himself from the web of metal bars that held up the platform at the apex of the rock formation. As he did, he saw Picard clambering back up from where he'd tumbled during their hand-to-hand struggle with Soran. "I thought you were going for the launcher," Kirk said to him. In fact, by returning when he had, Picard had prevented Kirk's death at the emitter end of Soran's hand-held energy weapon.

"I changed my mind," Picard said. "Captain's prerogative." Together, they started back down from the summit, heading for the trilithium missile that sat poised to take flight. As they reached that level and approached the launcher, though, Kirk heard a low whooshing sound from ahead, and he looked over to see the bronze missile fade into nothingness, obviously cloaking. More important, the launcher and its control panel also vanished.

Suddenly, Kirk heard another noise, above and to his left. He peered over and saw Soran falling down the side of the cliff face at the end of a rope, which he'd evidently grabbed hold of when he'd fallen. Now, he slid down fifteen meters, then jerked to a stop. A small object flew from his hands, clattered along the rocks, and landed atop one of the metal bridges constructed here.

"We need that control pad," Picard said, clearly concluding that Soran had used it to cloak the missile. They started for the device at once, Kirk in the lead. As he reached the bridge, though, Picard said, "Captain, look!" Kirk glanced up and immediately saw the source of Picard's concern. "Where's Soran?" Against the sheer rock face, the rope now hung empty. Either Soran had fallen or he'd found his way to safety.

It didn't matter. With time running out, they had little choice in how to proceed. Kirk turned and pointed back toward the location of the missile. Picard nodded and started for it, while Kirk hurried across the bridge toward the control pad.

Suddenly a pulse of green light flashed from below. It passed beneath the bridge, and Kirk turned to see it strike the rocks behind him, creating a momentary fireball. Before he could do anything, Soran corrected his aim and sent a pair of energy bursts slamming into the center of the bridge in front of Kirk. He felt the blasts as they rent the metal structure in two. Kirk reached for a pole at the side of the bridge, wrapping one arm around it as the surface beneath his feet fell. Both ends of the bridge remained attached to the rocks, though, depending from them at steep angles.

Expecting another blast from Soran's energy weapon at any moment, Kirk didn't wait, but began pulling himself up along the chains that hung between the poles at the sides of the bridge. As he did so, he saw Picard rushing back down from the missile platform, obviously to help him. Kirk pulled his knees in and used his feet to push himself upward from one of the poles. Above, he saw Picard positioning himself at the end of the bridge and preparing to reach down to him. Kirk took hold of the upper chain with his left hand and maneuvered himself onto his back, then reached his right hand up toward Picard.

Only centimeters separated their fingertips, but it might as well have been parsecs. Kirk strained, as did Picard, and the gap narrowed, but not enough. At the same time, he felt his hold on the chain slipping.

A terrifying instant later his hand came completely free. Kirk began sliding down the bridge. "No!" he yelled, elongating the word as he descended toward a fall that would likely kill him.

But then Picard's hand slapped down hard atop his wrist, the captain's fingers closing around it in a strong grip. Kirk reached again for one of the chains, found it, and began hauling himself up again. With Picard's help, this time he made it.

The two captains dropped onto the rocks at the end of the bridge, Picard no doubt as hot and exhausted as Kirk. The twenty-fourth-century captain peered down to the location from where Soran had fired his weapon, and then up at the sky. Kirk followed his gaze and saw a whirling, weaving band of fiery energy he remembered well from the main viewscreen on the bridge of the *Enterprise*-B. He'd also seen it up close, when it had torn through the outer bulkhead of the deflector control room. Kirk had been ascending a ladder when he'd been blown out into space amid a coruscation of brilliant light. As though through a fog, he'd seen for just a moment the massive form of the *Enterprise* above him, and beyond it, the pinpoints of the brightest stars, Sol among them.

And then he'd been with Edith on Earth in 1930. And with Gary on Delta Vega, with Sam on Deneva, with David on Regula, with Spock down in main engineering. He'd prevented Governor Kodos from giving the order to execute four thousand colonists on Tarsus IV, had avoided contracting the rapid-aging disease on Miri's planet, had reached the *S.S. Huron* before it had been attacked by Orion pirates. He'd spent time with Carol and Ruth, Areel Shaw and Janice Lester. He'd served under Captain Bannock aboard the *Republic* and under Captain Garrovick aboard the *Farragut*. He'd interacted with different people, visited a myriad of places, experienced events both old and new to him . . . dozens of times, hundreds, *thousands*.

"We're running out of time," Picard said in an odd counterpoint to the apparent wealth of time that had crashed in on Kirk. "Look," Picard said, peering back toward the splintered bridge. "The control pad. It's still on the other side."

Kirk saw it, wedged against a post support on the far half of the bridge. "I'll get it," he said, knowing that Picard would be better suited to disarming the missile with its twenty-fourth-century controls. "You go for the launcher."

"No, you'll never make that by yourself," Picard said, and then he gazed at Kirk. "We have to work together."

"We *are* working together," Kirk told him. "Trust me. Go."

Picard followed his direction without further protest, getting to his feet and heading for the missile platform. "Good luck, Captain," he said.

"Call me Jim," Kirk said as he stood and started back down the bridge. He took hold of the upper chain on the left side and made his way along the grated surface, which now hung down at nearly a forty-five-degree angle. As he moved, so too did the bridge, shaking and shimmying beneath his weight, its connections to the rocks strained. The stressed metal groaned as it shifted, and small pieces fell off and rattled to the bottom of the chasm below.

Two-thirds of the way down, the chain in his hands snapped. Kirk fell onto his side and skidded down the bridge toward where its charred, broken metal surface ended in midair. He reached for another chain and found it just in time.

Cautiously, he pulled himself up to a standing position, as close to the wrecked edge of the bridge as possible. He peered across the meters-wide gap and saw the other section moving too, appearing as though it could fall at any moment. He had no idea if it would bear up under his weight, particularly after a jump, but he had not come this far to play it safe. As he gazed at Soran's lost control pad, Kirk knew that he must risk his life to do this, for if he didn't, he would condemn the two hundred thirty million inhabitants of Veridian IV to certain death. He bent his knees in preparation, took a deep breath, and leaped.

He landed hard on the other side. He wrapped the fingers of one hand around another chain, while he sent those of his other hand through the grated surface to take hold there. That section of the bridge shook even more, and then Kirk heard the snap and creak of metal parts. The surface dropped to an even steeper angle, and he quickly let go of the chain and slammed that hand through the grating as well.

Above him, he heard a clatter, and he looked up just in time to see Soran's control pad falling toward him. Letting go of the bridge with one hand, he managed to catch the device. He examined it for a moment, then pointed it toward the cloaked missile. Over the shriek of failing metal, he pushed a button. In the distance, he saw Soran's trilithium weapon reappear on its platform, even as Picard raced up the ladder to it.

Not wanting to give up possession of the control pad, Kirk tucked it into his waistband. Then he reached again for the chain, intending to try and pull himself up to the rocks. Above him, he heard the report of metal splitting, and he knew he didn't have long to get to safety.

That was when the bridge fell.

Kirk held on tightly as it careered down the rocks. Metal ground against stone, and then the bottom edge of the bridge struck an outcropping, which sent Kirk and the entire structure spinning into open air. He felt instant, blinding fear in a way he rarely had. He didn't open his mouth, but in his mind, he screamed.

Seconds later, he crashed to the ground beneath the twisted mass of metal.

Kirk didn't know how much time had passed or whether he'd remained conscious throughout, but he became aware of the scrabble of footsteps in the dirt. He attempted to move, but he could not sustain the effort for more than a moment. The wreckage of the bridge had pinned him on his back, but even had it not been there, Kirk doubted that he would've been able to stir. Though he felt nothing, he knew that he'd been crushed, that within him, his organs had been damaged beyond repair. He could still see and hear, and the sharp taste of iron filled his mouth, but he could do little else but wait to die.

He heard more movement in the dirt, and then seemingly in the metal ruins about him. A bar shifted then, and a chain, rattling away from him. Then, filling that space, Picard leaned in and peered at him.

Kirk blinked, once, twice, trying to make sure of what he saw. "Did we do it?" he asked, the whisper of his own voice barely audible even to him. "Did . . . we make a difference?"

"Oh, yes. We made a difference," Picard told him earnestly. "Thank you."

"Least I could do," Kirk managed to say, "for the captain of the *Enterprise*." He looked away from Picard and into the past, to his successes, to his failures, and he found that it pleased him a great deal that his death would be in the service of saving others—beings he hadn't met and who would never know of his sacrifice. "It was . . . fun," he said, feeling the sides of his mouth curling upward in a faint smile.

He gazed back at Picard, and then past him. In the patch of sky visible over his right shoulder, Kirk saw heading rapidly toward them the winding, thrashing energy ribbon—but not *just* the energy ribbon. All about it, the sky fractured soundlessly, space-time ripping apart in mute devastation. "Oh, my," Kirk said as the black wave of destruction cleaving to the ribbon expanded in all directions, up toward space and down to encompass the planet's surface. In the blink of an eye, the earth and the air shattered in the distance, annihilated in some fundamental, irrevocable way.

At last the sound came, a rumble sonorous and dark, like the voice of death itself. Picard spun toward it as the ground beneath them began to quake. Like a tsunami, the ribbon and the dark maelstrom reached far above them, a vast imposing threat from which there clearly could be no escape.

The rumble increased to a roar, the ground shaking intensely. And then all of it descended upon them. The structure of existence in that moment, in that space, disintegrated. Kirk saw a coruscation of brilliant light and then—

Reality ceased to exist.

I

Many Things I Thought of Then

Dully at the leaden sky
Staring, and with idle eye
Measuring the listless plain,
I began to think again.
Many things I thought of then,
Battle, and the loves of men,
Cities entered, oceans crossed,
Knowledge gained and virtue lost,
Cureless folly done and said,
And the lovely way that led
To the slimepit and the mire
And the everlasting fire.
And against a smolder dun
And a dawn without a sun
Did the nearing bastion loom,
And across the gate of gloom
Still one saw the sentry go,
Trim and burning, to and fro,
One for women to admire
In his finery of fire.
Something, as I watched him pace,
Minded me of time and place,
Soldiers of another corps
And a sentry known before.

—A. E. Housman,
"Hell Gate"

ONE

Kirk stood beneath a hazy sky, feeling hazy himself. Around him rose trees and brush. A light breeze blew, causing the switchgrass to sway against the legs of his black uniform pants. The strong scent of Solomon's plumes wafted through the air, though in his mouth, he still tasted the tang of metal.

Metal? Still?

He reached his left hand to his lips, and his fingertips came away stained with blood. Kirk peered down at himself and saw dark patches on his crimson vest, and streaks of red on his long-sleeved white shirt and on his right hand. The material of his uniform had been covered with dirt and torn in numerous places. He struggled to recall what had happened—and then did.

Soran. Veridian Three.

Kirk remembered falling, remembered gazing out from beneath the misshapen remains of the bridge that had crushed him and knowing that he had only seconds to live. He'd seen the flaming ribbon of energy, racing toward him and bringing the obliteration of space and time with it. The ribbon and the ruin had extended down to the planet, had engulfed him and Picard—

Picard!

Kirk looked left and right, then turned in a circle, searching for any sign of the Enterprise *captain. He didn't see him, though, nor did he see the rocky desert locale where they'd fought Soran. Instead, he found himself once more among the rolling, wooded hills of Idaho, in the area where he and Picard had last spoken prior to their mission on Veridian Three.*

Except that they hadn't really been in Idaho, but in some type of temporal nexus that had allowed Kirk to imagine himself there. Picard had told him that, but Kirk had really known the truth of it even before then. He'd ridden Tom Telegraph out here from his uncle's barn sensing that it had been the day he'd met Antonia, but also knowing that it could only be an imitation of that time.

Movement caught Kirk's eye. He looked across the ravine to the hilltop, to where Antonia sat on horseback. Beneath the filmy sky, another horse and rider ascended the slope, approaching her. Only when they arrived at the summit of the hill and neared Antonia did Kirk recognize the second rider: himself, dressed not in the clothes he had worn on that long-ago day, but in the black slacks, white pullover shirt, and crimson vest of his Starfleet uniform—the same uniform he wore right now, though neither ripped nor coated with the soil of Veridian Three.

What's happening? *Kirk thought, and with an absurdity he realized a moment later, he actually patted the front of his own body in a visceral attempt to verify his own physical existence. He reasoned that he must be witnessing some sort of reproduced scene, since clearly he could not exist both here and there— or could he? Could his presence here, in this spot, simply be a later version of himself than the one right now appearing to meet Antonia for the first time? Could he be standing here minutes after he and Picard had stopped Soran sometime in the 2370s, viewing a period in his life that had taken place in 2282?*

He didn't know. That hadn't seemed to be how the nexus had functioned before. In his previous spell within the mysterious region, he hadn't been a witness to events, but a participant in them. He remembered preparing breakfast for Antonia on that day when he had been about to break the news to her of his intention to return to Starfleet, and then having his change of heart and telling Picard about it. He remembered stranding Gary Mitchell on Delta Vega but not being forced to kill him; finding a different way of dealing with Apollo on Pollux IV that did not require the self-styled god to spread himself thinner and thinner upon the wind, until only the wind remained; sharing a birthday meal with his son as David turned forty; and living or reliving so many other events of his life, some old, some new, many modified in ways clearly born of his own desires. But this . . .

He began walking forward, in the direction of the ravine, and beyond it, toward the hill where some version or replica of himself even now had that initial conversation with Antonia. As he moved through the switchgrass, he realized that it had been from this pre-cise location that he and Picard had departed the

nexus to reach Veridian Three. What did it mean, if
anything, that he had returned to this place when he'd
been swept back into the strange temporal confluence?
Had he even really left the nexus?

Kirk stopped, unsure how he should proceed. He
had intended to approach Antonia and the other Kirk,
but now he didn't know if he should. He looked to his
left, then moved that way, until he stood concealed be-
hind the foliage of a low-hanging tree branch. For
now, he decided, he would simply observe, in the hope
of gaining more information before choosing a course
of action.

As he peered through the leaves of the tree to the
top of the hill, Kirk could not help remembering the
original version of this day in his own life.

After waking up and eating a light breakfast, Jim
Kirk knocked around the one-story farmhouse for a
few minutes. Clad in blue jeans and a gray short-
sleeved shirt, he paced aimlessly through the few small
rooms: from his bedroom on the right side of the
house, past the refresher, down the short hall to the
kitchen, out into the living room, and into the second
bedroom, which he'd more or less set up as an office,
though he rarely spent any time there. With his years
of starship service—and consequently the requirements for written and recorded reports to Starfleet—at
an end, he found little need for a desk or any sort of
a sit-down workspace. He'd had a com/comm unit—a
computer and communications station—installed when
he'd moved in, but he almost never used it. During his

first few months here, Spock and McCoy and others had contacted him a number of times, but he supposed that he must've made it abundantly clear that he intended to disconnect from his former life and keep to himself in the Idaho wilderness. At this point, after residing here for nearly two years, days would pass between when he checked for messages, and only infrequently did he find one waiting for him.

Now, standing before the self-contained terminal, Kirk leaned forward and touched a control surface. It responded with a buzz, and the declaration 0 MESSAGES appeared on the display. Kirk felt a mixture of relief and disappointment.

If you want to talk with Spock or Bones, he told himself, *you can just go ahead and contact them.* He could, of course, but what would he say to them? That he'd made a mistake in leaving Starfleet? He knew that most of his friends and colleagues had believed that very thing when he'd stepped down, and they probably still believed it now. But while there might have been some truth to that view, he also knew that it would have been a much greater mistake for him to have stayed.

Kirk didn't want to discuss any of that, though, and what else could he tell his friends about his current life? Each day, he tended the horses, then often rode or hiked across the Idaho hills, even during the cold and sometimes snowy winter months. He occasionally went into Lost River for supplies, or farther afield, to Blackfoot or Pocatello or Idaho Falls. Twice, he'd visited the lava flows and cinder cones of Craters of the

Moon Monument and Preserve. Last summer, he'd tried his hand at cultivating his own fruits and vegetables, but had discovered that he possessed little interest in the activity, not to mention something less than a green thumb. Now as then, he thought that some Orion joke must've hidden in that last observation, but it still eluded him.

Leaving the office, Kirk walked back out into the living room. A sofa and a pair of easy chairs, all old and timeworn, formed a cozy sitting area about the hearth. The mantel and the two end tables on either side of the sofa remained bare, though, and no personal photographs or artwork adorned the walls—not just in this room, but throughout the house. Since he'd come here, Kirk had done little to make this place his own. He'd brought with him several crates of books and personal, naval, and antique artifacts that he'd collected through the years, but he had for the most part left those items packed up and stored down in the cellar. Every so often he would descend the old wooden stairs and rummage through one of the crates to find one volume or another to read—and usually to *re*read. At the moment, a black, leather-bound edition of *Great Expectations* lay on the sofa, a gold ribbon halfway through marking his place in it, but the book hardly qualified as decoration.

Kirk padded across the living room to the front door and opened it, knowing that he needed to take care of the horses. The spring had been exceedingly mild so far, and the dull sky—more gray-blue than blue—promised another cool day. Kirk grabbed his light-blue jacket from where it hung beside the door and pulled it on. As he stepped outside, he hoped that the sky would clear and that by the afternoon the mercury would climb.

Great expectations, he thought, but the phrase resonated less with respect to the weather than to his own life. On his way to the barn, he considered the classic novel, which he had already read several times before, and he suddenly faced a moment of self-revelation. *Have I become Miss Havisham?* he asked himself. Jilted at the altar, her heart broken, the Dickens character had subsequently locked herself away, spending the rest of her life in her manse, Satis House, which she had then allowed to decay around her.

And me? he thought. *Have I locked myself away?* Kirk had not been abandoned on the day of his wedding, but fifteen years ago he had watched as Edith Keeler had been killed. The death of the woman he'd believed his one true love had affected him deeply, and though he hadn't physically sequestered himself away as Miss Havisham had—at least not then— hadn't he isolated himself in other ways? After his loss of Edith, he had become involved with other women, and for a couple of them—Miramanee, Lori Ciana—he had developed strong feelings. But he had lost his memory prior to his romance with Miramanee, and in the end, he'd found that his relationship with Lori had been something less than healthy, something less than real. Yes, after Edith, he had become enamored of other women, perhaps even fallen in love with one or two, but in truth, he had kept the fullness of his heart locked away from all of them.

And now, he thought, *like Miss Havisham with Satis House, I'm letting my uncle's old farm crumble around me.* He knew he exaggerated that last point, even as he pulled at the barn's plank door and it creaked open in apparent support of the assertion. But while he hadn't let this place fall completely into disrepair, neither had he truly lived here. He had *survived,* but not *lived.*

I need to change that, he thought. He had no desire to go back to Starfleet, but he wanted to regain his equilibrium, to return to being the entire man with whom Edith had fallen in love—and then he wanted to move past that. With a sense of determination, he resolved that when he returned to the house later in the day, he would bring some of his crates up from the cellar and dress the house with his belongings. He would also sit down at the com/comm station and contact Bones and Spock.

Feeling more positive than he had in quite some time, Kirk hauled bales of hay from within the ragged old barn and out to the corral, where he broke them down. Then, after cleaning and refilling the watering troughs there, he went back into the barn and checked the two horses he kept—Tom Telegraph and Fellow Jacob—for signs of illness or injury. After verifying their apparent health, he cleaned their hooves, then led them outside. While the horses ate and watered in the corral, Kirk mucked out their stalls.

Later, he walked Fellow Jacob around the grounds for a while, then let him out to pasture. He then saddled up Tom Telegraph and rode him out into the hills.

There, he broke the horse into a gallop. The chill of the dawn had burned off now, the temperature rising nicely, and the rays of the midmorning sun warmed Kirk's face. Tom Telegraph's hooves beat rhythmically along the ground, accompanied by the whisper of the switchgrass through which they moved. As always, it felt good to ride.

Tom Telegraph moved well and seemed strong today, and Kirk decided to take him over to the ravine. He directed the horse into a moderately wooded area, and amid the trees and bushes, they picked up speed as they neared the meters-wide chasm. Kirk loosened the reins, leaned forward out of the saddle, and grabbed hold of Tom Telegraph's mane.

At the ravine, the horse leaped up and forward. As it always did, Kirk's heart beat faster in his chest as they crossed the wide gap in the earth. No matter how many times he had made this leap, it still scared the hell out of him whenever he did so again. A break in stride, a bad approach, a short landing, all could have spelled trouble for Kirk and the horse. But Tom Telegraph landed in stride and continued on up the rise on the other side. Kirk glanced back over his shoulder at the ravine, a last look at an old foe once more vanquished—

"That was foolish," declared a voice.

Kirk peered forward again as Tom Telegraph reached the crest of the hill. There, in a saddle atop her own horse, sat a woman Kirk had never before seen. Tall and attractive, she had deep brown eyes, a Roman nose, and a wide mouth, all framed by full, dark hair that fell in waves past her shoulders. She appeared perhaps ten or fifteen years younger than Kirk, but the lines around her mouth suggested that the two of them might actually be about the same age.

As he brought Tom Telegraph to a halt in front of the woman, Kirk said, "Pardon me?"

"I said, 'That was foolish,'" the woman repeated.

"Oh, I heard you," Kirk said with a slight grin, naturally flirting with her. "It just seemed like a curious way to say hello."

"Maybe that's because I wasn't actually trying to say hello," the woman told him. She offered no expression on her face, and Kirk couldn't gauge the seriousness or lightness of her disposition.

"I see," he said. "You just wanted to administer a scolding."

"No, not a scolding," the woman said. "More a judgment about your poor horsemanship. I suppose I was just trying to protect a life."

"Thanks," Kirk said, his grin widening as he contemplated the number of times his life had been in far greater jeopardy than when he'd taken Tom Telegraph over the ravine. "But I don't think my life really needed protecting."

"Maybe, maybe not," the woman said with a shrug. "But I wasn't talking about *your* life. I was talking about the horse's."

"Of course," Kirk said, feeling the smile fade from his face. At first, he'd thought the woman difficult to read, but now her attitude seemed both clear enough and harsh enough.

"Look, I'm not trying to start an argument here," she said after a moment, her tone at least somewhat conciliatory. "It's just that I watched you ride at full gallop and jump that gulch. You must've seen it, and yet you didn't bother to pull up and examine it in order to make sure that your horse could make it safely across."

"We've made this jump before," Kirk said, reaching forward and patting Tom Telegraph on the side of the neck.

"Not today, you haven't," the woman persisted. "I've been around here for a while, so I know this is your first time out this morning. Which means that even if you have made this jump before, you didn't know if the conditions had changed, if maybe the gulch had widened, its banks eroded by the weather. Maybe you made the jump two weeks ago, but this week, it's half a meter wider. Your horse could've fallen and been very badly injured or even killed."

Kirk nodded as she spoke. "Actually, I was out here two days ago," he said when she had finished. "We haven't had any rain since then, and no earthquakes or tornadoes or other serious weather events. And before I jumped, I took note of the plank." He pointed back down toward the ravine, and the woman peered in that direction. "I actually placed that there myself as an obvious visual measurement of the ravine's width. When I saw it there, I knew that the gap hadn't grown."

The woman looked back over at him. A bit sheepishly, she said, "I suppose that's logical."

Kirk burst into laughter, surprising himself with the

force of his amusement. The woman tilted her head to one side and looked at him with obvious curiosity.

"I'm not entirely sure why you find that funny," she said.

"It's a long story," Kirk said. *Really long,* he thought, since Spock had served as his first officer for more than a dozen years. "For what it's worth, though, I do appreciate your concern."

"Remember," the woman said, "my concern was for your horse."

"That's why I appreciate it," Kirk said. "This is Tom Telegraph." He brushed his fingers along the horse's mane.

"Interesting name," the woman observed.

"It has an old history," Kirk said.

"Well, this is Romeo," she said, gesturing to her own steed. "Also an old history."

Kirk nodded in understanding. *"The Most Excellent and Lamentable Tragedy of Romeo and Juliet,"* he said, naming Shakespeare's play. Then, quoting when Romeo first laid eyes on Juliet, he added, "'The measure done, I'll watch her place of stand,/And, touching hers, make blessèd my rude hand.'" He leaned forward in his saddle and offered his own hand to the woman. "I'm Jim—" He hesitated, not wanting to reveal his renowned identity. Too often, people judged him by his reputation and not by their own experiences with him. Still, he had already started to introduce himself, and he would not lie. "Kirk," he finished.

The woman reached over and shook his hand. "I'm Antonia . . . long pause . . . Salvatori," she said.

"Sarcasm?" he said. "So early in our relationship?" He also noted with satisfaction that Ms. Salvatori didn't seem to know who he was.

"Consider it a step up from scolding," she said.

"I'll do that," Kirk said, realizing that he felt an attraction to this woman. "I take it that you live around here."

"All right."

Kirk blinked. "Uh, that was a question," he said.

"Oh," Salvatori said. "Well, then, yes I live around here."

"What do you do?" Kirk asked.

"I live around here," Salvatori said with what seemed like willful obtuseness.

"This conversation isn't going well, is it?" Kirk said. "Why do I get the feeling I'd have more success chatting with your horse?"

Salvatori shrugged again, this time with just one shoulder. "It's your choice," she said. While her expression did not change, Kirk thought he detected a hint of mischief in her eyes.

"For now, I'll stick with you," he said. "So do you live a life of complete leisure, or do you provide some benefit to society other than with your beauty?"

"Flattery will get you nowhere," Salvatori told him. "But I'm a hippiater." When he furrowed his brow at the word, she said, "It's an old term for a horse doctor. I'm a veterinarian, but I specialize in our four-legged friends here." She stroked the side of Romeo's neck.

"No wonder you were worried about that jump,"

Kirk said, motioning back toward the ravine. "You didn't want another patient."

Salvatori peered down the hill, her features tensing. "I hate to think what a fall into that gulch would've done to Tom Telegraph."

"Not to mention to me," Kirk teased.

"That jump was your choice, not the horse's," Salvatori said, seemingly serious again. She regarded Kirk for a long moment before working the reins and pulling Romeo around to her right, heading him away from the ravine. "Well, safe riding, Mister Kirk," she said.

"Wait," Kirk called, struck by the impulse that, beyond the attraction he felt for this woman, he actually wanted to get to know her. "You didn't even tell me what town you live in." Although this section of Idaho remained only moderately populated, a number of towns and small cities spread across the hills and plains within riding distance.

Salvatori peered back over her shoulder at Kirk. "No," she said, at last offering him a smile. "I didn't." Then she took Romeo into a gallop and raced away.

For just a moment, Kirk considered riding after her. Her smile had given him the impression that, after he'd effectively proclaimed his interest in her, she had sped away as something of a challenge to him. He liked that. He liked challenges, but he also liked bending them to his own terms. If Dr. Salvatori did indeed practice veterinary medicine in the area, he should have no trouble locating her.

Kirk turned Tom Telegraph back the way he and the

horse had come. It had been an interesting morning, and he found himself for the first time in a long time open to new possibilities—and not only *open* to new possibilities, but *anxious* for them.

Halfway down the hill, Kirk urged Tom Telegraph into a gallop. Once more, they successfully leaped the ravine. This time, Kirk's heart beat faster not simply from fear, but from the memory of Antonia's smile.

TWO

Kirk observed from the cover of the foliage as his other self descended the hill and jumped the ravine again atop Tom Telegraph. The horse and rider passed his location without taking any apparent notice of him—if he even could be noticed. Kirk still lacked an understanding of how the nexus functioned.

He moved to watch his alter ego gallop away, presumably back to the farmhouse, but as Kirk turned, his surroundings changed. Once more, he felt disoriented. As had been the case when he'd looked around from the door of his vacation home and suddenly found himself in his uncle's barn, he experienced no transporter effect or anything that suggested a loss of consciousness, he spied no flashes of light or any morphing of objects. He simply no longer stood outside in the Idaho daylight. Instead, a white marble column rose before him, all the way up to an ornate ceiling. Reflexively, he looked back to where the ravine had been, but now he saw only a three-walled recess. A long, narrow table there contained a collection of busts carved from some dark green stone. Above the table hung a colorful tapestry depicting what appeared to be a chariot race, and to either side, in the corners of the space, statues perched atop pedestals. The column behind

which Kirk stood paired with another to form an en-
trance to the recess.

The setting seemed familiar, though he could not
quite place it. He peered cautiously out from behind
the column to the rest of the room. At its center, five
chairs encircled a small table, its surface covered with
dishes of fruit and meat, golden goblets, and a gold-
accented glass vessel containing a dark red liquid. The
skins of animals spread across the floor, and artwork
and plush red drapes provided additional ornamenta-
tion. A brace of columns had been erected at the cen-
ter of each of the room's other three walls; those to
the left and right bordered double doors, while those
on the far side led into a sleeping alcove.

But while Kirk's location had changed, the presence
of the other Kirk had not. He no longer rode Tom Tele-
graph, but instead sat on the bed in the alcove, still
wearing his jacketless Starfleet uniform. Kirk decided
to step out from behind the column and attempt to
speak with his alternate self in an effort to determine
the full nature of his—of their—circumstances. Before
he could, though, he saw another person across the
room. A woman with long blonde hair emerged from
the alcove, wearing a gleaming gold outfit that cov-
ered only select portions of her anatomy.

Drusilla, Kirk recalled. She had been a slave on the
fourth world of planetary system 892, where an in-
dustrialized version of the Roman Empire existed in a
stunning instance of Hodgkins's Law of Parallel Planet
Development. Kirk and the Enterprise crew had
tracked the debris of the long-missing survey vessel

Beagle *back to that world. There, Kirk had led Spock and McCoy on a landing party to the surface, where they had discovered that the ship's captain, R. M. Merrick, had transported down his entire crew of forty-seven, where many of them had died in forced gladiatorial combat. In further violation of the Prime Directive, Merrick had also become a significant part of the planet's pre-warp society, taking the position of first citizen.*

While the other Kirk lay back on the bed, Drusilla crossed the room to one set of doors and exited the room. The moment she had gone, the other Kirk bolted up and began searching his surroundings. Kirk remembered that once Drusilla had left, he'd hunted through the room for anything that might be of use to him. He, Spock, and McCoy had been taken captive by the Romans and sentenced to die by their leader.

As Kirk watched, though, he noticed that the alternate Kirk appeared very focused in his search, as though he sought not simply anything that could help him, but something specific. After a short time, he seemed to find what he'd been looking for: a writing implement and a paper tablet. This had not happened during Kirk's actual visit to planet 892-IV.

The other Kirk began writing at once, and Kirk speculated that he outlined directions for Merrick. Looking back on the entire incident now, Kirk recalled that the traitorous captain had stolen back from the Romans one of the Enterprise *landing party's commu-*nicators, indicating his change of heart about what he had done. Later, in fact, he had helped Kirk, Spock, *and McCoy escape the despotic civilization, though at the cost of his own life. Kirk regretted that he hadn't been able to bring Merrick back to the Federation to stand trial, not just for violating the Prime Directive, but also for his betrayal of the* Beagle *crew and his hand in their deaths. If Kirk could relive those events, knowing how they had ultimately transpired, he thought he would do what he supposed the other Kirk did now, namely detail a plan for Merrick that would see him leave this world with the landing party.*

When the other Kirk finished writing, he tore a small piece of paper from the tablet. After replacing the writing implement and tablet back where he'd found them, he folded the note into a small square, then tucked it into the fleshy crook at the base of his thumb. He then returned to the sleeping alcove and lay back on the bed.

Minutes passed, and Kirk tried to recollect how long he had pretended to sleep. While he hadn't written a note to Merrick, he had searched the room and looked for a means of escape. He remembered now that he had eventually heard somebody approaching, which had driven him back into bed, where he had feigned slumber.

Now, Kirk heard a set of doors open, and he carefully peered from behind the column to see two armed guards step into the room and take up positions there. A moment later, the Roman leader entered. Heavyset and garbed in a glittery green tunic, Proconsul Claudius Marcus moved and acted with the confidence of an egocentric dictator. A coat of arms emblazoned *the front of his left shoulder. Once in the room, he gazed around, then crossed to the sleeping alcove, where he lifted a boot onto the bench at the foot of the bed. "Captain," he said.*

The other Kirk started and looked up, as though just roused from sleep. He quickly sat up on the edge of the bed, but he said nothing.

"I'm sorry I was detained," said Claudius Marcus. "Shall we have our little talk now?" He swung his foot to the floor and walked toward the table at the center of the room, and the other Kirk followed. "So far on this planet we've kept you rather busy. I don't wonder you slept through the afternoon." Kirk recalled the proconsul's curious attempt at discretion, considering that the Roman leader had known that Kirk could've dozed for only a few minutes, after Drusilla had left.

Claudius Marcus sat down and poured red wine into a goblet. He offered it to the other Kirk, who shook his head. "Uh, by the way, one of the communicators we took from you is missing," the proconsul said. "Was it my pretty Drusilla by any chance?" As he spoke, First Citizen Merikus—the erstwhile Captain Merrick—entered and approached the table. "See if he has it," the proconsul ordered. While the slight-of-stature Merrick patted the other Kirk down, performing a cursory search for the device, Claudius Marcus added about Drusilla, "Not that I would have punished her." With a laugh, he said, "I would blame you. You're a Roman, Kirk, or you should've been." He then asked Merrick, "It's not on his person?"

"No, Proconsul," Merrick said.

With an expansive wave of his arms, Claudius Marcus said to the other Kirk, "I am sorry I was detained. I trust there was nothing further you required."

Behind the column, Kirk remembered how Drusilla had wanted to pass the time with him, claiming that she had been told to act as his slave. The sensitivity the proconsul tried to project seemed overdone and even juvenile.

As Kirk had all those years ago, the other Kirk said, "Nothing, except perhaps an explanation."

"Because you're a man, I owe you that," the proconsul said. "You must die shortly, and because you are a man." He peered up at the first citizen and said, "Would you leave us, Merrick? The thoughts of one man to another cannot possibly interest you." Although Claudius Marcus had evidently received help from Merrick during the former Federation captain's six years on the planet, the proconsul's words clearly indicated his contempt for him.

As Merrick turned to go, the other Kirk shifted his weight and seemed to accidentally brush against him. The Enterprise *captain appeared to reach up automatically to steady himself, his hands briefly touching the first citizen. Though from his vantage behind the column, Kirk could not see it, he had no doubt that his alter ego had just passed his note to Merrick.*

As the old Beagle *captain departed, the other Kirk looked after him. "Because you are a man, I gave you some last hours as a man," Claudius Marcus said, obviously explaining the rationale for Drusilla's presence during Kirk's detention here.*

"I appreciate that," the other Kirk said.

"Unfortunately, we must demonstrate defiance is intolerable," the proconsul said.

"Of course," the other Kirk said.

"But I've learned to respect you," Claudius Marcus told him. "I promise you, you will die easily, quickly."

"I thank you," the other Kirk said. "And my friends?" Kirk recalled that Spock and McCoy had been taken back to a jail cell after surviving a turn in the gladiatorial arena.

"When their time comes, the same, of course," the proconsul said. He held his goblet up to the other Kirk as though offering him a toast, then drank from it. "Guards!" he called. The two uniformed, helmeted men marched from the door to stand on either side of the other Kirk. They both carried automatic projectile weapons. Claudius Marcus rose from his chair. "Take him to the arena," he said. "Oh, we've preempted fifteen minutes on the early show for you, in full color. We guarantee you a splendid audience."

"Before I go," the other Kirk said, "may I have a few moments to myself, to make peace with my god?" Still observing from behind the column, Kirk recognized the ploy, which likely confirmed the nature of what his counterpart had written to Merrick.

"Your god, Kirk?" said the proconsul. "I must confess to surprise. The gods are simply tools we use to manipulate the masses. Haven't your people advanced beyond the need for religion?"

"So much for respecting me as a man," the other Kirk said. The words and tone had been perfectly de-

livered, Kirk thought, *to exact the action needed of the proconsul.*

"Very well," Claudius Marcus said. "I grant you your time." He gestured toward the sleeping alcove, and the other Kirk started toward it. "You have a few moments only," the proconsul said, "so speak to your god quickly."

The other Kirk acknowledged Claudius Marcus with a nod before stepping over beside the bed. There, he kneeled down and folded his hands together, bowing his head as though in prayer. The proconsul and his two guards waited, speaking among themselves as seconds passed, then a minute, then two. Kirk thought that perhaps the other Kirk's plan had failed, but then he heard the telltale whine of the transporter beam. Clearly Merrick had followed the instructions he'd been passed, which doubtless had told him to use the purloined communicator to contact the Enterprise and provide Scotty with the relative locations of Kirk, Spock, and McCoy in order to beam them all up to the ship.

Kirk watched as his alter ego's image sparkled gold with the transporter effect. "Guards!" Claudius Marcus yelled, pointing, but too late. As the armed men moved into position and raised their weapons, the outline of the other Kirk had already begun to fade.

And then with it, so too did the entire scene, a different setting gradually starting to appear in its place. It felt to Kirk as though his surroundings had begun to dissolve about him and then re-form. In an instant, he recalled the first time he had ever beamed anywhere, and how, as a child, he'd actually believed that the transporter had functioned by breaking down the universe, moving it, then reconstituting it about him. With reminiscence came memories of his parents, still a force in his life despite having died so many years ago.

As the next reproduced locale within the nexus solidified into existence, Kirk expected to see the family farm where he'd grown up in Iowa, or maybe the scene of his grandfather's funeral, the event that had necessitated his first trip by transporter. But Kirk clearly no longer controlled what he experienced within the nexus, if he even ever had. Rather, as he shook his head in an attempt to clear it, he saw lush vegetation forming all around him. Through it, at the edge of a clearing, he saw the other Kirk—still in his crimson uniform, still without his jacket—along with Spock, Pavel Chekov, Yeoman Landon, and security guards Marple and Kaplan. All those members of the landing party wore the uniforms Starfleet had issued them during Kirk's original command of the *Enterprise*, Spock in the blue of the sciences division, Chekov in the gold of command, and the others in the red of engineering and services.

In the clearing, the hum of the transporter grew once more, and then McCoy materialized, along with two more security officers, Hendorf and Mallory. As they approached the first group, Kirk looked away. *What is this?* he thought. *More mistakes that I've made in my life?* He recollected very well this mission to Gamma Trianguli VI, when all four of the security

guards had been killed, when Spock had very nearly
lost his own life when he'd been struck by a directed
bolt of lightning, and when Kirk, in order to save the
ship and crew, had been forced to deactivate the machine that had ruled and supported the native population. Before that, planet 892-IV, where although he'd
managed to escape with the lives of the members of
the landing party, he'd failed to bring Merrick back to
the Federation and to justice. And before that, in his
previous time in the nexus, the day he'd broken off his
relationship with Antonia, and before that—

How long has this been going on? he wondered.
How long have I been in the nexus trying to "fix" my
life?

As he heard the other Kirk talking with the members of his crew, he turned away and walked deeper
into the tropical landscape, out of earshot of the landing party. He did not wish to see how this re-created
sequence would allow his alternate self to undo the
mistakes he'd made in his career, in his life, because
it achieved nothing. No matter if Hendorf and Kaplan,
Mallory and Marple survived this replayed incident,
they had not survived in the real universe. Whatever
happened here, Kirk could not obviate his role in their
deaths.

And yet, when he had previously been in the nexus,
when he had himself experienced these repeated incidents from his life rather than just observing them, he
had taken solace, even happiness, in reliving them and
being able to alter the outcomes. But even so, he asked
himself now, what point had there been to that? Kirk

had hardly lived a perfect existence, but in carrying
out the many missions he had been assigned, he had
always striven to protect the lives of his crew, even
though he had not always been successful in doing so.
Despite his failures, he knew that he had accomplished
a great deal in his years. Beyond the value of the many
exploratory, first contact, and diplomatic missions he'd
led aboard the Enterprise, Kirk had helped to protect
the Federation and to foster peace throughout the
quadrant. On quite a few occasions, he had saved
lives—sometimes many lives, even whole populations.
He had lived an existence that had mattered not only
to himself, but to others.

Whole populations, Kirk thought. He recalled the
threats to Deneva and Ariannus, and those posed by
Lazarus and Gary Seven, Nomad and the doomsday
machine, the Guardian of Forever and V'Ger and the
probe that had wanted to communicate with humpback
whales. Kirk hadn't acted alone, but he had acted.

He also remembered another population and another world that had been at risk: the more than two
hundred million of Veridian IV. Kirk believed that he
had left the nexus and worked with Picard to defeat
Soran and prevent the annihilation of the Veridian star
and its planets. But then the ribbon of energy had
reappeared in the sky, bearing with it utter devastation. Had that been confined to the third world in the
system, or had it spread farther and imperiled the
fourth as well? He assumed that he'd been spared the
destruction expanding into space and raining down on
the planet because he'd been pulled back into the

nexus an instant before it had reached him. Had that destruction ended, or did it continue even now back in the "real" universe?

In the middle of the jungle on this imaginary Gamma Trianguli VI, Kirk questioned whether the term *now* actually carried any meaning here. He had seen only the past, repeated—and sometimes altered—again and again, but Picard had spoken of being from the future. Once more, Kirk wondered just how long he had been in the nexus.

"You've been here a long time," a voice said behind him.

Kirk spun around, startled, his arm rushing through the fronds of a tall plant as he did so. As he heard an explosion somewhere in the distance, he saw somebody standing before him—somebody not a member of the *Enterprise* landing party or a native of this world. "Guinan?" he said even before he realized he would speak. He didn't consciously recognize the woman he addressed, though clearly he must have known her on some level.

"We've met before," she said. She possessed a distinctive appearance: rich, chocolate skin; dark eyes; a wide nose; and prominent, rounded cheeks. Black braids emerged from beneath a violet cloth headdress that had a thick, flat brim at its crown. She wore a long, sleeveless robe, also violet, atop an auburn gown.

"Are you reading my mind?" Kirk asked. The two statements she'd made had seemed to speak directly to what he'd been thinking.

"No," Guinan said. "I'm just very . . . intuitive."

"And you know where we are?" Kirk said. "You know what's going on here?"

"You know where we are too," Guinan told him. "You've been here before."

"In the nexus," Kirk replied.

"Yes."

Kirk attempted to puzzle it all out. He glanced past Guinan and into the distance, back toward the clearing where he'd seen the Enterprise landing party, though he could see them no longer. He felt the need to move, and so he took a few paces away, pushing through the tropical greenery. "I was here before," he said. "And then I left the nexus."

"Yes," Guinan confirmed. "You left and you returned."

"Is that why there seem to be two of me here?" Kirk asked.

Guinan furrowed her brow, as though in thought. "Do you remember where you and I met?" she asked him at last.

"No," Kirk admitted.

"Right here," she said, raising her arms in an inclusive motion.

"On Gamma Trianguli Six?"

"In the nexus," Guinan said. "I was onboard the transport ship Lakul when it became trapped in the energy ribbon. That was when I was drawn into this place."

Kirk looked down for a second, reminded again of another failure. Peering back up at Guinan, he said, "We didn't rescue you," he said. "I'm sorry. We tried."

"But you did rescue me," Guinan said.

Kirk stared at her without comprehension. He felt as though he had missed some fundamental piece of information. "I don't understand," he said.

"I was one of those transported safely aboard the Enterprise," Guinan said.

"But you're still here," Kirk said, feeling as though he had stated the obvious.

"I think of myself as an echo of the person who was pulled off the Lakul and out of the nexus," she said. "I was beamed back into the universe you and I know, but the essence of who I am also remained here, duplicated in some way."

"And that's what I am?" Kirk asked. "An echo?" That didn't seem quite right to him.

"In some ways, we're all echoes, reverberations one moment of who we were in the previous moment," Guinan said. "But you are James T. Kirk. You entered the nexus when the energy ribbon penetrated the hull of the Enterprise-B, and when you left to go to Veridian Three with Captain Picard, an echo of you remained behind. When you returned to the nexus, that echo was still here."

Kirk felt his mouth open as a sense of realization washed over him. "That's who I've been watching," he said. "An echo of myself."

"That is how I see it, although you and he are both as real as the other," Guinan said. "But while he has accepted being here, has even experienced great joy from being here, you have not."

"I did," Kirk said. "When I first entered the nexus."

"Yes," Guinan agreed. "But not now. Why?"

Kirk considered that. As best he could recall, when he'd initially come into this temporal other-space, he'd immediately begun reliving and remaking the events of his life. When he'd reentered the nexus, though, he hadn't attempted to prevent himself from existing in some remembered or imagined moment; he'd simply found himself observing one of those moments rather than participating in it. He supposed that he could even now select some blissful event to experience again, remake some painful incident into something positive, or invent some wonderful new circumstance for himself, but—

"Guinan, just before I returned to the nexus, something happened to the energy ribbon," he said. "It moved at much greater speed than when I'd previously seen it, and it appeared to expand in a way that destroyed the universe all around it. I'm concerned about the population of a world that might be in its path. Millions of lives may be at risk." He paused, wanting to emphasize the importance of his next question. "Do you know what happened to the energy ribbon?"

A pall seemed to pass over Guinan's visage. "Yes, I do," she said. "You happened to it."

THREE

"There," Guinan said, pointing past Kirk. He turned to follow her gesture, and once again, everything changed. Where he had one moment been standing amid the lush growth of a jungle, he now stood on a rocky mountaintop. The still, temperate climes of Gamma Trianguli VI had given way here to a cool, blustery wind.

Kirk waited for his sense of dislocation to pass as he peered down from the high tor across a wide, wooded plain. At first, he neither saw nor heard the object of Guinan's attention, but then a growing roar reached his ears. He raised a hand to shield his eyes from the sun, and in the distance, he spied something that he could not immediately identify. A flat, circular object glided low over the land, headed in their direction. As it drew nearer, Kirk realized that he had underestimated its size, and as the noise increased in volume, he also understood that the object did not fly above the ground, but slid across it. Trees splintered in its path and vanished beneath its mass as—

Kirk felt a surge of emotion course through him as he recognized the object: the saucer section of a Starfleet vessel. "Where are we?" Kirk asked Guinan, unable to take his gaze from the disaster playing out *before him.* "What is this?" He could hear the dismay in his own voice.

"We're still in the nexus," Guinan said. "This is Veridian Three. And that's the Enterprise. Picard's Enterprise. While you and he fought Soran, the ship was attacked by rogue Klingons and suffered a warp-core breach. The Enterprise crew separated the saucer, but the explosion of the core forced them down."

Now Kirk turned to Guinan. "How do you know this?" he asked her.

"All of this exists within the nexus," Guinan said, regarding him levelly. "But I was also on the ship."

"You—?" Kirk started, but so many questions occurred to him that he allowed the single word to convey his perplexity.

"I was just one of a number of civilians aboard who worked in a capacity to support the crew and their families," Guinan explained.

"Civilians?" Kirk said, stunned. "Families?" He looked back at the saucer as it continued crashing across the planet's surface.

"Yes," Guinan said. "The ship carried the families of some of the crew."

Kirk felt a twist in the pit of his stomach as he watched the great hull grind past the mountain atop which he and Guinan stood. Bad enough for the crew to be placed in harm's way, but for civilians—families!—to be there with them . . . Kirk shook his head. He didn't know if he could've commanded effectively in such an environment, and he had no idea how Picard managed to do so.

Down just past the base of the mountain, the saucer finally came to rest, close enough that Kirk could just make out the letters and numbers of its designation: NCC-1701-D. The vast hull had to be at least four hundred meters across, greater than the entire length of any of the ships that Kirk in his day had commanded. In the vessel's wake, it had left a wide swath of destruction, a long, dark trench that stretched back as far as Kirk could see, and about which the remnants of trees had been strewn like brittle twigs.

"They managed to level off during their descent," Guinan said. "Amazingly, their casualties were light."

"That is amazing," Kirk said. He looked over at her again. "And you obviously survived."

An expression appeared on Guinan's face that Kirk could not read. He could not tell whether in that moment she felt peace or sorrow, acceptance or resignation, or something else altogether. "No," she told him. "I died shortly after the crash."

Kirk didn't think he would've felt more surprised if Guinan had reached out and pushed him from the mountaintop. Not having any notion of how to respond, he peered back down at the saucer. Dust billowed up from the edges of the disc, but he saw no smoke from fires. Still, the ship appeared inert, and even if most of its crew had endured the downing of their vessel, it seemed obvious that this Enterprise *would never journey through space again. He could not help remembering standing on the Genesis Planet with Bones and Scotty, Hikaru and Pavel, watching his own* Enterprise *plummet through the atmosphere in the last blazing throes of its existence. "Why are you showing me this?" he asked Guinan.*

"This is why," she said, and she reached up and took his arm. As he turned the way she led him, the nexus again transformed their surroundings, from outside the wrecked ship to what surely must have been its interior. Once his disorientation passed, he saw a large, circular area rimmed with inactive control stations, some of them smashed, others showing evidence of being subjected to intense heat, though if any fires had burned here, they had by now been extinguished. Fiber-optic lines, conduits, and structural beams littered the decking, and a dome at the top of the compartment had shattered, revealing clouds high up in the sky overhead. Sunlight streamed in through the opening, illuminating a small area at the center of the bridge, the rest of which remained in shadows.

From his location with Guinan in a recess beside a pair of doors in the upper, outer bulkhead, Kirk saw people moving about, all uniformed in ways reminiscent of Picard. He saw dirt and blood on the officers who moved through the light, but nobody present seemed to have suffered grievous injuries. Guinan motioned to the lower area of the bridge, just past a long, curving structure, toward where a tall, bearded, dark-haired officer spoke to a yellow-eyed, sallow-complected individual. "What have you got, Data?" the taller man said.

"I am reading nine hundred thirty-seven discrete humanoid life signs, Commander," Data said, consulting a compact device that must have been a tricorder.

"Some are faint, but most are strong. There may even be more."

"Nine hundred?" Kirk whispered to Guinan.

"The total number of people aboard ship was just above a thousand," she explained. The figure initially surprised Kirk, but then, he had noted the size of this Enterprise.

Suddenly, he detected a considerable vibration in the decking. At first, he thought that the saucer must be shifting its position on the ground, but the trembling not only continued, it intensified. A low rumble grew in the enclosed space.

"Data, what is that?" the commander asked.

"Scanning," Data said as he adjusted his tricorder. "I am detecting the energy ribbon."

"Where?" the commander asked.

"Moving now along the surface of the planet," Data said.

"It's returned here?" The commander clearly hadn't expected that information.

"Yes," Data said, and then, "No, not precisely. I am reading a massive shock wave driving it along its path."

"A shock wave from what?" the commander wanted to know, even as Kirk understood that it must be the same destructive phenomenon he had seen before being carried back into the nexus. "Did Soran's weapon launch?" Kirk knew that it hadn't.

Again, Data operated his tricorder. "Negative," he reported. "Solar energy levels indicate that the Veridian star is intact, but . . . I am reading a complete breakdown of the space-time continuum along the course of the shock wave."

"Caused by what?" the commander asked again.

"It is unclear, but it appears to be emerging from the past," Data said, raising his voice as the rumbling increased in volume. Kirk recognized the character of the sound, having heard it before. It chilled him.

"From the past?" the commander said, also speaking louder, the skepticism in his voice plain.

"The shock wave matches a theoretical concept known as a converging temporal loop," Data reported. "Two significant and identical sets of chronometric particles, connected by a conduit of some sort, essentially merge across time and space, annihilating everything between them. It seems to have been triggered within the last few minutes." Data looked up from the tricorder and over at the tall man. "Commander, the shock wave is destroying the planet."

"What can we do?" the commander asked, yelling now as the noise grew louder still.

In response, Data peered upward. Kirk lifted his gaze to the center of the overhead too, to where the dome had been smashed, and saw that it was already too late. In the scrap of sky visible there, the intense radiance of the energy ribbon appeared, and then about it, existence began to crumble. Kirk quickly looked around and saw confusion mingling with fear on the faces he could make out.

And then both darkness and light collapsed upon them. Those few touched by the bright energy of the ribbon seemed to fade away, but for one gruesome in-

stant, Kirk saw the wave of blackness tear apart the rest of the crew. He turned away, slamming his eyes closed, unable to bear it. The great din pushed in on him like a physical force, threatening to crush him, until—

It all faded.

Kirk opened his eyes. Though Guinan still stood beside him, the nexus had taken them to yet another time and place. Once more, they stood atop a mountain, one of many in a chain of spectacular snow-capped peaks. Directly below Kirk and Guinan spread a crystalline city of surpassing beauty. Slender spires reached up elegantly toward a vibrant twilit sky, while artfully crafted structures reflected the light as though delicately dancing with it. On the horizon to the left, opposite the setting sun, a string of prismatic pearls arced across the heavens. The glittering dots swirled from one color to the next, like a spinning chain of self-contained rainbows. Kirk had never seen anything quite like it.

"What is that?" he asked, transfixed, the horror of what he'd just witnessed on Veridian Three slipping from his mind with the change of scene.

"Geysers on the moon," Guinan said. "They discharge water beyond the pull of the low gravity, sending it into space. The ice freezes there and reflects the sun as it falls to the planet."

"It's beautiful," Kirk said. "Where are we?"

"This was the world of my people," Guinan said. "This was Lauresse, the city I called home."

" 'Was?' " Kirk asked.

"This place . . . most of my people . . . were destroyed by invaders," Guinan said. "I managed to escape, but . . ." She did not complete her thought, but offered a different one. "In the nexus, I spend much of my time here."

"I can see why," Kirk said as he gazed out over the city. It saddened him to hear of Guinan's loss, of the extermination of her people. It also reminded him of the awful events he'd just seen replayed on Veridian Three, as well as of the potential threat to the population of the neighboring planet. "Guinan," he said, "the converging temporal loop, caused by the two identical sets of chronometric particles—"

"That was you," she said. "In twenty-two ninety-three and twenty-three seventy-one."

"Me?" Kirk said, attempting to work out what Guinan claimed and taking into account what Data had said. "My body contained a unique set of chronometric particles both before I entered the nexus and after I left it." Back during the five-year mission, McCoy had detected a discrepancy in Kirk's M'Benga numbers, a measurement comparing the expected and actual energy of the humanoid nervous system. That had ultimately led to the identification of chronometric particles within his body. "So once I exited the nexus, two identical sets of particles existed at two different points in time and space."

"And they were connected by the nexus," Guinan said, distinguishing the "conduit" that Data had mentioned. "Your departure with Captain Picard to Veridian Three then initiated the convergence loop."

"But it didn't happen right away," Kirk noted.

"I'm sure it did," Guinan said. "But it must have taken time for the loop to close across a span of seventy-eight years and scores of light-years."

Kirk nodded his head as he tried to fathom the extent of the devastation about which he and Guinan spoke. "So every point in time and space between my location in twenty-two ninety-three on the Enterprise-B and my location in twenty-three seventy-one on Veridian Three—"

"And obviously in neighboring time and space," Guinan pointed out.

"Was completely obliterated," Kirk finished.

"Yes," Guinan said.

The idea staggered Kirk. Not only had Veridian IV and its population likely been wiped out, but the same must have been true of other worlds, not to mention starships, beginning with and including the Enterprise-B. Kirk stood in silence as he tried to come to terms with the enormity of the situation.

Then, from the city below, the graceful sound of bells began to play. The gentle ringing seemed to Kirk an appropriate accompaniment to the fragile-looking structures from which it rose. He listened for a few moments, allowing the lilting notes to calm his troubled mind. But then something else occurred to him.

"Why me?" he asked Guinan. "Why couldn't it have been Picard? He entered and exited the nexus too."

"It was you," Guinan said. "Data stated that the converging temporal loop required a significant set of identical chronometric particles."

"Right," Kirk said, not knowing how Guinan knew this about him, but comprehending the wealth of information available to her within the nexus. He recalled again his exceedingly high M'Benga numbers, and that Spock and McCoy had ultimately used that quantity to distinguish chronometric activity within his body. As far as Kirk knew, his numbers, which had grown sizably during his time in Starfleet, had been by far the highest ever recorded. Some of that had been attributable to his various travels through time, but his readings had always remained greater even than those of individuals who had time-traveled as much as he had. Bones had theorized that other unusual experiences must have contributed to his high numbers, possibly including some unexplained forms of instantaneous transport, such as when Trelane had whisked him from the Enterprise bridge or when the Providers of Triskelion had pulled him through space across more than eleven light-years; or possibly his exposure to other universes, such as when he had slipped through a place of interphase in Tholian space or when the ship had reached the "magical" realm of Megas-Tu; or possibly the transference of his mind out of his body, such as when he had permitted Sargon to switch consciousnesses with him or when Janice Lester had forced him to do so. Whatever the cause or causes, the chronometric activity within his body had been extremely high by the time he'd entered the nexus.

"Guinan," Kirk said, "the crew aboard Picard's Enterprise, were they pulled into the nexus?" He'd seen some of them vanish from the bridge when the *bright light of the energy ribbon had touched them.*

"Some of them were drawn into the nexus," Guinan said, "but most were not."

"Why?" Kirk asked. "Why not all of them?"

"It just depended on who was touched by the energy ribbon first," she said, "and who was struck by the shock wave."

Kirk nodded. The luck of the draw, *he thought. He could just as easily have been ripped apart by the converging temporal loop as pulled back into the nexus.*

But you didn't die, *he told himself. And that meant that he had a responsibility to do everything he could to find a way to undo the destruction that had been wrought on the universe. Many of the crew aboard Picard's* Enterprise *had been killed, probably many of those aboard Harriman's* Enterprise *as well, not to mention the hundreds of millions on Veridian IV and whatever other worlds had been impacted by the loop.* "Guinan," he said, "Picard left the nexus to go back to Veridian Three in the minutes before Soran launched his weapon. Where can I go?"

"Time has no meaning here," Guinan said. "You can go anywhere, any time." She paused, then asked, "But where would you go?"

Kirk looked at Guinan and asked himself the same question: Where would I go? *But then he realized that he had asked the wrong question. He needed to determine not where he could go, and not even when, but what he could do.*

Turning away from Guinan, Kirk peered out over the magnificent city below. The peal of the bells still

*drifted upward, a fragile melody that sounded almost
as though the notes had been generated from the crystal buildings themselves. Now, though, Kirk stopped
listening, stopped even seeing the great city, instead
turning all of his senses inward.*

After a few minutes, he bade Guinan good-bye.

FOUR

(2267/2276)

Kirk strode purposefully through the corridors of the Enterprise—his Enterprise. On the promontory over-looking the city of Lauresse, he had taken his leave of Guinan. He'd realized that she had come to him in order to help, and he'd told her how much he appreciated it. But as he'd begun to consider what actions he could take to reverse the devastation caused by the shock wave of the converging temporal loop, he'd discovered that he needed to do so alone. Guinan had understood, and she had reminded him that he had all of the nexus—essentially the entirety of his life, real or imagined—in which to find solitude.

When Kirk had reentered the nexus, he hadn't chosen or participated in the events in which he'd then found himself: meeting Antonia for the first time, escaping the clutches of the proconsul on planet 892-IV, transporting down with a landing party to Gamma Tri-anguli VI. Prior to that, though, before he'd left the nexus with Picard, he had lived or relived much. Standing with Guinan above her city, he had harked back to those experiences, then turned from her—

And stepped out of a turbolift and onto deck seventeen of the Enterprise.

Now, he walked among the crew of his first com-

mand, the familiar vibration of the ship telling him that it traveled at warp. Headed aft, he passed Yeoman Atkins and Ensign Nored, Crewman Moody and Lieutenant Leslie, offering each a curt nod. Nostalgia welled up within Kirk, along with the unexpected sentiment that these had been simpler, happier times in his life. He knew that hadn't been the case, though. He remembered well the weight of responsibility that came with leading a crew, as well as the terrible cost that his position had claimed from him. He had loved Edith as he had loved no other woman, either before or after. For the most part, he had found fulfillment each day that he'd been able to step onto the bridge of the Enterprise *or the* Enterprise-A *as its commanding officer, and he still felt that there had been something special about his first captaincy, but he could not deny the great scar it had placed permanently on his soul.*

Kirk reached his destination and proceeded through the pale blue doors, which glided open at his approach. He marched down a short corridor, then turned right through a pair of irregularly shaped hexagonal entryways and onto the empty observation deck. Not wanting to deal with the more intense recollections that it might bring him if he spent time in his quarters, he had opted to come here, to this place he had occasionally visited during his years aboard ship. He'd selected this time, after the crew's encounter with the Elluvex and before they reached the Pyris system, because he'd recalled having a few days of light duty. He also remembered coming here alone during that period and remaining undisturbed by any of the crew.

To his left, starting a meter or so above the deck and rising to the overhead, a pair of wide ports angled away from the bulkhead, allowing a view directly into the hangar deck. Kirk went to one of the ports and peered down. Situated on the combination turntable and lift at the center of the bay, a shuttlecraft—the Aristarchus, NCC-1701/9—*sat ready for flight should it be needed. For just a second, the sight triggered thoughts of Kirk's piloting drills back at the academy, but he quickly disregarded them. He hadn't come here to reminisce.*

Turning away from the hangar deck, Kirk looked across the narrow observation compartment at the viewports in the outer bulkhead. Through them he saw the stars, many stationary because of the Enterprise's *great distance from them, others seeming to move as the result of parallax. Even by this point in his career, Kirk had visited numerous planetary systems, but the vastness of the galaxy had always provided him new frontiers.*

Some of that expanse had been destroyed now, though, and with it, lives lost. Kirk himself had evidently been the source of that destruction, albeit inadvertently. Regardless of his role in the catastrophe, though, he wanted to do something about it.

But it's even more than that, *he thought.* Because of his part in what had happened, he might be the only person *capable of taking action in these circumstances. Even if somebody outside the nexus could determine precisely what had taken place, what could they possibly do to counteract the damage that had been done?*

Based not only upon what Guinan had told him, but also upon his experience with Picard on Veridian Three, Kirk believed that he could exit the nexus at any place and, of even greater import, at any time. More specifically, he could travel into the past, meaning that he could at least theoretically prevent the shock wave from ever occurring. Considering the nature and apparent cause of the converging temporal loop, Kirk reasoned that there could be only two ways of precluding it from developing: either he must stop himself from entering the nexus in 2293 or from exiting it in 2371. By accomplishing either of those goals, he would avert his existence—and that of the substantial set of chronometric particles within his body—at two distinct points in time with a conduit connecting them. Without those requirements, the temporal loop would not converge and the shock wave would not arise.

But if I don't enter the nexus in twenty-two ninety-three, *he thought,* then the *Enterprise*-B and its crew and passengers would be destroyed by the energy ribbon. *Kirk supposed that he might be able to travel back in time and find a means of saving the* Enterprise *without having to be down in the deflector control room, but if he did that, then he would not vanish and be presumed dead. In that case, he would alter the timeline, something he must avoid doing; he had already sacrificed his own happiness to preserve history, and he would not allow time to be changed now.*

And there's another problem, *Kirk thought. If he didn't enter the nexus in the first place, then clearly he would never leave it. That would provide another* means of preventing the temporal loop, but if he didn't leave the nexus to assist Picard on Veridian Three, then Soran would succeed at launching his weapon and the population of two hundred thirty million on Veridian IV would die. The calculus seemed impossible to negotiate.

Kirk paced across the compartment and over to an exterior viewport. He peered out at the stars burning hot in the deep, never-ending winter of space. People die, he told himself, reciting a fact he knew all too well. Since he'd been five years old and had lost his grandfather, death had been a regular companion in his life. His parents, gone. His uncle, his brother, his sister-in-law, gone too. David, the son he had barely known. Miramanee, carrying his unborn child. Captain Garrovick and two hundred of the Farragut crew. Gary Mitchell. Lee Kelso and Scott Darnell and so many others from the crews he had led through space, whose names he could recount because they had perished on his watch and he could do no less than remember them.

And Edith.

Once, when he thought he had lost Spock, he had admitted to David that he had never truly faced death, but that had not been quite true. Kirk had lived beneath the specter of loss for most of his days; he'd simply grown far too weary of it. Back then, he had grasped at the scant hope provided by Spock's father, Sarek, and amazingly, through a confluence of amazing circumstances, he had managed to help resurrect his friend.

And how many times have I skirted my own death

by the narrowest of margins? *he thought. He had been torn from within the* Enterprise-B *and thrown out into space and had still survived. Not that long ago, subjectively, he had fallen scores of meters and been crushed by a metal bridge on Veridian Three, yet he survived even now.*

I've faced death, *Kirk thought,* and I've railed against it. *Occasionally, he had succeeded in beating it back, saving the lives of his crew, of his friends and of strangers, of himself. But the end had still come often enough, plucking the people he cared about from his life like petals from a dying flower. Ultimately, he knew, entropy, disorder, and death would win out over all—over those he loved, over himself, over the inhabitants of Veridian IV.* I should just let go of all this, *Kirk told himself.*

But he wouldn't. He couldn't. *That simply wasn't who he was.*

Standing alone in the observation deck of the old Enterprise, *Kirk stared out at the unfeeling void, unwilling to allow it to dictate the terms of life and death. Then he began to formulate a plan.*

The black hole hung invisibly in the sky among the countless points of light that formed the Milky Way. Below, the surface of the planet-sized metal sphere extended away from Kirk in all directions, bathed only in the scant illumination provided by the distant stars. The fourth of seven "worlds" in this artificial solar system, the almost-featureless globe approximated the circumference, mass, and gravity of Earth.

Kirk had come here from the Starfleet archives, which he had visited with the echo of Picard still in the nexus. After Kirk had cobbled together the most workable strategy he could for stopping the converging temporal loop, he had gone to the archives from the Enterprise's shuttlebay observation deck, coincidentally to check the record of the Enterprise-B's own shuttlecraft. After that, he had prepared to depart the nexus. He hadn't known precisely how to do that, and neither had Picard. Like everything in this timeless region, though, it seemed reasonable to assume that it could be effected simply by an effort of will. He had no comprehension of the physical aspects of the nexus, but he envisioned it as a limitless blank canvas upon which minds drew their own realities. So thinking, he had then found himself, alone, on the largely empty shell of the Otevrel's fourth orb.

The crew of the Enterprise had first encountered the sociocentric, quasi-nomadic species during the ship's exploratory journey to the Aquarius Formation. Kirk had never walked the surface of the Otevrel "planet" like this—he, Bones, and Scotty had traveled here from the ship in a shuttlecraft—but as he had already learned, events within the nexus often bore only passing resemblance to their counterparts in reality. In further verification of that, Kirk realized that he did not currently wear the environmental suit he had donned before boarding the shuttle on this particular mission, but rather one of the old life-support belts that Starfleet had introduced during the final year or so of his first command. The belts generated a personal *force field for the wearer that maintained the appropriate atmosphere, temperature, and pressure about them. Kirk had liked the greater freedom of movement that the belts had provided over traditional environmental suits, but Starfleet had stopped using them when concerns had arisen regarding the long-term effects that prolonged proximity to the force fields would have on living tissue.*

Now, Kirk peered down at the wide white band encircling his waist and the soft yellow glow it produced about his body. When he did, he also saw something that he hadn't thought about since he had first returned to the nexus: his uniform, still covered with the dirt of Veridian Three, still torn, still showing streaks and smudges of his own blood on his white shirt and crimson vest. He remembered falling after he'd retrieved Soran's cloaking control pad, whirling through the air with the distorted section of the metal bridge, until he had landed on the ground, crushed beneath the deformed mass. In that moment, he recalled, he had known as surely as he had ever known anything that he had only seconds left to live.

But then the energy ribbon had swallowed him up once more, bearing him back into the nexus—where time had no meaning. The seconds remaining in his life had never come, nor obviously had his death. Clearly, too, his existence within the nexus had been a function of his mind and not his body, for even without the flow of time, the injuries he'd suffered on Veridian Three should have rendered him incapacitated.

But what happens when I leave here? *Kirk asked*

himself. *The answer seemed manifest: back in the physical universe, he would be immediately debilitated by the damage done to his body. Seconds later, he would be dead.*

Kirk considered his dilemma. He saw absolutely no means of preventing the temporal shock wave without exiting the nexus. He also could conceive of no way to return to the physical universe without dying. Even if he appeared in sickbay directly in front of McCoy and ordered the doctor to place him in a stasis field at once, and even if McCoy could then repair his injuries, doing all of that could easily alter the timeline.

No, Kirk thought. *I can't do this.*

Then he realized that he knew somebody within the nexus who could.

FIVE

The plasma blast seared the air beside the left ear of
Lieutenant James T. Kirk. Though he didn't see the
pulse as it rocketed past him, he did feel its heat, did
hear the low, menacing hum it generated. He flinched
and dived down to his right, throwing himself to the
outpost floor behind a dense tangle of wrecked equipment. On the far side of the room, the plasma shot exploded against the wall, sending up a thunderous report
and leaving behind a scorched, smoking scar in whatever type of metal had been utilized to construct the
Pelfrey Complex here on Beta Regenis II.

Next to Kirk, Lieutenant Commander Leslie
DeGuerrin sat with her back against a broken console
that had crashed onto its side. Tall and strongly built,
she calmly studied the gauge on her laser pistol. "Almost drained," she told Kirk. It didn't surprise him.
They'd been engaged in this firefight for more than an
hour, and for the last half of that time, they'd abandoned the stun settings—and the correspondingly
lower power requirements—of their weapons. When it
had become apparent that the landing party faced a
force at least three times their number, DeGuerrin had
made it clear that the odds of their getting out of the
complex alive would increase dramatically if they

could permanently eliminate enemy fighters, rather than just rendering them unconscious for a short time; Tholians typically recovered quickly from the stun effect of Starfleet lasers.

Kirk raised his own pistol and examined the power indicator. "Mine's down to nineteen percent," he said. "What do we do now?" DeGuerrin had led their four-member team here from the *Farragut*. While the starship completed a badly needed delivery of medicine and medical personnel to the New Mozambique colony, Captain Garrovick had sent the shuttlecraft *Dahlgren* to Beta Regenis II. There, in the domed Pelfrey Complex that had been constructed on the inhospitable surface of the class-K planet, Dr. Mowry—the ship's assistant chief medical officer—would administer the annual physical examinations to the outpost scientists, as required by Starfleet regulations. At the same time, DeGuerrin, Kirk, and Ensign Ketchum would collect research materials and reports that needed to be conveyed to Starfleet.

DeGuerrin looked up from her laser pistol. "I'm not sure what we *can* do," she said. "How many of them did you count?"

"There have to be at least fourteen," Kirk said, basing the figure on what he had seen and heard of the Tholians since the *Dahlgren* crew had come under attack. Because the nonhumanoid aliens wore environmental suits, it had been particularly difficult to tell one from another, but Kirk felt confident that he'd identified as least that many distinct individuals.

"I thought at least eighteen," DeGuerrin said, "in-

cluding the two we killed. That leaves no less than sixteen." Kirk didn't dispute DeGuerrin's assessment,
trusting her expertise in security matters. He also understood what she hadn't said: that, given the circumstances, the quartet of *Farragut* crewmembers had
virtually no chance of defeating a Tholian contingent
of that size. "We're going to have to make a run for
the *Dahlgren*," DeGuerrin said, clearly choosing re-
treat over continuing the battle.

But while Kirk would've gladly considered escape
a victory at this juncture, he also knew two facts that
made such a course problematic. To begin with, this
facility had been erected for the purpose of allowing a
scientific team to investigate both the planet's atmosphere and its volatile crust; the former inhibited the
use of transporters, sensors, deflector shields, and
communicators, while the latter contained unusual
compounds that might provide useful in power generation and the manufacture of weapons. Kirk didn't
know what the researchers and scientists had learned
so far, but he did know that any knowledge they had
gleaned needed to be kept out of the hands of the bel-
ligerent Tholian Assembly.

He also knew that if the *Farragut* crewmembers attempted to reach the *Dahlgren* in the complex's
hangar, they would find a group of Tholians waiting
for them. He said as much to DeGuerrin. "Even if we
managed to get to the shuttlecraft and were able to
launch," he added, "they must have a ship somewhere
nearby." Since the Tholians could not have beamed
through the atmosphere, they must have landed at the

complex at some point, but when Kirk had set the
Dahlgren down in the hangar—he'd piloted the shuttle here from the *Farragut*—he had seen no craft there
other than the scientists' two workpods.

In fact, the first indication of there being something
wrong at the facility had come when DeGuerrin's team
entered and found it silent. Within the small pressure
dome, the Pelfrey Complex consisted of a series of
concentric, interlocking rings. The hangar and life support machinery occupied the perimeter and encircled a
loop of hydroponically grown crops. Next came living
quarters and common areas for the dozen scientists and
support personnel stationed on Beta Regenis II. At the
center of the complex, a series of laboratories had been
set up. It had been there, in one of the labs, that the
Farragut crew had found the twelve bodies. DeGuerrin had ordered the team back to the shuttlecraft at
once, but too late; the Tholians had already cut off
their escape.

"Our only other choice is to try to find a way of destroying the complex," DeGuerrin said. Suddenly, two
more plasma weapons fired, one pulse striking the far
wall and the other slamming into the heap of ruined
equipment behind which Kirk and DeGuerrin had
taken cover. He automatically recoiled, but the security officer only reacted by climbing to her knees and
firing her laser pistol from behind the pile of equipment.

When she finished, Kirk said, "This place is en-
cased in a pressure dome. It shouldn't take too much
effort to make it fail."

"No," DeGuerrin agreed, but then she shook her head. "The Tholians are wearing environmental suits, though. They could potentially survive a catastrophic failure of the dome."

"They could," Kirk said. "The scientists here also kept their own environmental suits back in the hangar, but we could never reach them." He shrugged. "I wasn't thinking about saving us or killing the Tholians, though. I was only thinking about protecting the research that's been done here. Even if the data or the samples or whatever work has been accomplished isn't wiped out, the collapse of the dome atop the complex would make retrieving any of it more than a simple operation."

"That would give Captain Garrovick enough time to realize that we're overdue and bring the *Farragut* here," DeGuerrin said.

"And stop the Tholians," Kirk concluded.

DeGuerrin peered around the lab. "Do you think they would have put dome monitors and controls in here?" she asked.

"My guess is that if they did, the panels are through there," Kirk said, pointing to a pair of closed doors to their left, perhaps ten strides away. "That's the hub of the complex. Besides having controls out by the life support equipment, I think the support personnel would want to be able to check and operate those systems from a secondary, centrally located area."

"Makes sense," DeGuerrin said. Kirk also knew that it didn't much matter whether it did or not. The Tholians had allowed the four of them to reach the heart of the complex before closing ranks around them. Completely contained now, the *Farragut* crewmembers could realistically only attempt to hold their ground or move farther inward.

DeGuerrin looked directly ahead, and Kirk followed her gaze to an open doorway. The two had left Dr. Mowry and Ensign Ketchum in the adjoining lab, giving them a respite while Kirk and DeGuerrin had returned here to reengage the Tholians. "Can you get back to them?" asked the lieutenant commander. "Tell them what I'm going to attempt?"

Kirk nodded. He did not relish the idea of informing two of his crewmates that they would shortly die, but he understood that he had to tell them. About to make the sacrifice they knew might be required of them when they had joined Starfleet, they deserved to be treated with honesty and respect. "I'll make it," Kirk said. "I'll tell them."

"All right," DeGuerrin said. She rose up onto her haunches, obviously preparing to break for the inner labs to their left. "Cover me," she said. "And wish me luck."

"Luck," Kirk said as he set himself at the edge of the smashed equipment behind which he and DeGuerrin hid. He raised his laser pistol and asked, "Are you ready?"

"Yes."

"Then here I go," Kirk said. Low to the floor, he looked out toward the positions from which the Tholians had been firing—two open entryways into the room—and saw the shimmer of their green environ-

mental suits from just beyond. He opened fire. He
saw one of the Tholians duck away, but another
returned a spate of plasma bolts in Kirk's direction.
The heap of wrecked equipment shook as the shots
rocked it.

Kirk continued to fire, but glanced over toward
DeGuerrin. He saw her sprinting across the room toward the doors, which opened at her approach, but
then a plasma bolt slammed into her shoulder. Kirk
heard her cry out briefly. Her momentum carried her
forward as her body spun around from the force of the
shot. DeGuerrin made it into the next room, but just
past the threshold, she collapsed. The doors slid shut
behind her.

Kirk stopped firing and took cover once more. He
looked to his left again and saw two more blasts from
the Tholian weapons, these hammering into the doors.
He didn't know what he should do. Lieutenant Commander DeGuerrin had been hit, he'd seen that, he'd
seen her go down, but if she'd only been wounded, she
still might be able to carry out the actions she'd intended.

But she might not be, Kirk told himself, and the
thought made his decision easy. He quickly made his
way to the other side of the shattered equipment, then
prepared to follow DeGuerrin. As he did so, he spotted her laser pistol lying on the floor two-thirds of the
way to the doors. She must've dropped it when she'd
been hit. Kirk thought that the lost weapon might just
allow him to safely navigate his way to the hub of the
lab complex.

Reaching out quickly, Kirk fired blindly toward the Tholians, then raced out from his cover and toward the doors. After three steps, he stopped abruptly, waited for an instant, then resumed running again. He heard, felt, and saw plasma bolts all about him. Five strides along, Kirk lunged forward, bringing his right shoulder down toward the floor. He saw DeGuerrin's laser at close range as he flew over it, but he did not reach for it. As his shoulder struck the floor and he rolled, he saw a blast of plasma surge into the weapon and send it flying.

Amid the salvo of the Tholian weapons, a small squeak reached Kirk's ears: the doors to the inner labs opening. He soared past the jamb and came to rest on his back. As the doors glided closed behind him, he quickly pushed himself up. Beside him lay Lieutenant Commander DeGuerrin, her eyes closed, smoke rising from a charred wound in her shoulder, the stench of her seared flesh sickeningly strong. Kirk reached two fingers to her neck, searching for a pulse. He found one, weak but present.

Knowing that he didn't have long, that the Tholians would close in soon enough, Kirk rose, touched a control beside the doors to lock them, then examined his new environs. He stood in a large room shaped like one quarter of a circle, having entered it through the outer, arcing wall. Consoles lined the periphery of the room, and several large machines he did not recognize filled the interior of the space. Dashing from one panel to the next, he searched for anything that resembled environmental controls for the dome.

He found nothing.

Weapons fire pounded into the doors, and Kirk looked back in that direction, over at DeGuerrin. If the Tholians penetrated this lab, he knew that they would immediately kill her, and so he felt the temptation to return to her and move her to a safer place. The thought made no sense, though, for if Kirk succeeded in bringing down the pressure dome, they would all die anyway. Saving Lieutenant Commander DeGuerrin now would be a foolish waste of time.

Another pulse struck the door, the percussive sound pushing Kirk back into motion. He rushed across the room and through a single door, this in one of the two straight walls. He found himself in a lab shaped identically to the last one, but oriented and equipped differently. Various stations lined the walls, but two very large machines sat in the middle of the room, their purposes a mystery to Kirk. Bordering one of them, a low platform contained an enormous slab of metallic rock, at least five meters long, five meters wide, and two deep. It had obviously been carved out of the planet's surface and brought here for study.

As he had in the previous lab, Kirk locked the doors, then hied from panel to panel, hunting for the controls of the pressure dome. He'd only checked two consoles, though, before he stopped and turned back to regard the mass of native stone. Then he peered at all three entrances into the room, a single door in each of the two straight walls and a set of double doors in the curved wall. The great rock would have fit through none of them, he realized; it must have been *beamed* here.

Kirk returned his attention to the panels, but now he began looking for transporter controls. He knew that the planet's atmosphere inhibited transport *through* it, but within the Pelfrey Complex itself, within the pressure dome, it must have been possible. The scientists must have employed a workpod to drag the mammoth stone into the hangar, and then from there beamed it into the lab.

At the fifth console he came to, Kirk saw a symbol composed of two outward-pointing arrows on either side of a square. A series of dots formed the bottom half of the square, as though the shape was dematerializing. Kirk scrutinized the controls and saw that they did indeed conform to those of a transporter.

Activating it, he found the targeting sensors and scanned for human life signs. Four sets of coordinates appeared on the display, confirming that sensors, useless within the planet's atmosphere, still functioned within the pressure dome. As quickly as he could, Kirk beamed the colossal stone from atop the platform and onto the floor of the lab. Once he'd done so, he locked onto the other three *Farragut* crewmembers and transported them here.

Once they'd materialized, Kirk went to the platform and, without explaining the situation, pointed out DeGuerrin's wound to Dr. Mowry. Together, Kirk and Ketchum lifted the security officer and lowered her to the floor, where the doctor took the medkit hanging at his side and began examining her. Kirk then returned to the transporter controls and scanned for *all* life signs. He saw only the four in this room and un-

derstood that the sensors clearly hadn't been cali-
brated for Tholians. "Doctor," he called back over his
shoulder, "this transporter doesn't recognize Tholian
life-forms. I need to know distinguishing characteristics I can scan for." Mowry didn't respond right away,
no doubt continuing to minister to DeGuerrin. "Doctor," Kirk said, "I need to know *now* or we're all going
to die."

"They have two arms and six legs," Mowry said.
"They have an exoskeleton. They—"

"I need something I can scan for easily," Kirk said.

Mowry did not respond for a moment, but then said,
"They have body temperatures of over two hundred degrees."

"Now that I can scan for," Kirk said, more to himself than to the doctor. He did so, and found not the
sixteen Tholians that DeGuerrin had estimated, but
twenty-one. He started to adjust the sensors to target
their plasma pistols, intending to transport the weapons
here, but then something else occurred to him: even
unarmed, twenty-one Tholians might be able to overwhelm just four Starfleet personnel. "Doctor Mowry,"
he asked, "can Tholians survive in normal human temperature ranges? At say twenty or twenty-five?" It
couldn't be any warmer than that within the complex.

"No," Mowry said. "At one hundred, a Tholian's
exoskeleton will begin to crack."

Kirk operated the targeting sensors again, fine-
tuning his goals. He hesitated to take the action he'd
planned, though, reluctant to cause such loss of life.
The Tholians invaded this complex, Kirk reminded

himself. *They killed the twelve personnel stationed here, and they're trying to kill us too.*

As though providing corroboration of his thoughts, weapons fire suddenly battered the door through which Kirk had entered the lab. He reached forward and triggered the transporter. Kirk heard the familiar whine of the materialization sequence, and he turned to see the green environmental suits of the Tholians appear on the platform, along with any other equipment they'd been holding, including their plasma weapons. The suits hung in the air as they formed, holding the shapes of their wearers, then with the other equipment fell in a clatter to the platform.

From the neighboring lab rose a horrible shriek and a series of frantic chirps and clicks. Kirk didn't need to understand the language of the Tholians to differentiate their cries of pain. He took no pleasure in what he'd done, but he accepted the necessity of it.

Peering back at the transporter console, Kirk checked the readings of the twenty-one Tholians. Some of them continued to move, mostly in haphazard fashion, but not for long. Within a minute, all motion had ceased.

Kirk walked back over to where Mowry treated DeGuerrin. Standing beside Ketchum, he asked the doctor, "Is she going to be all right?"

"Yes," Mowry said, looking up at Kirk. "And I guess we will be too."

"We've got a fighting chance, anyway," Kirk said. "But I still need to take the *Dahlgren* into space and get a message to the *Farragut* about what's going on here.

There's got to be a Tholian ship around, so I'm going to have to elude it, but I'm confident that I can. The planet's atmosphere will provide good cover for me."

"We're not all going?" Ketchum said.

"I think you'll be safer here," Kirk told him. "There's only one way into the complex, and that's through the hangar. If any more Tholians try to enter, you'll be able to defend yourselves the way I just did. Let me show you."

Kirk escorted Ketchum back over to the transporter console, where he demonstrated for the ensign how he had scanned for the Tholians and beamed away their environmental suits and weapons. Kirk then returned to the platform and pulled the Tholian equipment from it and onto the floor, selecting one of their plasma pistols to go along with his own, nearly depleted laser. Then he stepped up onto the platform and told Ketchum to transport him to the hangar. "If I'm not back in—" He calculated the amount of time it should take him to get into orbit, send a message to the *Farragut*, and return to the complex, then added in a buffer for any evasive maneuvers he might have to take if he encountered a Tholian vessel. "If I'm not back in three hours, you'll have to take one of the workpods into orbit and attempt to reach the *Farragut*," he told Ketchum.

"Yes, sir," the ensign said.

"Energize," Kirk ordered. As he dematerialized, the lab faded from view, and then a subjectively indeterminate amount of time later, the hangar appeared in its place, the shuttlecraft directly in front of him. Kirk hurried to board the *Dahlgren*, and only as the hatch hummed closed after him did he see through a viewport the half-dozen Tholians scattered about the hangar. The dark red, multilegged beings, about the same general proportions as a humanoid, had crumpled to the floor, their carapaces ruptured, a bright ichor pooling about them. Despite their being adversaries, Kirk wished that their attack on the research station had not made his actions necessary.

Knowing that he had a duty to perform, Kirk allowed himself only a moment for such thoughts, then put them out of his mind. He took a seat at the shuttlecraft's forward console, quickly bringing the *Dahlgren* up to power. As he engaged the antigravs to lift the shuttle and take it out of the hangar, he hoped that he would not be detected by the Tholian vessel— or vessels—when he cleared the atmosphere, or if he did, that it would turn out to be a single transport or scout ship with minimal armaments. The *Dahlgren*, he knew, had no weaponry of any kind.

With no other choice, Kirk pointed the bow of the shuttlecraft upward and began the ascent to orbit.

Not knowing to what place or time he should go, Kirk had instead concentrated on an identity, then turned in place on the metallic plain of the Otevrel's artificial world. As he'd hoped, the nexus had changed about him, taking him where he needed to go. Now, he stood in the cramped body of an old Starfleet shuttle, peering ahead to where another version of himself piloted the craft—the same version he'd seen meeting

Antonia for the first time, escaping with Merrick from planet 892-IV, and leading a landing party down to Gamma Trianguli VI.

Kirk took a step forward and opened his mouth, but then didn't know how to address this other Kirk. He peered through the bow viewport for a moment, where he saw a thick planetary atmosphere giving way to stars above. Finally, he simply said, "Jim."

The other Kirk—Jim—spun around in his seat, drawing an outmoded laser pistol from his side. "Who—" he started, but then stopped, obviously shocked to see Kirk standing there. He stood up then, slowly, still brandishing his weapon. "Who are you?"

"You know who I am," Kirk said. As best he could tell, at one point in time, they had been the same person, deciding to abandon the chimera of the nexus in order to help Picard prevent the deaths of the inhabitants of Veridian IV. And Kirk had left, but according to Guinan—and as Kirk also somehow perceived—this echo of himself had been left behind, no less real, but now with a life that had diverged from his own path.

"You can't be me," Jim said, though in a less-than-authoritative way that suggested he sought to convince himself of his assertion.

"Not anymore I'm not," Kirk agreed, "but until a short time ago, yes, we were the same person." He recalled how Picard had phrased the situation, and he repeated it now. "We are both caught up in some type of temporal nexus." Kirk considered how best to convince his alter ego of their circumstances, but then he saw awareness dawn on Jim's face.

"Picard," he said as he lowered his laser.

"Yes," Kirk said. *"I left the nexus with him. We stopped Soran, but then—"* The shuttlecraft jolted hard, as though struck by something. Kirk staggered to his right and almost went down, but righted himself against the bulkhead. When he looked back toward the bow, he saw through the viewport a small vessel that seemed as though it had been constructed out of a collection of triangular hull components. He recognized its origin immediately—Tholian—and knew the time period to which he had come. For his actions down on Beta Regenis II and out here in space, Starfleet had awarded him the Grankite Order of Tactics.

"Hold on," Jim yelled, now back at the forward console. Kirk grabbed onto the handle of an equipment door as the shuttle veered to port, the inertial dampers taking a fraction of a second to compensate for the rapid movement. Through the viewport, Kirk saw a bolt of plasma energy streak past.

As Jim operated the helm controls, Kirk made his way forward until he dropped into the chair beside him. *"Jim,"* he said, *"stop this. I need to talk with you."*

"You don't understand," Jim said, not looking away from where his hands darted across the panel. *"I have to—"*

"You have to evade the Tholians while you transmit a message to Captain Garrovick aboard the Farragut," Kirk said. *"Down at the research complex, all of the scientists are dead, killed in an unprovoked attack by the Tholians."*

Jim looked up at him but said nothing. Then another Tholian weapon landed, shaking the cabin violently, and he began working the controls again. Kirk remembered that this hadn't happened before, that while he'd been spotted by the Tholian vessel in orbit, he'd managed to evade it after taking only a single blast of its weapons fire. But then, when he'd piloted the shuttlecraft all those years ago, he hadn't been distracted by an unexpected passenger. "If you know where we are and what's going on," Jim said, "then you know I have to do this."

"No, you don't," Kirk said, but Jim continued taking the shuttle through evasive maneuvers. Kirk reached over and took hold of his counterpart by his upper arms, turning Jim to face him. "You don't *have to do this," Kirk insisted. "This isn't even really happening."*

Another plasma bolt struck the shuttlecraft. The forward control console exploded, bathing the two men in a shower of sparks. Smoke filled the cabin, and then Kirk heard the low moan of overstressed metal. He saw a thin crack zigzag up the bulkhead, and then the shuttle fractured, bursting apart around them. For a moment, they floated in the frightening totality of space, the insensate stars peering coldly down on them, the planet hanging off to one side, the Tholian vessel looming above them.

Kirk had not let go his grip on Jim's arms, and now he called to mind another location, a safe place where he'd been alone. With the stars still surrounding them, Kirk felt something beneath his feet. He peered down-

ward as he felt the pull of gravity, and he saw grass below him. Looking up, he saw that he and Jim now stood amid trees and other modest growth, in what looked to be a wide parkland. An airpod sat nearby, its gull-wing hatch propped open.

Before him, Jim turned in a circle, inspecting their new locale. Three-quarters of the way around, he stopped and raised an arm, pointing. "That's Mojave," he said. Kirk looked that way and saw the towers and spires of the California metropolis, saw the stylized four-posted arch that rose majestically from the lake at the city's eastern end. "I was only here once."

"After reading a biography of Christopher Pike," Kirk said.

"Yes," Jim agreed. "When I was chief of Starfleet Operations." He continued looking toward the city. "Captain Pike was born and raised there," he said. "He used to ride horses out here when he was a boy. They've got a memorial to him at the city center."

Kirk stepped forward, interposing himself between Jim and the city. "Except that's not really Mojave," he said, "and we're not really on Earth. We're in some type of—"

"Temporal nexus," Jim said along with him. "Yes, I heard you." He turned and paced away, but then peered back at Kirk. "I remember Picard," he said. "I remember deciding to leave the nexus and help him, but then . . . then I didn't. I stayed, got caught up again in the events of my own life . . ." The realization appeared to agitate him.

"It's all right," Kirk said. "But now I need your help."

"You *need* my *help?*" Jim said. "Here in the nexus?"

"No. Back in the real universe where we lived our life," Kirk said. "When I left here with Picard, we were successful in stopping Soran, but then something else happened."

"Something else?" Jim said.

"Something that I—that we—essentially caused," Kirk said. "A phenomenon known as a converging temporal loop." He explained what he had witnessed on Veridian Three, as well as the concept of the loop as described by Data. "It's destroyed a sizable volume of the space-time continuum and taken many lives, perhaps millions, perhaps even many more than that."

Jim padded back across the grass until he stood directly in front of Kirk. It should've seemed like gazing into a mirror, Kirk thought, but it didn't. The image he always saw when he peered at his reflection showed him the reverse of his features, which didn't happen here as he looked at this echo of himself. "And you think what?" Jim asked. "That we can go back in time, somehow stop it from occurring."

"Not we," Kirk told him. "You." And then he explained his plan.

SIX

Jim Kirk trod back and forth across the grass in the parkland adjoining the city of Mojave. He had just listened to—

Myself? *he thought, the very notion absurd on the face of it.* Except not all that absurd, *he amended, thinking of the incident back during the* Enterprise's *five-year mission when a transporter malfunction had produced two versions of him.*

And yet this doesn't seem like that, *Kirk thought. Back in orbit of Alfa 177, where the transporter accident had taken place, neither of the two Kirk identities that had been created—and he could still remember existing as each of them—had felt entirely like himself. Right now, though, he did feel whole, and he suspected that his doppelganger did as well.*

Kirk glanced over at his double, who appeared to match him precisely, but for the visible effects of the fall he said he'd taken on Veridian Three. Both dirt and blood covered his hands and face as well as his uniform, which had been ripped in many places. According to him, he had been crushed by a metal bridge and on the verge of death when he had been swept back into the nexus. He also believed that he had beheld a powerful destructive force called a converging tempo-

ral loop. He now wanted to leave the nexus and go
back in time to prevent the loop from ever developing,
though he claimed that he could not do so himself as
he would, upon exiting this timeless place, die as a result of his injuries.

As fantastic as Kirk found the collection of details
he'd just been given, all of it seemed to make an internal kind of sense, but for one thing. He stopped pacing about and addressed that now. "You said that the
convergence loop was caused by there being two large,
identical sets of chronometric particles in our universe,
connected by the conduit of the nexus," he said.

"That's right," the other, bloodied Kirk said, nodding.

"And that those particles were in our body," Kirk
said. Again, his duplicate nodded. "So if I leave the
nexus, won't that unleash another temporal loop?"

"I was concerned about that myself," the other Kirk
said. "But right now, neither of those sets of chronometric particles exists in our universe because the converging loop destroyed them. If you leave and succeed
in preventing the loop, then the conditions that caused
it in the first place—the two sets of particles joined together by the nexus—will never arise."

"Right," Kirk said. He understood the logical argument that the other Kirk had just put forward, but
thinking about these time-related concepts seemed
dizzying. It's more than dealing with time, Kirk
thought. It's also about not wanting to leave the nexus.
"Why should I trust you?" he said, hunting for a reason to stay here, but as soon as the words had left his
mouth, he knew they carried no weight.

"I think you do trust me," the other Kirk said. "I think you know who I am. I think you know that I'm you."

Kirk nodded, unable to do anything but agree. He looked away, toward the beautiful city of Mojave off in the distance, then back at his other self. "What if I don't want to leave the nexus?" he said, choosing to speak more plainly. He remembered refusing and then acquiescing to Picard's request for assistance in stopping Soran, but he also recalled all of the joyous times of his life that he had lived and relived here, mostly before that, but also afterward. He had agreed to exit the nexus with Picard, but then he hadn't done so, instead experiencing that first meeting with Antonia all over again.

"What can you tell me that I haven't already thought of myself?" the other Kirk said. "We both know that none of this—" He spread his arms wide, taking in the extent of their surroundings. "—is real. We've been through the same events here."

"Not all the same events," Kirk said. "I got to meet Antonia for the first time again, and it was different. I made it different. I can go back to our relationship and this time make it work."

The other Kirk walked over to him. "You made it different how?" he asked, his tone almost combative. "You know, because I know, that no matter what you did, no matter what you changed, it would still never work out."

"I told her who I was," Kirk said. "This time, I didn't hide my identity from her." In the real universe, Kirk had simply given Antonia his name, but here in

*the nexus, he had also mentioned that he'd retired from
Starfleet. "I told her flatly that very first time that my
life in the space service was over," Kirk continued. "I
didn't wait until later, and this time, I won't act in a
way that allows her to doubt my commitment to her.
This time, I'll keep all of those implicit and explicit
promises I made and I'll stay with her. This time, I
won't let myself desire a return to Starfleet."*

*"'Desire a return to Starfleet?'" said the other
Kirk. "Jim," he went on, the name sounding odd coming from his lips, "you know you didn't leave Antonia
because you wanted to go back to Starfleet. You went
back to Starfleet so that Antonia would leave you."*

*Kirk said nothing, recognizing the hard truth of the
other Kirk's words.*

*"You lied to her—we lied to her—from the begin-
ning," the other Kirk continued. "But then, we lied to
ourselves too."*

*A deep sense of shame threatened to overwhelm
Kirk because he knew that his counterpart was right.
He had lied to Antonia, even when she had pleaded
with him for honesty. No matter what he did here in
the nexus, he would not be able to alter the reality of
what had really happened between them.*

*And although he didn't want to, he couldn't help re-
membering the day that he'd first begun to betray her.*

Outside, snow dusted the Idaho hills. Kirk stood at
the window in his living room, holding open the curtain with one hand as he gazed into the night. He
squinted out at the darkness, unable to see past the re-

flections in the glass. Cupping his free hand over his eyes, he leaned in to the windowpane, which felt cold to the touch. His vision now shielded from the indoor lighting, he saw snowflakes still drifting lazily down from the autumnal sky, as though the heavens had chosen to sprinkle the stars down upon the Earth.

He heard footsteps behind him and knew that Antonia had returned from her self-appointed task in the kitchen. "Here we go," she said as she came up behind him. He turned to see her holding two ceramic mugs, steam curling up from each. "My famous hot-buttered rum to go with the first snow of the season."

Kirk accepted the mug Antonia offered and sipped at the concoction within. The sweet scent of the drink gave way to a taste that seemed almost like apple pie, though with a kick he hadn't expected. He pursed his lips at the strong flavor of the rum. "You make drinks like a ship's chief medical officer," he said.

Antonia offered him a quizzical look. "All right," she said. "I'm not exactly sure what that's supposed to mean, so I'll just choose to take it as a compliment."

"It means that some doctors love to kill the pain, no matter how much alcohol it takes," Kirk joked. "My CMO on the *Enterprise*—"

"Bones?" Antonia said.

"Right," Kirk said. "He made a drink called a Finagle's Folly that he claimed was known all the way to Orion." He sipped again at the rum. "Somehow I think they probably know Salvatori's Hot-buttered Rum there too."

Antonia smiled at him, but quickly and thinly, as

though filling a moment she didn't particularly enjoy. It surprised him, but he decided not to address it. Perhaps he'd mischaracterized her expression, and if he hadn't, if something troubled Antonia, he doubted that it had anything to do with him or their relationship, which seemed to be unfolding very well. If something weighed on her mind, though, she would tell him only when she felt ready to do so. If he'd learned one thing about her during the months that they'd been seeing each other, it had been that she couldn't be pressured into doing anything she didn't herself elect to do, even simply talking.

Antonia moved away from the window and over to the sofa. She wore long dark slacks that flattered her athletic figure, and a red and blue sweater that reflected the onset of the wintry weather. She sat down on the sofa and peered at the crackling fire in the hearth.

Kirk went over and settled in beside her in the cozy setting. She put down her mug on the end table, then wrapped her hands around his arm and leaned in against him. They sat that way for a while, quietly, comfortably—an apt description for all the time they had spent together in the spring and summer and now into the fall.

After their initial meeting, Kirk had tracked her down through her veterinary practice to the nearby small town of—appropriately enough, given her profession—Antelope Brook. He'd made no pretext about visiting her office because his horses needed her care, but had instead simply gone there and asked her out, his impression being that Antonia would appreciate a forthright approach. She had, and they'd begun seeing each other once or twice a week, a frequency that had increased with time.

They had spent many days together riding through the Idaho hills, occasionally taking in a film in town or heading into one of the bigger cities for dinner or a concert or a sporting event. Mostly, though, Antonia liked staying home, playing games or reading or making love. Their physical relationship had actually taken some time to progress, but once it had, they enjoyed each other fully. Kirk found her energetic and playful, both in bed and out. Though she took some things very seriously—such as her practice and the general good care of animals—Antonia for the most part maintained an air of lightness about her.

As Kirk drank his rum with Antonia by his side, his gaze came to rest on the mantelpiece, atop which he had placed three handcrafted models of old sailing vessels. Several other antique pieces dressed the shelves he'd built on either side of the fireplace, including a clock that his uncle had left to him, a sextant, an orrery. On the very day he'd met Antonia, he'd vowed to himself that he would start living his life again, that he would do his best to forge past the memories of sadness and loss that for so long had held him back. With the personal adornments he'd added to the house and with his new romance, he felt that he had in large part succeeded in those efforts. He had even lately thought about taking the next step with Antonia.

Kirk finished his rum, then reached past Antonia to

set his mug down next to hers on the end table. Once
he had, he didn't lean back on the sofa, but remained
leaning over her. Peering into her dark brown eyes, he
said, "Doctor Salvatori, what would you think about
moving in here?"

Antonia wrinkled her brow. "Is that a hypothetical
question," she said, "or are you really asking me to
move in with you?" She had a penchant for reacting
to certain situations in a deliberately obtuse manner,
but Kirk had learned to bully his way through such tactics.

"I'm asking," he said. He bent forward and kissed
her lightly on the lips. "We've been seeing each other
for months now and things seem to be going well between us."

"Oh, you think so?" Antonia said, without any in-
flection to indicate a blithe spirit behind her remark.

"Yes, I do," Kirk said, refusing to be denied.

"Well . . . yes," Antonia finally agreed, but she appeared less than pleased by the admission. Abruptly
she pushed past Kirk, stood up, and walked toward the
corner of the room. "It's been wonderful," she said,
facing him, but when she continued, she looked down
at her hands, which she nervously twisted together.
"It's just that I'm not so sure that we have a future together."

"What?" Kirk said, unprepared for Antonia's assessment. He rose from the sofa but did not try to approach her, instead gazing at her across the room.
"I . . . I thought we were growing closer," he said. "I
thought we had a good thing going and that we were

moving forward together." It had been some time since he'd been seriously involved with a woman, but it shocked him that he could have been so mistaken in his evaluation of their relationship. With Edith it had been so easy—

Kirk cut himself off in midthought, wanting to prevent himself from comparing Antonia to Edith. Besides being unfair to Antonia, it also did him no good. Edith was gone, and she always would be.

Across the room, Antonia raised her eyes and looked at him. "We *have* grown closer," she said. "We *do* have a good thing going. I really enjoy your company and we always have a fine time with each other, but . . . I'm just not sure that we're moving forward together."

Kirk looked away from Antonia and over at the logs burning in the fireplace. He didn't know what to say or think, and he told her so. "I'm shocked," he said, "but I guess maybe that just illustrates how badly I misjudged our relationship."

"No, no, you didn't," Antonia said. "But . . . tell me, what were you looking at through the window before?"

"What?" Kirk said, completely nonplussed by the question. "I was just looking to see if it was still snowing." The more he considered what she'd asked, the less sense it made to him. "Why?" he said. "Is there something else you thought I was looking at?"

"Another woman," Antonia said.

"What?" Kirk couldn't believe her claim. He had been seeing no one but her, though he now felt a pang of guilt for his errant thought of Edith.

"The stars," Antonia said.

Kirk shook his head. "I don't understand," he said. Antonia couldn't possibly know about Edith. Other than Spock and Bones, he didn't think anybody did. Even when he'd sought counseling after Sam and Aurelan's deaths, which had immediately followed his loss of Edith, he hadn't spoken of her to his psychiatrist.

"I think you do understand," Antonia said. She took a step toward him, but then seemed to consciously stop herself from coming any closer. "Jim, I really have enjoyed being with you. You're fun and funny, a good companion and an interesting man. Certainly you've lived an interesting life." She paused, then added, "Maybe too interesting."

"What does that mean?" Kirk wanted to know.

"It means that I don't want to get too involved with a man who's eventually going to leave me," Antonia said. She spoke without anger or bitterness, but with a conviction that suggested she believed her opinion of their future to be fact, not conjecture.

"I have no intention of leaving you," Kirk said. "Why would you think that I would?"

"Tell me when you were at the window that you weren't looking at the stars," she said.

"Honestly, no, I wasn't," Kirk said. He recalled comparing in his mind the snowflakes to the pinpoints of light in the sky, but that seemed immaterial. "I was just looking out at the snow."

"I believe you," Antonia allowed. "But I *have* seen you looking at the stars."

"Well, yes, of course," he said. "Doesn't everybody? Don't you?"

"Sure, but not in the same way that you do," she said. "When I look at the stars, all I see is a beautiful night sky. When you look, I can tell that you're remembering alien worlds you've already visited and imagining the exotic places you've yet to explore."

"Antonia," he said. He started to move toward her, but she held her hand up, and he halted a few steps from her. "Yes, I admit that I can recall the different planets I've been to, the strange landscapes I've walked, but that doesn't mean that I'm going to leave you."

"It also doesn't mean that you're going to stay," she noted. "That you won't decide at some point to go back to Starfleet."

"I've been retired for two and a half years now," Kirk said. "Why do you think I'm suddenly going to want to return to space? Have I ever given you any indication of that? Other than looking at the stars, which as you said, you do yourself?"

Antonia did not answer immediately, and Kirk suspected that when she did, the future of their relationship—or the lack of a future—would turn on her answer. Finally, she said, "No, you haven't acted like you want to go back to Starfleet. But when you do look up at the stars, it just seems like we don't connect."

"Then that's my fault," Kirk told her. "I never meant to make you feel disconnected from me. I'll make sure that doesn't happen again."

"It's all right," Antonia said. "I don't want to change who you are. I like who you are. I just don't want to be involved in a long-distance, part-time relationship. I've had a couple of those in my life and I don't like them. I want a partner who will be here with me."

"Antonia," Kirk said, and this time when he went to her, she didn't try to stop him. When he reached her, he put his hands on her arms and looked her directly in the eyes. "I'm not asking you to be in a relationship while I board a starship and go running off through the galaxy. I'm asking you to move into my house with me, right here in Idaho."

"And what happens when you go back to Starfleet?" she asked quietly.

"That's not going to happen," he promised her.

"How can I be sure of that?" she asked him. "How can *you* be sure of that?"

Kirk chuckled. "Next year I'll have lived half a century," he said. "I think by now I ought to know myself."

"You *ought* to," Antonia said, peering at him in an almost pleading way. "But *do* you?"

"Yes," he told her. "I think I do."

Antonia nodded, and then she actually smiled. She moved to the side, and Kirk let his hands drop from her arms. She passed him and crossed the room, back over to the window. Holding the curtains open, she looked outside. "I like it when it snows," she said. "When there's an accumulation, there's a surreal quiet, like a thick blanket's been draped over the land."

Kirk walked over to Antonia and sent his arms

around her midsection, hugging her to him. "I told you that I've got a house up in the Canadian Rockies," he said. "We should go. Lots of snow up there."

Antonia let the curtains fall back into place and looked back over her shoulder at him. "Are you trying to bribe me to move in with you?" she said, her tone now playful.

"If that's what it takes," Kirk said.

She turned in his arms to face him, reaching up and putting her own hands on his shoulders. "Jim, I'm serious about this," she said. "I like being with you and I can even see us together in the future, but I don't want to get completely involved only to have that taken away from me."

"I'm not going back to Starfleet," Kirk said. "I love you, Antonia." And he did love her, even if she was not the love of his life—

Once more, he put a quick end to such thoughts.

"I love you too, Jim," Antonia said. She kissed him, and he kissed her back.

Later, he would try to tell himself that he had never lied to her, not really, because at the time, he really hadn't planned on going back to Starfleet. But then, that hadn't been the worst of his lies.

SEVEN

Jim Kirk looked at his bloodied counterpart, the city of Mojave in the background, and he found that he couldn't argue anymore. On a superficial level, on a selfish level, he wanted to remain here in the nexus. He wanted to undo the pain that he had caused Antonia, wanted to find happiness with her.

But the other Kirk had been right. Anything he did here would not be real. More than that, though, even if he could change the past that he had shared with Antonia, even if he could prevent himself from returning to Starfleet, it would make no difference. Starfleet had indeed been his excuse to break off his relationship with Antonia—to compel her to break it off with him—but there had been another reason that he hadn't been able to stay with her: she wasn't Edith.

"I'll go," Kirk said. "I'll try to stop the converging temporal loop."

"Thank you," the other Kirk said.

He would try to stop the loop, but he also knew that he would need to do more than that. In addition to traveling back in time to attempt to prevent the shock wave, he would also have to ensure that the Enterprise-B *still escaped the energy ribbon, and that Picard still managed to stop Soran from wiping out the population of*

Veridian IV—and he would have to accomplish all of that without altering the timeline. He understood the plan that the other Kirk had devised, but not the logistics of how to accomplish all of it. "When I leave the nexus," he asked, "how do I reenter it?"

"You don't," the other Kirk said. "I only ended up here again by chance."

"But your plan involves me taking action in twenty-two ninety-three and twenty-three seventy-one," Kirk said. "If I can only exit the nexus once—"

"You'll have to use another means to move safely and surreptitiously through time," the other Kirk said.

"But how?" he asked. He had traveled in time on a number of occasions, most often by employing the light-speed breakaway factor, taking a starship racing at excessive speed toward a star, circling around it deep within its gravity well, and then pulling away from it in a slingshot-like movement. Even if after leaving the nexus Kirk could somehow acquire a vessel powerful and strong enough to achieve such a maneuver, he could hardly do all of that with any realistic expectation of remaining unobserved. The only other means he had used to travel through time—

And suddenly he knew what had been planned by his alter ego, who then confirmed it: "The Guardian of Forever."

Kirk could see it. The Guardian's remote location, during a time prior to when it had been discovered, would allow him to move stealthily through time. Except that he foresaw a problem. "I'll need to enter the Guardian in twenty-two ninety-three," he said. "But—"

"I know," the other Kirk responded. "The Klingons."

On the bridge of the *Enterprise*, Kirk peered from his command chair at the main viewscreen. The view astern showed Starfleet's now-empty Einstein research station receding into the distance as the ship sped away from it. A central, compacted sphere formed the main body of the facility, on the top and bottom of which extended a tapering spire. Its hull glistened blue, as though constructed of colored crystal. An arc of the brown planet about which it orbited showed in a corner of the screen.

Visible beyond the station, the gray shapes of the Klingon vessels *Goren* and *Gr'oth* continued their pursuit of the *Enterprise*. Each had a bulbous control section at the forward end of a long, narrow neck, which extended from an angular main body, on either side of which hung its shortened engine structures. The two warships would pass close to the Einstein station.

"Ten seconds," announced Lieutenant Haines from the sciences station. Several minutes ago, Spock had gone down to engineering to assist Scotty in restoring the weapons and the shields. "Five seconds."

"Now, Chekov!" Kirk ordered, leaning forward in his chair. At the navigation console, the ensign worked his controls. On the main viewer, Kirk watched as the Einstein station blew apart. The two Klingon vessels vanished for a moment behind the fiery explosion, which immediately began to die in the vacuum of space.

Kirk waited to see if his actions had brought his crew any closer to safety. The irony did not elude him that on the voyage back to Earth, the ship and crew might not make it on this, the last leg of their five-year journey. He held his breath as he gazed at the viewscreen.

The *Goren* emerged from the fading conflagration in pieces, the forward control section no longer attached to the main body of the ship. The two hulls spun through space, until they each exploded. In almost no time at all, nothing remained of the warship.

"Got him!" Chekov said, throwing a clenched fist into the air.

"Easy, mister, we're not out of this yet," Kirk told him. In mute testimony of that fact, the *Gr'oth* became visible on the viewer, still pursuing the *Enterprise*. But then blue bolts of energy suddenly erupted on the hull of the Klingon vessel.

"A piece of the station penetrated the *Gr'oth*'s hull," Haines said, and Kirk saw part of one spire jutting from beneath the main body of the ship. "I'm reading heavy casualties. They've lost most of their systems, including shields and weapons, and their life support is faltering."

"They're now drifting," Lieutenant Sulu said from the helm. On the viewscreen, the *Gr'oth* glided askew of its flight path. Clearly, the *Enterprise* and its crew had won the battle.

"Sulu, reverse course," Kirk said. "Close to within

transporter range." With no weapons and no shields, with life support failing, the crew of the *Gr'oth* had transformed from dangerous attackers into survivors who needed rescue. He leaned in over the intercom on the arm of his chair, the channel still open from a few moments ago. "Mister Kyle, have our guests escorted to quarters—" Just before the destruction of the Einstein station, its seventeen personnel had been beamed aboard. "—and then have security report to the cargo transporter. We may be taking on some prisoners."

"*Aye, sir,*" Kyle said.

"Kirk out." He pushed a button beside the intercom, closing the channel.

"Captain," Lieutenant Uhura said from the communications station, "we're being hailed."

Kirk felt both frustration and anger swelling within him. "Now they want to talk," he said. If the Klingons had been willing to do so before beginning their attack, then all of this—the destruction of the Starfleet vessels *Minerva* and *Clemson,* of the Einstein facility, and of the Klingon ships *Rikkon, Vintahg,* and *Goren,* along with the loss of hundreds of lives—could have been averted. "Put them on screen, Lieutenant," he said.

"Aye, sir," Uhura said.

On the main viewer, the image of the wounded *Gr'oth* disappeared, replaced by the interior of its bridge. Standing amid clouds of smoke colored green by their alert lighting, the Klingon commander glared forward. Kirk recognized him at once, not just from Starfleet security briefs, but from an encounter he'd had with him a couple of years ago aboard Deep

Space Station K-7. The executive officer of the *Gr'oth* back then, Korax now commanded the ship. He had dark brown hair and a goatee, and he wore the regulation black and gold uniform of the Klingon Imperial Fleet.

"Kirk," Korax said loudly. He smiled at the same time that his eyes seemed filled with hatred. *"You managed to conduct a battle without the help of the Organians."* The issue of the powerful incorporeal beings had concerned and confused Starfleet Command, Kirk knew. They had prevented a war between the Federation and the Klingons three years ago, essentially forcing a ceasefire upon both parties, but they had taken no action since then, even when conflicts such as this one had broken out. *"Could it be because the Organians don't approve of Starfleet attempting to build a new weapon to use against us?"*

Before her ship had been rammed and obliterated by the *Vintahg,* Captain Chelsea of the *U.S.S. Clemson* had warned Kirk that this had been the Klingons' claim, their justification for sending a quartet of warships here. The charge had no merit, but he also knew that the Klingons must have detected the waves of time displacement emanating from the nearby planet. Although Starfleet had not created the Guardian of Forever, nor intended to employ it as a weapon, Kirk could not dispute its potential use in such a manner. Still, he said, "There is no weapon, Korax."

"Then you won't mind me sending a landing party down to the planet to investigate for myself," the Klingon said.

"Not at all," Kirk told him, bluffing. He could afford the pretense. With most of the *Gr'oth*'s systems down, the heavy casualties it had sustained, and its life support on the verge of failure, the Klingon crew would be fortunate simply to escape the current circumstances with their lives.

Amazingly, Korax actually laughed. *"Funny,"* he said. *"The captains of the* Minerva *and the* Clemson *didn't seem quite so accommodating as you."*

Though he did not reveal the fact, just the mention of the two Starfleet vessels that had been lost to the Klingons enraged Kirk. To cover his fury, he stood from his command chair. "I'm an accommodating fellow," he said equably. "Let us transport your crew aboard the *Enterprise* before your life support fails."

Korax threw his head back and laughed loudly. *"You are an amusing fellow, Kirk,"* he said when he'd finished. *"I look forward to bringing your ship back to the Empire. A minor trophy, to be sure, but still a trophy."*

In Kirk's head, a red alert sounded. Along with what Korax had just said came the realization that, although the *Gr'oth* had lost weapons and shields and many other systems, its transporters might still be functioning. In that instant, aware that his own ship's shields remained down, Kirk knew that Korax meant to board the *Enterprise*. "Uhura!" he called. The lieutenant immediately cut communications with the *Gr'oth*, and the image of the enemy vessel floating through space returned to the main viewscreen. "Chekov, fire torpedoes!"

The ensign operated his controls, to no effect. "Captain, weapons are all offline."

Damn! "Clear the bridge!" Kirk ordered. Korax would send a boarding party here and to engineering first, he knew. He looked around and saw Haines rising from her position at the sciences station, Uhura from communications, and Lieutenant Leslie from the primary engineering console, but Sulu and Chekov still sat at their posts. "Now!" he yelled, and the two men finally moved. Kirk waited for the young ensign to pass him, then followed him up the steps to the outer section of the bridge.

By the time Kirk arrived at the turbolift, the entire bridge crew had entered before him. As he himself stepped inside the car, he saw Sulu's eyes widen, the lieutenant peering past him, back onto the bridge. Kirk guessed in that moment that the Klingons had begun to materialize behind him. He reached for the lift's activation wand, but Leslie already had his hand on it. "Deck two," the lieutenant said. Kirk expected a disruptor bolt to blast him in two at any moment, but then the doors squeaked closed behind him. As the turbolift started to descend, he realized that they'd actually made it.

And then an explosion rocked the lift, knocking it sideways. Kirk hurtled forward, raising his arms to protect not just himself, but his crewmates. His head struck the side of the lift, and then—

Everything went dark.

Kirk sat in an easy chair, a hardcover novel—the twenty-first-century classic *Renaissance and Blues*—

open on his lap. He'd read the same sentence half a dozen times and now decided to give up altogether. So many thoughts filled his head, though one image in particular kept returning to his mind.

After closing the book, Kirk reached forward and set it atop the bed, then rose and crossed the quarters that Commodore Stocker had assigned him here at Starbase 10. Kirk had been released from the station's infirmary only this morning, after spending sixteen days there in recovery. The explosion that had demolished the *Enterprise* bridge and killed the members of a Klingon boarding party had sent the turbolift plunging down its shaft until it had become wedged between decks. All six members of the bridge crew had survived, though Kirk had struck his head and fallen into a coma. During the three days he'd remained unconscious, Scotty and his engineering crew had repaired the ship enough to get it back to base.

When Kirk had finally left Starbase 10's infirmary this morning, Bones had accompanied him here, to these guest quarters. Later, Spock had arrived with Commodore Stocker to discuss with him all that had happened during and after the *Enterprise*'s battle with the Klingons. They hadn't stayed long, promising to return tomorrow after he'd gotten some rest. Spock had seemed oddly reticent to Kirk, but he simply ascribed that to all that his first officer and the rest of the crew had recently endured, perhaps an indication of post-traumatic stress. He imagined that even Vulcans—and particularly *half*-Vulcans—might not be immune to such disorders.

Kirk reached the computer terminal on the far side
of his quarters and sat down before it. Of all that Spock
and Stocker had revealed to him today, one thing continued to come back to him. He'd watched with them
the visual recording made by the security team aboard
the *Enterprise* shuttlecraft *Kepler,* and what it had
showed deeply disturbed him. He knew that he had no
real reason to view it again now, but he found that he
couldn't stop himself.

He worked the terminal console, providing the computer with his security clearance and a request for the
Kepler recording. After a moment, the display filled
with a frozen split-screen image. On the left, an aerial
view showed the Guardian of Forever, standing alone
on a vast, broken plain. The irregular, coppery ring
stood as he'd always seen it, a strange and inexplica-
ble alien object of great power and potential. Fractured
columns and other archeological artifacts littered the
ground around it, but since he and the crew of the *Enterprise* had discovered the place three years ago, the
landscape had changed, even if the Guardian had not.
When he had first gone there, mounds and walls of
rock had surrounded the time vortex, and in the distance, the ruins of a long-dead civilization had provided an eerie backdrop.

After the *Enterprise*'s initial visit to the world of the
Guardian, Starfleet had attempted to construct a research facility there. All such efforts, even those made
on the other side of the planet, had failed, wrecked by
violent seisms that had altered the landscape. Ruins
had been buried, the ground had cracked open in

places, rock formations had toppled. The Guardian itself had refused to confirm or deny any part in producing the earthquakes, but Starfleet had believed it responsible, unwilling to allow any construction on the planet's surface. As a result, the Einstein research station had been built in orbit.

On the right side of the computer display, the Klingon vessel *Gr'oth* hung frozen within the planet's atmosphere, the forward edges of its hull blazing red from the friction with the air. While Spock and Scotty and the rest of the crew had fought to fend off Klingon boarders in main engineering, and then had worked to repair the *Enterprise,* Korax had done this. Kirk raised his hand and touched a blinking green button on the computer panel. The recording began to play on the monitor.

Kirk watched as the Klingon battle cruiser dived toward the surface—toward the Guardian. Seconds passed, and the glowing sections of the *Gr'oth*'s hull grew hotter still, shifting from red to white. Finally, the D7 warship appeared on the left side of the monitor, its body obstructing the view of the Guardian as the ship raced toward the alien object.

The *Gr'oth* crashed directly into the Guardian of Forever. The split-screen ended, replaced by a single view. The display dimmed as a brilliant fireball burst from the point of impact. A huge mushroom-shaped cloud rose at great speed, reaching high into the sky.

Kirk touched another control, and the recording skipped ahead to its end. He halted the image there and beheld an enormous crater carved out of the ground where once the Guardian of Forever had stood. Kirk saw no signs of either the *Gr'oth* or the Guardian, but clearly both had been vaporized by the great heat of the blast. Nothing could have survived the explosion.

For a long time, Kirk sat and stared at the devastation. When he and his crew had discovered the Guardian, he had been awed by its power and abilities and enraptured by the amazing possibilities it offered. But after chasing McCoy through it and back into time, the vortex had become a symbol of profound pain for him, a reminder that the best part of his life had come and gone and would never return.

Now, as he gazed at the image of the ruined landscape, at the place from which the Guardian of Forever had delivered to him the love of his life and then stripped her away from him, he felt terrible anguish. Somehow, it was as though he had lost Edith all over again.

EIGHT

1930

In the encompassing darkness carried in with the deep of night, Kirk could have lain awake and fixated on the burden of his responsibilities, could have intentionally eluded sleep in order to lament the unthinkable possibility that Spock had delivered to him four days ago. He could have done those things, just as he had in nights past, but he didn't. Instead, he found the will to drift above his fatigue and his concerns, concentrating now on the warmth of Edith's bare form lying against his own, on the relaxed cadence of her breathing, on the now-musky scent of her flesh. In these perfect moments, he shut out the rest of the universe.

Just a few minutes ago, Edith had reached away from him to switch off the lamp on the nightstand. Then she'd rolled back over to him, and he'd enfolded her in his embrace. He held her now, his arms encircling her as though they'd been designed specifically for that purpose.

In the twenty-five days since he and Spock had arrived in Earth's past, Kirk had attempted to resist the feelings that had begun to develop within him from the first instant that Edith Keeler had walked into his life. It made no sense for him to fall in love with a woman with whom he could have no possible future. Whether or not her death would be required in order to preserve the timeline, as Spock had suggested might be the case, Kirk intended to right the flow of history, after which he and his first officer would return to their own time in the twenty-third century. At that point, Edith would necessarily be gone from his life forever.

But even though he had tried to keep a rein on his emotions, he'd failed completely. With a rapidity he almost couldn't believe, he had fallen for Edith, and day by day, even hour by hour, his love for her had grown deeper and deeper. He found her beauty, both within and without, singular. From virtually the moment he'd first seen Edith, descending the wooden stairs into the basement of the 21st Street Mission, he had been taken with her—with her dark hair and eyes, her delicate features and pearlescent skin, her quiet confidence and certain, almost regal bearing.

When the two of them had met, Kirk could not possibly have known how similarly they viewed life. But in a world beset by wars, by disease, by poverty and starvation, Edith somehow possessed the soul to gaze up at the stars and see the same things that Kirk did: a better tomorrow, an advanced humanity, hope, wonder. Edith perceived a positive future she did not simply long for, but one she worked to bring about as best she could. Where Kirk traveled the galaxy seeking out new knowledge, encountering new species, mediating disputes, keeping the peace, Edith fed the poor, with food for their bodies and a great vision for their minds.

You see the same things that I do, Edith had said

earlier, and he did. He always had, from far back in his life. When he'd been a boy, his family had sometimes taken walks at night out on the farm in Iowa. Sometimes his mother had gone, sometimes his brother, but most often it had been just Kirk and his father. They'd gazed together at the stars and seen the future—Jim's future, mankind's, the universe's.

"A penny for your thoughts," Edith said, her words quiet and soft in the darkness.

"I was just thinking about my father," he said, the ease with which he spoke surprising him. While his parents had greatly influenced his life, always fostering and supporting his dreams of space exploration, he almost never spoke of them to anybody. His mother's death from disease when Kirk had been just nine years old had left him heartbroken and traumatized, and the day just two years later, when he'd found his father's lifeless body out in the fields one summer afternoon, had hardened him. Afterward, he had more or less sealed off that part of his life, not only not speaking of his parents after that, but pushing away any recollections of them.

"What about your father?" Edith asked. Kirk could hear in her voice a thirst for information about himself, just as he too yearned to learn more about her. He also discovered that, with Edith by his side, he did not feel the need to turn away from his childhood memories, nor to avoid talking about his parents.

"I was thinking about the nights when I was a boy that I used to walk with my father out into fields and look up at the stars," he said.

"Were you raised on a farm?" Edith asked. He could feel her adjust the position of her head on his shoulder as she raised her face toward his in the darkened room.

"I was," Kirk said. "In Iowa." He knew that he shouldn't reveal too much about himself, but he could not see how Edith knowing the place of his birth would cause any disruption.

"In England, I grew up on a farm too," Edith said, her tone conveying her pleasure at this additional point of commonality between them. "After my mother died," she went on, quieter, "my father just couldn't maintain the land anymore, and we lost it." A few nights ago, Edith had spoken of the close relationship she'd had with her father, particularly after her mother had passed away. After years of living a difficult life, her father had at last chosen to make a new start for himself and for his daughter, and he'd believed that relocating to America would allow them the best chance to do that. That had been eight years ago, and he'd died only days after he and Edith had arrived in their new country.

"My father died when I was eleven," Kirk said. "I found him out in our north field, working the corn. It was a strong sun that day, and it turned out that he had a weak heart . . ." He thought to say more, but he'd never before said aloud the words he just had, and whatever would have come next caught in his throat. Tears welled in his eyes, and for just a second, he felt grateful that the lightless room concealed his weakness.

But he didn't feel weak, he realized. He felt . . . free. Free to reveal to Edith—to *share* with her—his deepest wounds, his greatest fears, his most desperate hopes and desires. He would be utterly vulnerable to her, and yet he found that he trusted her so completely that he had not the slightest doubt that she would never betray his faith in her. He knew that, for all her days, she would love and nurture and even protect him.

A tear spilled from his eye and down the side of his face. Kirk didn't know how she knew, but Edith reached up and gently traced one finger along his cheek. "It's all right, Jim," she said. "I understand."

He knew that she did understand—what he felt for his lost parents, what he saw when he peered up at the stars, what he wanted and worked to make happen for the human race. Edith understood that and more, much more. "I get through my days by not thinking about it," Kirk admitted, "but I miss my mom and dad."

"I know," Edith said, placing her hand lightly against the side of his face. "But they would want you to go on. They would be proud of you for doing so." The words could have sounded like a hopeful fantasy or even a sort of appeasement, but delivered by Edith, they rang true.

Kirk reached up and took Edith's hand in his own, squeezing it in a wordless display of the emotion he felt for her. She squeezed back, then pushed up from bed. Before he knew what she was doing, her lips brushed tenderly against his own.

Tonight, after he had walked her home from the mission, she had invited him here, into her one-room apartment. They had swept easily, naturally into each other's arms, their movements sure and effortless, like those of longtime dance partners. Their lovemaking had developed at its own pace, by turns languorous and slow, then fevered and full of energy. She could not have been more right for him, nor he for her.

In the darkness, Edith lowered herself back to his side, back into arms. She again rested her head on his shoulder. After a moment, she said, "Do you have any sisters or brothers?"

"I do," Kirk said. "I have an older brother, Sam. He and his wife have also given me three nephews."

"That's wonderful," Edith said, and Kirk perceived in the assessment the sense that she had no family of her own left to her.

"They're good boys," Kirk said, though Sam's two older sons had both reached their twenties. "I haven't seen my brother and his family in almost two years." He could hear the wistfulness in his own voice. It had been just before Kirk had taken command of the *Enterprise* that Sam and Aurelan had brought their family on a surprise visit to see him off on his first captaincy. He had been deeply touched by their gesture, and he realized now how much he missed them all—especially Sam. "I'd love for you to meet them," he said without thinking.

"I'd like that too," Edith said.

For a moment, Kirk cursed himself for his foolishness, but he could not maintain his anger. Even though he knew that Edith would never meet Sam, that she would never be more a part of his life than she was right now, his sentiment remained true: he *would* love for her to meet his brother. In fact, he wanted to share all of his life with her.

Edith raised herself up again, this time onto her elbows, her hands resting on Kirk's chest. "Where is your brother?" she asked. "What does he do?"

"He's a scientist," Kirk said with the exuberant pride of a younger brother. "He's—" *On Deneva,* Kirk thought, but he knew he could not say that. "—out of the country doing research right now," he finished, prevaricating but not actually lying. He didn't think that he *could* lie to Edith.

"Well, when he gets back," Edith said, "I'll have to ask him about you . . . perhaps about what you were like as a boy."

"Whatever he tells you, don't believe it," Kirk joked, despite the impossibility of such a meeting ever occurring. "They'll just be the musings of a man jealous of his younger brother."

"Oh, I see," Edith said. "And what reason does Sam have to be jealous of you?"

Kirk felt the smile on his lips fade as he stared up into the darkness where he knew Edith's face to be. "For one thing, because I have you." He knew that this relationship with Edith would end, that it *must* end, and yet in this isolated time with her, none of that mattered. "The entire universe should envy me because I have you in my life." Even though his time with her would end up measured merely in days, he still believed that.

"You are very sweet, Mister Kirk," Edith whispered.

Again, he felt her lips touch his. They kissed slowly, passionately.

When at last their lips parted, Kirk said, "I love you."

"And I love you," Edith responded.

Kirk's heart had never been so full, and even though he knew that it never would be again, right now, he didn't care. If he could freeze time, preserve this moment in amber, he would, but he ignored the fact that he couldn't. He threw himself wholly into this instant, opened himself up to experience every trace of emotion within him.

"Edith," he said, loving even the sound of her name. He pulled her down on top of him, and once more, they moved together in the darkness of her room. He wished the night would last forever.

NINE

(2271/2276)

*In the parkland outside Mojave, California, Jim Kirk
peered at the other version of himself and wondered
which one of them had gone mad. His wounded double had suggested a plan to prevent the converging
temporal loop by using the Guardian of Forever in the
year 2293, despite that the mysterious artifact had
been annihilated in 2270 when Korax had crashed his
battle cruiser into it. "Yes," Kirk said, agreeing with
his bloodied counterpart about the flaw in the plan.
"The Klingons."*

"I'm hoping it won't matter," said the other Kirk.

*"Hoping?" Kirk said, uncomfortable with the idea
of leaving anything to chance. But then his alter ego
explained why he believed that his plan would work,
despite—perhaps even because of—Korax's final destructive act. It would require an action, the success of
which could not be guaranteed, but Kirk also felt confident that it could be achieved. If not, then there would
be one other possibility for success, though it would be
arduous and risky. Of course, all of this posed a risk.*

*"So where do I begin?" he asked. "How do I leave
the nexus?"*

*"Here," the other Kirk said, and he held out his arm
as though ushering Kirk into a room.*

Kirk looked to where his counterpart motioned, and there he saw not the spires and edifices of Mojave, but a dim, open plain. Above, a sunless sky provided only the faint illumination of the stars. He peered about and saw only a flat, empty expanse stretching away in every direction. It took him a moment, but then he recognized their location: one of the artificial worlds of the Otevrel.

He gazed over at the other Kirk and noticed him bathed in the yellow glow of the old self-contained life support belts. Glancing down, he saw a similar radiance about his own body, one of the belts encircling his own waist. He knew that by the time the Enterprise had encountered the Otevrel, the life support belts had fallen out of use in Starfleet because of health concerns, but then he had already learned well that what had occurred in the real, physical universe often did not get reproduced precisely in the nexus.

"Why are we here?" he asked.

The other Kirk shrugged. "This seems to be the place from which you or I can leave the nexus," he said. "I'm sure it doesn't have to be this place, but this is what my mind conjured up when I first intended to depart."

Kirk nodded. That explanation made no more or less sense than anything else within this timeless, unreal domain. "So where should I begin?" he asked. "And when?"

"You remember the historical research done on the Guardian's world, the efforts made to identify the origin of the time vortex," the other Kirk said. Though he had offered a statement of fact rather than asking a question, his tone invited a response.

"Yes," he said. The scientists had discovered that, at least according to the record provided by the Guardian, the planet on which it had stood had existed, essentially without change, since almost the beginning of the universe. The Guardian's own genesis had remained unknown, though, since the vortex had never shown the period of time in which it had initially appeared on the planet.

"And you recall the first words the Guardian uttered when we discovered it," the other Kirk said.

"Yes," he said. " 'Since before your sun burned hot in space and before your race was born, I have awaited a question.' "

"That's where you're going," the other Kirk said. "That's when you're going."

"You're talking billions of years ago," Kirk said.

"Yes," the other Kirk said. "Otherwise you would contradict what the Guardian said, and thereby alter history."

Kirk nodded slowly. He understood. "How do I do it?" he asked.

"I think you just need to imagine when and where you want to go."

Kirk did. He envisioned the time vortex, thought as best he could about the age before Earth's sun had ignited in space. He turned to his left, away from his counterpart, and suddenly a gleaming white light began to shine before him, as though growing out of the nexus itself. The black sky, the white specks of the *stars, the steel gray of the Otevrel world, all blurred and paled. Kirk stepped forward, and the field of white enfolded him. For a subjectively immeasurable span of time, he could see nothing, could hear nothing, could sense nothing. Even the feel of his own body vanished, as though he existed only as thought. He wanted to run but had no legs, wanted to scream but had no voice—*

II

Under Twilight Brooding Dim

Onward led the road again
Through the sad uncolored plain
Under twilight brooding dim,
And along the utmost rim
Wall and rampart risen to sight
Cast a shadow not of night,
And beyond them seemed to glow
Bonfires lighted long ago.
And my dark conductor broke
Silence at my side and spoke,
Saying, "You conjecture well:
Yonder is the gate of hell."

—A. E. Housman,
"Hell Gate"

TEN

Before Sol Burned Hot in Space

Beneath the leaden sky, the land looked different than it would five billion years from now, but only marginally so. Several new—*Or old,* Kirk corrected himself—rock formations climbed from the rugged soil, while others he had once seen here had yet to take shape. This long ago, a number of fissures had not opened in the ground, though some looked to him as though they would remain essentially unaltered in the millennia to come. In the distance, where he and Spock and the rest of the *Enterprise* landing party had observed archeological ruins during their initial visit here, Kirk now saw nothing.

The Guardian of Forever appeared completely unchanged. The sepia-toned ring stood on edge a dozen or so meters ahead of Kirk, the irregularly flowing shape perhaps two and a half times his height and looking just as it had on the day he'd first set eyes on it. The scientists and historians who had studied the enigmatic artifact had reported its seemingly fixed nature even across eons, but Kirk had no idea how that could be possible. *Doesn't everything change with time?* he asked himself, and then he supposed that his question had its own answer embedded within it: time.

The Guardian clearly had a significant measure of control over time in a fundamental way, a control that could be readily witnessed, but that had yet to be explained.

Kirk remembered discovering the Guardian. From the moment that the mysterious entity had confirmed its nature as a gateway through time and space, Kirk's imagination had been sparked. He'd found the idea of stepping into the past and losing himself in another world tantalizing and compelling.

And then he had done just that, chasing McCoy into Earth's twentieth century. Kirk and Spock had restored the timeline that Bones had accidentally altered. After they had reset events to avoid a Nazi victory in World War II, the Guardian had returned the three of them to their own time. *It will be as though none of you had gone,* the Guardian had said of a successful attempt to repair the damage done to history, but that hadn't been the case. Time had indeed resumed its shape, but the experience had changed the rest of Kirk's life.

He hated this place. Coming here had led him to his one chance for true happiness, but then that chance had been stolen back from him in the cruelest way. Even when he'd next visited this nearly empty world, the wonder and potential of the Guardian had been eclipsed by the effortlessness with which its use could bring about unexpected and lethal changes to the universe. On the third and final occasion when Kirk had approached this planet, he hadn't made it to the surface, but had led the *Enterprise* crew into a deadly battle with the Klingons that had caused hundreds of deaths and very nearly his own.

Despite all of that, though, he had come here now seeking the Guardian's aid. Kirk wanted to use the time vortex for a positive, useful end while avoiding any repercussions, any modifications to the timeline. The best chance he had of accomplishing all of that would depend not only on his own abilities and actions, but on the will of the Guardian itself. The situation put Kirk in mind of tales belonging to the literary subgenre of protagonists attempting to forge a deal with the devil.

"Guardian," he said, pacing forward to stand directly in front of it. "Do you remember me?"

It offered no response. Kirk recalled that, during his preparations for his second visit to this place, he had read through the documentation of the researchers who'd worked here. The reports had stated that the Guardian did not reply to every question asked of it, and also that it sometimes spoke without being addressed in any way. More than that, the researchers had noted, just as Spock had, that much of what it said came "couched in riddles."

"Guardian," Kirk said again. "Are you machine or being?" This had been one of the first questions he'd asked when he and the *Enterprise* landing party had initially encountered the Guardian. It had responded by claiming to be both machine and being, and neither machine nor being.

Now, though, it remained silent. Kirk decided to attempt to engage it by way of a different tack, at the same time addressing an important issue. "Guardian, do you know when your existence will end?"

"I am my own beginning, my own ending," it said, its deep voice booming and full even in the open space. Synchronized with its words, different portions of the ring glowed from within.

"No, you are not," Kirk asserted, though he made an effort to keep any hint of defiance or hostility from his tone. "You are not your own ending. I know this because, in the future, I witnessed your destruction." He waited for a reply. When none came, he opted to continue. "I saw a starship plunge from space and through the atmosphere of this—"

"I am the Guardian of Forever," the vortex proclaimed. *"I am the union and the intersection of all moments and all places. I am what was and what will be. Through me is eternity kept."*

"How can you possess eternity when you are not yourself eternal?" Kirk asked. "Five billion years from now, a starship commander will intentionally crash his vessel on this world, on this very spot. A powerful detonation will result, creating a massive crater and vaporizing both the ship and you."

Again, Kirk waited. He heard the howl of the wind, though about him, the air remained still. Through the center of the Guardian, in the distance, he saw dirt kicking up and blowing across the land. Finally, he went on. "I tell you this for your own sake," he said. "I tell you this so that you will be able to avoid the end that I have seen. If you do not listen to me, if you do nothing, you will cease to exist."

"Time bends," the Guardian said cryptically. *"The end is but the beginning."*

"What does that mean?" Kirk asked, but he knew better than to expect a straightforward answer—or any answer at all. When indeed the Guardian said nothing, Kirk turned and paced away from it. His boots scraped noisily along the hard terrain, and now he felt the chill movement of the air. It struck him that he had no protective garments, no clothing whatsoever beyond that which he wore right now. He had no shelter in this desolate place, no food, no water. In order to achieve his goals, he would therefore have only so much time—

But of course he had access to time. He glanced back over his shoulder at the Guardian. If Kirk needed anything at all, it waited for him just on the other side of the vortex. He had only to call up a time and place, and then leap to it.

Virtually any *time and place,* Kirk thought. The researchers had found few limitations on what they could observe of the past beyond the time surrounding the actual origin of the Guardian. *That means that it must be possible to access the moments when the* Gr'oth *had plummeted to the surface of this world.* Persuading the Guardian of the reality of that event might or might not be critical in securing its compliance, but back in the nexus, the other Kirk had believed attempting to do so to be the right choice. Kirk himself had agreed. *And maybe the Guardian can convince itself of its own demise,* he thought.

Kirk turned and headed back to the Guardian. When

he reached it, he said, "I wish to see tomorrow." He knew that in the accounts that he had read of the research done at the Guardian, no mention had ever been made of the vortex displaying future events or allowing anybody to travel forward through time. He and the other Kirk had been aware that it might not be possible to find a direct route through the Guardian to 2293 or 2371—or in this case, to 2270, the year when the *Gr'oth* had slammed into the planet. He chose to see if being more specific in his request would make a difference.

"Guardian," he said, "I wish to see the thirteenth day of June in the Earth year twenty-two seventy." Once again, Kirk received no response, and so he decided to try an indirect path to the event. "I wish to see yesterday."

Still nothing.

For an instant, panic gripped Kirk. He had expected that the Guardian might be either unwilling or unable to present the future to him, but he had no reason to think that it would not replay the past. It had done so before. In his previous trips here, it had shown him the history of humanity on Earth, the dawn of Orion civilization, and a recent day on the planet Vulcan.

Now, though, the vortex stood empty.

"'Since before your sun burned hot in space,'" Kirk said to himself, quoting the Guardian. "'Since before your race was born.'" When Kirk had exited the nexus, he had come five billion years into the past—or at least he had wanted to do so. He assumed for the moment that he had, despite having no real means of confirming that fact. But if he had arrived here that long ago, then Earth's sun had yet to form in the cold reaches of space, and the evolution of humanity lay even further ahead in the future than that. Kirk had asked to see yesterday, but for human beings, right now, at this moment, *today* did not exist. *With no today, how can there be a yesterday?* Kirk thought. *Have I come too far into the past to make use of the Guardian?* He wondered too if he had inadvertently condemned himself to living his final days on this barren world, while at the same time being unable to do anything to prevent the destruction caused by the converging temporal loop.

But today exists for me, Kirk told himself. *And so does yesterday.* Once more, he would shift from the general to the specific. "Guardian, I wish to see *my* yesterday."

"*Behold,*" it said. "*A gateway to your own past, if you wish.*"

A white mist spilled down from the top of the wide, roughly circular opening through the center of the Guardian's ring. Then images began to form: Kirk's mother giving birth, his brother Sam holding him as an infant, Kirk sleeping in a crib. This had been one of the ways in which the historians had learned to refine their requests of the Guardian. If it showed a thousand images of a ten-thousand-year epoch, it would present just ten scenes per century, making it difficult to view or navigate to particular points in time with much precision. Observing the course of a single life, though, because of its relative brevity, allowed for

greater granularity: a thousand images displayed of
Kirk's sixty-year life would produce one scene for
every three weeks he'd lived. The numbers worked out
differently than that, and the Guardian didn't always
show moments spaced evenly apart, but the principle
remained that you could see far more detail of a single life through the vortex than you could of a longer
period.

Kirk continued to watch as his existence unfolded
before him. He smiled when he saw himself tottering
across the family living room and into Sam's waiting
arms, perhaps taking his first steps, but he also felt a
deep melancholy as well; Sam had been gone now for
almost half of Kirk's life. Similar emotions played
through his mind as his mother and father appeared, as
his grandfather did, his uncle, all of them lost for so
long at this point.

He closed his eyes when the colony on Tarsus IV
materialized. At the age of thirteen, Kirk had been living there when the food supply had been all but wiped
out by an exotic fungus. Governor Kodos had seized
full power and declared martial law, then executed four
thousand colonists in a horribly misguided and ultimately unnecessary attempt to save the other four
thousand.

Kirk watched with interest, though, as he sped
through Starfleet Academy. He saw himself as a young
officer aboard the *Republic,* and then later, aboard the
Farragut. Aboard the *Enterprise,* he saw Spock and
Bones and Scotty.

And then the Guardian of Forever appeared. And then New York City in 1930. And then Edith.

Kirk turned away. He could not bear to see her. It occurred to him briefly that he could simply step through the time vortex and rejoin his beloved, save her from the traffic accident that had taken her from him—

But he had already made the decision once to sacrifice his own desires to preserve history. How could he in good conscience abandon that now? He had come here with a greater purpose than his own happiness, and he would see that effort through.

When Kirk peered back at the Guardian, he saw himself in gangster clothing on Sigma Iotia II. He fought the Kelvans as they commandeered the *Enterprise,* ferried the *Dohlman* of Elas to her arranged marriage on Troyius. He spoke with High Priestess Natira on Yonada, argued with the insane Captain Garth on Elba II, observed a glommer devouring a tribble.

As the period of the Klingon attack on the Einstein station approached, Kirk said, "Guardian, do you perceive yourself with the times that these images present?"

"I see all," it said, a pronouncement startling for its lack of ambiguity.

Kirk thought for a moment how best to phrase what he would say next. "Then you will see the time when you will cease to exist," he said. "I propose that you can avoid such an end by moving yourself through time."

"All that will be, has already been," the Guardian said inscrutably. *"All that has been, will be."*

"Does that mean that you have already escaped the destruction caused by the starship?" Kirk asked. He did not anticipate a direct answer, but he wanted as much as possible to try to divine the Guardian's intent, as well as any movement it might have made through time. When it did not reply to his question, he said, "In my lifetime, a temporal phenomenon has devastated a section of the galaxy between the years twenty-two ninety-three and twenty-three seventy-one, with a corresponding loss of life. I wish to prevent that from occurring."

Within the ring of the Guardian, Kirk saw himself lying in a coma in the *Enterprise*'s sickbay, and then unconscious atop a diagnostic pallet in Starbase 10's infirmary. It struck him that those times in his life had come *after* the *Gr'oth* had rammed into the Guardian of Forever. *Or had it?* Kirk thought. The recordings of the incident had shown the Klingon vessel as it had streaked through the atmosphere, and they had shown its intended target. But when the *Gr'oth* had gotten close to the planet's surface, its mass had obscured the view of the Guardian. Could it be that the time vortex had during those last moments taken itself away, traveling through time to a place and time of safety? *If the Guardian had been destroyed,* Kirk asked himself, *could it possibly be showing me events in my life that had taken place after that?* Though he could not be sure, he didn't think so.

As his life continued to unfurl within the Guardian, he said, "I will unintentionally cause the shock wave that will destroy a portion of the galaxy, and I need your help to keep that from happening." When the Guardian did not respond, Kirk explained precisely how and why the converging temporal loop had developed, then detailed his plan to stop it from occurring.

"Do you understand?" he asked when he had finished.

No reply.

"Will you help me?" he tried.

Nothing.

"Will you save yourself from the starship in the way that I have requested?"

"I am my own beginning, my own ending," repeated the Guardian. *"Through me is eternity kept."*

Kirk could not determine whether that answered his question, but he also realized that he would likely receive no reply more explicit than that, no matter what he asked. Strictly speaking, other than the Guardian allowing him to travel back into his own life right now, its participation would not be crucial to Kirk's efforts to avert the temporal loop. Being able to move through time via the vortex a second time would make it far easier to carry out his plan, but if necessary, he could succeed without that capability.

In the mists of the Guardian, moments from the *Enterprise*'s seven-and-a-half-year expedition to and from the Aquarius Formation flickered past. After that, he saw himself riding a horse on his uncle's farm in Idaho,

and he saw Antonia. He saw Khan Noonien Singh and
Carol Marcus. He saw his son, David.

While the images continued to fade into and out of
view, Kirk made additional attempts to converse with
the Guardian. He tried to learn if it would indeed protect itself from Korax's suicidal plunge to the planet,
and if it would be available to Kirk in his attempt to
thwart the emergence of the shock wave. The Guardian
spoke little and revealed less.

In the end, recognizing that he would learn no more
than he already had, Kirk decided to proceed. Either
the Guardian would survive beyond 2270 or it would
not, either it would assist him when the time came or
it would not. No matter, Kirk would do whatever he
could to prevent the converging temporal loop.

He waited quietly as the pictures within the vortex
moved on, showing the days aboard his last command,
the *Enterprise*-A. Eventually, he saw himself in retirement once more, this time not sequestering himself away in the hills of Idaho, but traveling the globe
and the galaxy: rappelling the Crystalline Trench,
climbing Mount Revek, diving the Alandros Caves,
rafting the lava flows of the Valtarik volcano, and
more. As he reflected on the feats of derring-do that
he'd undertaken during his second retirement, he realized how much he had been motivated to engage in
such dangerous activities by the general sadness that
had settled over his life.

At last, the images within the vortex reached the
days just before he had boarded the *Enterprise*-B for
its maiden voyage. He quickly reiterated his requests

of the Guardian, then took a step back with one foot, preparing himself to move quickly. When he saw himself walking along the streets of San Francisco, he knew that the moment had come.

Kirk sprang forward and leaped through the Guardian of Forever, back into his own past.

ELEVEN

A cool breeze blew in from the bay and across the Presidio, hardly unusual weather for San Francisco late on a summer afternoon. As Jim Kirk walked alongside the facilities building on the Starfleet Headquarters campus, he glanced north, past the international-orange towers of the Golden Gate Bridge to the Marin Headlands. There, he saw fog already beginning to roll in from the Pacific. It would doubtless be a cold, damp night.

At the intersection with Robert April Way, Kirk turned onto the wide pedestrian thoroughfare, which led up to the main administration building in the center of the grounds. Hugging the wall a little too tightly, he nearly tripped over a low bench situated against the wall. He quickly jogged to his right and skirted both it and a potted bush beside it.

Several people strode along the gray paving stones and amid the scattered greenery, most of them in groups of two or three, and so far as Kirk could see, all of the them in uniform. Dressed himself in civilian attire— brown slacks and a jade-colored shirt—he felt out of place. Although he had spent more than half his life—

Kirk heard a scuffling noise behind him and he looked around in that direction. Back past the bench

he had almost fallen over, he saw disappearing behind
the facilities building a black pant leg, its thin red
stripe distinguishing it as part of a Starfleet uniform.
Kirk turned around and continued on his way.

Although he'd officially retired from Starfleet only
earlier in the year, it already seemed strange to be back
here. He still lived close by, in Russian Hill Tower, and
he could even see the Presidio campus from the windows of this apartment. But merely seeing this place
did not equate with actually being here.

Twice, Kirk had declined this invitation. Fleet Captain Strnod had left messages asking to meet with
him, both times when Kirk had been off world. Once,
he'd been cliff diving into the garnet waters of the
Canopus Planet, and the other time, employing artificial wings to fly in the low-gravity environment of
Izar's Shroud. On each occasion, after the message
had been forwarded to him, he'd replied with the same
simple rejection: "Whatever it is, no thanks. I'm retired." He hadn't even wanted to know why Starfleet
had asked to see him. If their interest had related to
the assassination of Klingon Chancellor Gorkon and
the attempt on the life of Federation President Ra-
ghoratreii, if the admiralty had perhaps needed him to
provide additional testimony about his role in un-
masking the conspiracy, they would have made him
aware of that. Since Strnod hadn't specified the reason for calling him in for a meeting, though, Kirk had
assumed that they'd merely wanted to try to coax him
back into the fold.

He would never allow that to happen.

As he followed April Way around a curve that would bring the walkway across the front of the administration building, Kirk thought about the reasons he'd decided to leave Starfleet. In some ways, it had begun with the *Enterprise*-A, the ship he had commanded for eight years, and the namesake of which he had commanded for a dozen more. When Starfleet had decided to decommission the vessel after its decades of service—the ship had first seen duty as the *Yorktown* prior to its rechristening, when Kirk had been posted as its captain—the time had seemed right to step away. Many of the senior command crew with whom he had for so long served had aspirations beyond starship duty. Spock had initially returned to training cadets, but then he'd accepted an appointment as a full-fledged ambassador. McCoy had gone back to medical research, Uhura had taken a position with Starfleet Intelligence, and Scotty had retired. Kirk certainly could have assumed the captaincy of another ship, but he'd found little desire to command a vessel other than the *Enterprise,* and even less to do so without his friends by his side.

In addition to all of that, the space service in his estimation had become overly political in recent years. With so many interstellar tensions—with the Klingons, the Romulans, the Tholians, and others—missions of exploration had frequently given way to missions of diplomacy. Kirk understood and agreed with the efforts to maintain peace throughout the quadrant, but when he'd peered up at the stars as a boy, it had not been with the dream that he would one day mediate.

Kirk had also come to realize that he would not find what he needed out in space. He had found her once. He would not find her again.

Nearing the ten-story administration building, Kirk peered at the huge version of the Starfleet insignia adorning its façade. Years ago, when each starship had carried its own unique emblem, the asymmetrical arrowhead had belonged to the *Enterprise*. Later, when the policy of assigning distinct insignia had been discarded, Kirk had been proud that the distinguished record of his vessel had motivated Starfleet Command to adopt its symbol servicewide. Even now, seeing it so prominently displayed at headquarters prompted in him a glimmer of satisfaction.

When he reached the building, Kirk walked into its sprawling atrium. Beneath the transparent canopy that arced inward and upward from the doors all the way up to the top of the structure, he headed for the large circular desk located at the center of the space, to where a sign written in Federation Standard read VISITORS. Beyond the desk stood several banks of turbolifts. Kirk knew that automated sensors scanned every individual who entered the building, and that those identified as active Starfleet personnel could move freely about. Those not so identified and who did not check in with security would find themselves unable to leave the atrium; turbolifts containing unauthorized individuals would not function.

As Kirk approached the desk, a young security officer looked up at him. "Captain Kirk," he said, tapping at the controls of a console. "You can go right up to the tenth floor, office ten-thirteen," he said. "Admiral Sinclair-Alexander is expecting you." Kirk couldn't tell whether the officer had recognized him or the sensors had revealed his identity.

He thanked the security officer, who informed him that he could use either of the central turbolifts. Kirk hadn't needed to be told that; when he'd served as Starfleet's chief of operations, he'd occupied an office on the tenth floor himself. He headed past the desk and over to one of the lifts.

As the car started upward, Kirk wondered if he'd made the right choice in coming here. After Fleet Captain Strnod had tried and failed to persuade him to attend a meeting here at Starfleet Headquarters, Margaret Alexander—*Sinclair-Alexander now,* he reminded himself—had added her voice to the request. Kirk had known Madge Alexander for many years now, ever since she had served for a year aboard his first command. A lieutenant at the time, she had performed so well that she'd earned a field promotion during her time aboard the *Enterprise,* at the end of which she had transferred to the *Firenze* to serve as its second officer. Her rapid ascent through the ranks had continued when she'd been made a full commander and assigned to the *Freedom* as its exec. Later, she had served as captain of the *Freedom* through to its decommissioning, and then she'd taken command of the *Saratoga.* From there, she had eventually moved into Starfleet Command. When she had followed up Strnod's invitations to a meeting at Starfleet with one of her own, she'd also mentioned that she would consider it a personal favor. With the request phrased in such terms, he had been unable to refuse.

The turbolift arrived at the tenth floor, and Kirk stepped out into a reception area. Another young officer immediately greeted him. "Captain Kirk," she said, "I'm Ensign Teagarden, Admiral Sinclair-Alexander's assistant. Let me take you back there." She gestured vaguely off to her right.

"Thank you," Kirk said, and he followed Teagarden through several corridors, past his own former office. Finally, she led him through an anteroom—no doubt the ensign's own workspace—and into a large, comfortably appointed room. A sofa stood against the wall to the left, and a small conference table to the right. Artwork—mostly wooden carvings and masks, but also two paintings—hung on the walls and reflected the influences of Sinclair-Alexander's Jamaican birthplace. Across the room, before a row of tall windows, the admiral sat at a desk of blond wood.

"Jim," she said as she looked up from a data slate. She rose and came out from behind her desk to greet him, both hands extended. As the ensign left, Kirk moved to the center of the office, where he took Sinclair-Alexander's hands in his own, offering a warm squeeze.

"Madge," he said. "You're looking well." Tall and dignified, Sinclair-Alexander had beautiful coffee-colored skin, high cheekbones, dark eyes, and black shoulder-length hair. Though just a few years younger than Kirk, she had something of a timeless appearance that made it difficult to estimate her age simply by looking at her.

"Thank you so much for coming in," she said. Her voice carried the hint of a Caribbean accent. "Can I get you anything? A little Saurian brandy perhaps?"

"Is your plan to ply me with liquor before you tell me why you've called me here?" Kirk said with a smile.

"Ah, you're on to me," she said. "Here, let's sit." She let go of his hands and motioned toward the sofa. They sat down, and she asked again if he wanted anything to drink. When he declined, she said, "So how is life outside of Starfleet? Something I need to try for myself?"

"Oh, I don't know," Kirk said. "You seem to be doing pretty well right where you are. In fact, I understand that congratulations are in order, Admiral *Sinclair*-Alexander."

She smiled widely, exuding a radiance that bespoke her happiness. "We got married last year," she said. "You'll have to come over for dinner one night. Cynthia's a wonderful cook."

"So you're spoiled then?" Kirk joked.

"Completely," Sinclair-Alexander said. "No more food synthesizers for this old girl."

"That's reason enough to give up a starship command," Kirk said with a chuckle.

"If I'd have still been on the *Saratoga* when Cynthia and I met," Sinclair-Alexander said, "you can bet I would've jumped ship."

The notion of abandoning a captaincy for the right

person dredged up an all-too-familiar sadness within Kirk. *If only I'd been able to,* he thought, but he worked to keep the smile on his face. "Congratulations," he told Sinclair-Alexander. "I'm happy for you, Madge."

"Thank you, Jim," she said. "So how *are* you enjoying your retirement? No regrets?"

"Oh, plenty of regrets," Kirk said with a laugh. "Just none of them I can do anything about now." When Sinclair-Alexander peered at him just a bit askance, as though she had detected a seriousness in his jest, he quickly continued. "Actually, I'm enjoying retirement. I've been able to do a lot of things I never had time for."

"Like what?" Sinclair-Alexander asked.

Kirk shrugged. "I've caught up on my reading. . . . Done some horseback riding. . . . I dove the Alandros Caves. . . . I climbed—"

"The Alandros Caves?" Sinclair-Alexander asked, her eyes widening. "That's a little more demanding than riding horses or reading."

"And something Starfleet Command typically frowns on its captains doing on shore leave," he said. "Which is why I'm finally getting to do it now."

Sinclair-Alexander shook her head, on her face an expression that seemed to mix disbelief with appreciation. "Well, you'll have to tell me about that and all your other adventures when you come to dinner," she said. "Unfortunately, I've got a meeting in a few minutes, so I need to talk to you about the reason I asked you here."

He still fully expected the admiral to suggest that he return to Starfleet. "I've been afraid to ask," Kirk said.

"Which is why you twice turned down Captain Strnod's invitation to meet," Sinclair-Alexander said. "I appreciate that you agreed to come when it was me who asked."

"How could I refuse?" Kirk said with a lightness he did not entirely feel. "So what is it?"

"Jim, we're launching a new *Excelsior*-class vessel next week, with a new captain and a young crew," she said. "We'll be sending it out on a mission of deep-space exploration, and we're calling it the *Enterprise*."

Kirk felt a moment's indignation at the prospect before a sense of pride rose within him. "I'm glad that the name's being perpetuated."

"I thought you might be," Sinclair-Alexander said. "Because of the name, it's been suggested that perhaps you would be willing to don your uniform one last time and be a guest of honor at the launch. You could christen the ship, perhaps even board it for a quick jaunt around the solar system."

"Madge," Kirk said. Though she hadn't entreated him to return to the space service, he still felt uncomfortable with the idea of becoming involved again even on the level she had suggested.

"I know, I know," Sinclair-Alexander said, holding her hands up in front of her as though surrendering to his reluctance. "If it were up to me, Jim, I wouldn't even be asking. But you know as well as I do that Starfleet's image suffered a great deal when some of our own conspired to kill Chancellor Gorkon and Pres-

ident Ra-ghoratreii, to incite hostilities between us and
the Klingons." She shook her head as though in disbelief. Kirk understood. Much as he'd fostered an irrational hatred of the Klingons after the death of his
son, even he hadn't acted to foment war with the Empire. "It's believed that Starfleet could really use the
positive publicity it would bring to have you attend the
launch of this new *Enterprise*. With your record,
you're well known not only here on Earth, but throughout the Federation."

"That's another reason I left Starfleet," Kirk said.
"Peace and quiet and anonymity."

"I know this is an imposition," Sinclair-Alexander
said. "But I'm getting a lot of pressure to get you to
sign on for this." Kirk wondered who could possibly
be applying that pressure. It didn't sound like something Commander in Chief Smillie would do, and few
other admirals would have the power to bully Sinclair-
Alexander. "Frankly, I could handle the pressure," she
went on, "but for one thing: I think they're right. I
think this really would help the public's view of
Starfleet right now."

"I don't know," Kirk said. He felt a natural inclina-
tion to acquiesce for Sinclair-Alexander, but he really
didn't want to do what she'd asked of him.

"If it helps," she said, "I've already recruited two of
your old crewmates to come along: Captain Scott and
Commander Chekov."

"You got Scotty to agree to attend?" Kirk said, surprised. "I thought he'd headed for the Norpin Colony.
Is he coming all the way back to Earth?"

"No. He's booked passage to Norpin, but he hasn't departed yet," Sinclair-Alexander said. "He's consented to doing this first."

Now Kirk shook his head. "I can't believe neither one of them told me about this." He hadn't seen Scotty or Chekov in months, but they still could've contacted him to let him know.

"Don't blame them for that," Sinclair-Alexander said. "I swore them both to secrecy. Actually, in Commander Chekov's case, since he's still in Starfleet, I simply ordered him not to say anything. As for Mister Scott, I suggested that if he mentioned anything to you, then I might have to point the right authorities in the direction of his new boat, just to make sure that nobody had effected any illegal modifications to the engine."

"Spoken like somebody who's dealt with chief engineers for most of her career," Kirk noted.

"The ceremony and the launch are next Thursday," Sinclair-Alexander said. "We would activate you and Mister Scott for the day, transport you from here up to dry dock, and then somebody would hand you a bottle of Dom Pérignon."

Kirk looked at her, searching for a graceful way to turn down the admiral. He couldn't find one. "Just a quick trip around the system?" he said.

"And perhaps a tour of the ship," she said.

To his dismay, Kirk actually thought that he would enjoy that. "All right," he said.

"Thank you, Jim," Sinclair-Alexander said. "I appreciate it and so does all of Starfleet Command."

Kirk stood up, and the admiral then did so as well. "Make sure they all know that this is a singular occasion," he said. "The last thing I want to do is become the public face of Starfleet."

"One time," Sinclair-Alexander confirmed. "I completely understand. I'll have my assistant send an itinerary early next week."

"All right," Kirk said. "I'm only doing this because I want that dinner."

"And you'll get it," Sinclair-Alexander said with a smile. "I'll contact you after the launch and we'll set something up."

"Absolutely," Kirk said, but then he realized something. "You're not going to be at the ceremony?" he asked.

"Me?" Sinclair-Alexander said with a smile. "No, I've got more important things to do."

"That's why they made you an admiral," Kirk said with a laugh.

"I guess so," Sinclair-Alexander said. "I'll have people there to guide you through the ceremony, but you, Captain Scott, and Commander Chekov will be the stars of the show."

Kirk raised his hands, and the admiral took them. "That dinner had better be good," he said. He gave her hands a squeeze again, then headed for the door. On his way back down to the atrium, he remembered that he had scheduled an appointment for next Wednesday to go orbital skydiving. He would be propelled from a platform in orbit somewhere over the Arabian Peninsula and alight in the middle of North America.

With any luck at all, Kirk thought wryly, *I won't survive 'til Thursday.*

Kirk's left foot landed softly on the pavement, as though he'd just effortlessly jumped a stream out on his property in Idaho rather than leaping across hundreds of trillions of kilometers and five billion years of history. Despite having previously experienced the superficially simple transition, he still marveled at a journey that seemed as though it should've been impossible. As on the other occasions he had traveled through the Guardian of Forever, he felt no disorientation from the actual passage through space and time, though it did seem strange to bound from the barren surface of the Guardian's world to the modern civilization on Earth.

Finding himself in daylight, Kirk quickly looked about, surveying his surroundings. He stood on a wide pedestrian walkway, along which he saw several individuals in Starfleet uniforms, though none of them appeared to have taken any notice of his unusual arrival. Although he still wore his own uniform, sans jacket, he thought that he should probably—

Kirk saw himself. Clad in brown slacks and a jade-colored shirt, the Jim Kirk from this time period strolled away from him along the gray paving stones. Beyond him, in the distance, stood the main administration building on the San Francisco campus of Starfleet Headquarters.

At once, Kirk knew that he needed to avoid being seen by the other, earlier version of himself, that to do otherwise would be to risk altering the timeline. He turned quickly away from his counterpart and nearly tripped over a low bench sitting against the wall of a building. He scuffled for a second, but then righted himself and fled around the corner.

Kirk ran for only a few paces, then slowed to a walk, wanting to avoid drawing any attention to himself. He didn't need somebody happening to notice two Jim Kirks on the grounds of Starfleet Headquarters. Keeping his head down, he made his way from the campus and onto the streets of San Francisco proper.

As he strode along, Kirk determined the day on which he had arrived. Although he had by one measure spent seventy-eight years within the nexus, no time had seemed to pass for him during that period, at least subjectively. Consequently, he remembered well the last week prior to his being lost aboard the *Enterprise*-B. During those days, he had returned to Starfleet's Presidio campus twice: on the day he'd met with Admiral Margaret Sinclair-Alexander, when she'd recruited him for the *Enterprise*-B launch ceremony, and then on the day of the actual launch. *If today is when the* Enterprise *encounters the energy ribbon,* he thought, *then I'm too late.* But then he realized that his alter ego had been wearing civilian clothes and not a uniform, indicating that he'd been on his way merely to meet with the admiral.

Friday, Kirk thought. He'd gone to see Madge on a Friday, and the launch of the *Enterprise*-B had taken place the following Thursday. There would be five full days before then. *Enough time to figure out the pre-*

cise logistics of what I need to do and how to do it.

Walking along Lombard Street, Kirk felt conspicuous in his uniform. With Starfleet headquartered here in San Francisco, the sight of an officer dressed in official attire could hardly be considered out of the ordinary, but he still wished to invite as little scrutiny as possible. To that end, he casually unbuttoned his vest and removed it, leaving him in his black pants and long-sleeved white pullover.

Knowing that it would be a few minutes before his counterpart reached the tenth floor of the administration building and met with Admiral Sinclair-Alexander, Kirk headed for his apartment on Russian Hill. He would not stay long, just enough time to retrieve a couple of things he would be able to use over the next few days. When one of the historic cable cars wheeled past him in the street, he climbed aboard, hastening his journey.

Back at his apartment, Kirk's hand and retina prints allowed him access. He entered and quickly moved through the small foyer and the living room, then into the den. He spared only a moment's glance through the floor-to-ceiling windows that peered out on San Francisco Bay. Off to the left, toward the west, Kirk saw the great stanchions of the Golden Gate Bridge, their late-afternoon shadows falling onto the water.

Along the inner wall, Kirk activated the computer terminal. Calling up the personal calendar of his double, he confirmed today's date, then verified the details of next week's daytrip, all just as he remembered it. On Wednesday, the day before the *Enterprise*-B launch—

which had yet to be listed in the schedule—the Kirk of this time planned to leave early for Wichita, Kansas, where he would perform a survey of his landing zone. He would then travel from there to Tunis, Tunisia, where he would commence preparations for his orbital skydive. When ready, he would transport up to a platform in orbit, which would at the proper time be over the Arabian Peninsula, and from which he would be sent hurtling down through the atmosphere.

Kirk recalled the experience, which had been exhilarating and more than a little daunting. The only detail that would change between now and then, he knew, would be that his counterpart would invite Scotty and Chekov to meet him at the landing zone, which they would scout together the morning of the jump. Later that evening, after he'd landed, the three old friends would have dinner in nearby Wichita. *That'll be the time to act,* he told himself. With the Kirk of this time away for most of the day, Kirk himself could essentially assume his identity in order to accomplish what he needed to prior to the *Enterprise*-B launch and its deadly encounter with the energy ribbon.

After shutting down the terminal, he went into the bedroom and pulled out two changes of clothing, selecting articles at the bottom of the dresser drawers and hanging at the far side of the closet in the hopes that they would not be missed. He quickly changed into a pair of blue jeans and a light gray shirt. From the back of the closet, he picked out a small carryall that he knew the other version of himself would not be using that week, and he loaded his jacketless uniform and the other changes of clothes into it. He knew that he would need a complete Starfleet uniform on Wednesday, but rather than taking one of the three jackets from the closet right now, he decided to return here next week to get it.

Standing in the bedroom doorway, Kirk gazed around, wanting to ensure that he'd left everything the way he'd found it, save for the few items he would take with him. He then returned to the den to confirm that he'd deactivated the computer terminal. Finally, he left the apartment and rode a turbolift back down to the lobby.

Out on the street, he headed for the nearest public transporter. Until next Wednesday, he would need to hide himself away. Fortunately, he knew just the place to do that.

TWELVE

The old place didn't have a retina scanner, but Kirk's handprint opened the front door. He stepped into the living room, the air within stale and close. He had a caretaker, Joe Semple, who came out from Lost River a couple of times a year to open up the house and check for any problems that the weather or simple age might have caused, but Joe probably hadn't been out here since the spring.

By the time Kirk had arrived here, dusk had fallen on the Idaho hills. In the fading light of the day, he reached to the wall inside the door and tapped the control pad there. The overhead panels came on, revealing a roomful of Halloween ghosts: the sofa, the easy chairs, the end tables, all mere shapes beneath the white sheets that covered them. The mantel above the fireplace sat bare, as did the shelves he'd built on either side of it, as did the walls themselves. Where once the sentimental trinkets of his life—and later, of Antonia's—had enlivened this place, now only emptiness remained.

How appropriate, Kirk thought, struck by the lonely path his life had taken. *Why did I leave the nexus? I could've fixed this. I could've fixed all of it.*

But of course, he couldn't have, not really. The

nexus had been filled with joys, but imagined joys. What he had to do now, he had to do in the real universe.

Kirk closed the door behind him, then pulled the strap of the carryall from his shoulder and dropped the bag onto the floor. It landed with a soft thump, and he thought that he might just want to follow it down. Fatigue had washed over him, and he realized that he had no idea when last he'd slept.

Kirk decided to walk through the rest of the house. He ducked his head into the office he'd once set up off the living room, and which Antonia had then made her own once she'd moved in. Everything with which she had filled the room had gone now, leaving most of the space empty. Only the com/comm unit he'd had installed there now remained, draped like the rest of the furniture with a white sheet. Kirk padded over to it and gingerly gathered the covering from atop it, not wanting to stir up all the dust that had accumulated during the past months. After setting the balled sheet down on the floor, he tapped at the console's controls. It blinked to life with a chirp, confirming that he would be able to use it to record the message he needed for next week, for the *Enterprise*-B launch. He deactivated it, then continued on through the rest of the house.

Moving through the kitchen, down the short hall, past the refresher, and into the bedroom, Kirk saw only more signs of disuse. At one time he had loved this place back when he'd spent a couple of summers here as a boy. It had been here that his uncle had taught him how to ride horses, and just being away from home had made those trips seem like adventures. In the years since the property had passed to him, though, he had neglected it. His long duty aboard the *Enterprise* had certainly prevented him from visiting more than occasionally, but even when he'd been stationed on Earth as chief of Starfleet Operations, he hadn't come here much. Even during that first time he'd stepped away from the space service, when he'd actually come here to live, he hadn't really taken care of the place until he'd met Antonia.

And now look at it, he thought as he gazed at the unused furniture hidden beneath yet more sheets. As tired as he felt, he couldn't bring himself to lie down on the bed. He imagined it would seem like a betrayal of sorts to treat this place like home.

Too many regrets, he told himself. As little as he'd used this place over the years, he'd still been unable to divest himself of it. Kirk had rarely seen his nephews, owing both to his time on the *Enterprise* and their being scattered throughout the quadrant, so he supposed that holding on to his uncle's old house had provided a familial touchstone for him, however infrequently he'd visited it. Just knowing it was there, waiting for him, had probably helped him in ways of which he hadn't even been aware.

Kirk paced back through the house to the living room. He thought about checking outside for some wood, but then thought better of it, deciding that he didn't have the energy to build a fire. Instead, he carefully pulled the sheet from the sofa and sat down.

As he did, his hand struck something. Kirk looked

down and saw a hardcover book on the cushion beside him. He picked it up, the scent of its age reaching him, a smell he recalled from childhood; his mother had so loved books. Kirk examined the small, thin volume, bound in gilded leather. Its cover contained an ornate design, but no title. He turned it so that he could see its spine, and when he saw the words there, he read them aloud: *"The Tragedy of Romeo and Juliet."* His voice echoed slightly in the room, evoking the peculiar impression that no words had ever been spoken here before.

But of course many had.

Too many, Kirk thought.

He shook his head. He didn't remember leaving the book here, though clearly he must have on his last trip out to the house, before the nexus, before the *Enterprise*-B, before everything. It had been a gift from Antonia, on the second anniversary of their first date, just half a year or so before she would last speak to him. *She must've suspected when she'd given this to me,* Kirk thought. *A tragedy in the offing.*

He opened the cover of the book. On the front endpaper, he saw words flowing across the page in Antonia's delicate hand. *Dear Jim,* she had written, *Even though I don't care much for the story, I know how much you love old books. This is just to show how much I love old Jim Kirk. Always, Antonia.*

"'Always,'" Kirk said. She'd been wrong about that, and wrong about the tragedy too. Kirk had been the forlorn Romeo, but Antonia had not been his Juliet.

And I knew that, Kirk rebuked himself. *I knew it all*

along. He had done so much good in his life, but he would never forgive himself for what he had done to Antonia.

For a fleeting moment, Kirk considered contacting her now, telling her how sorry he felt for how badly he'd hurt her. He knew that he couldn't do that for fear of changing the timeline, for fear of disrupting his plans to prevent the temporal loop, but even if he could speak with her, he understood that it would do no good. Kirk craved absolution, but he also knew that he did not deserve it.

Kirk leafed through the book until he reached the first page of the play. He began to read, but before long, his eyelids fluttered closed. His head lolled back on the sofa and he drifted to sleep.

Unfortunately for him, his slumber did not lack for dreams.

As Jim Kirk slid the pan of Ktarian eggs onto the low heat of the cooking surface, he felt the chill of the morning air. Thinking that he should start a fire, he dashed around the island and out of the kitchen. In the living room, he peered down beside the hearth at the log basket there, which sat empty. He then went over to the front door, opened it, and looked out at several stacks of wood, some of it cut, some not.

Kirk paced outside to his right and up the curved stone stairs to the front clearing. There, he reached down for a few pieces of firewood, but as he did so, his gaze came to rest on the axe that he'd left sticking in the stump. Suddenly feeling the need for some physical activity, he went over to the pile of unhewn tree segments, grabbed one, and set it down beside the axe. He pulled the tool free, then swung it up and around, bringing the blade down squarely into the short length of tree trunk, which divided neatly in two, each piece falling to the ground. He bent, picked up one of the pieces, and placed it back in position to be split.

Before he brought the axe down again, Kirk breathed in deeply. Where before he'd found the air cool, he now appreciated its crispness. He gazed around at the evergreen trees holding court about the house, and past them, at the stately Canadian Rockies, clad in the white folds of autumn snow. *Beautiful day,* he thought, and he knew that his sentiment wouldn't last.

"You're stalling," he told himself. He peered over at the house, at the second-story window on the left, beyond which he knew Antonia still lay in bed. How could a man who'd once battled a Gorn in hand-to-hand combat, who'd by himself piloted a starship into the maw of a machine that devoured entire planets, who'd floated alone in a completely empty universe— how could he be scared to talk with the woman who loved him?

Because it's not fear stopping me, Kirk knew. *It's guilt.*

Kirk brought the blade of the axe down into the stump, then headed back into the house. In the kitchen, left over the low heat, the Ktarian eggs had almost finished cooking. From the far counter, Kirk retrieved the tray he'd already set for Antonia's breakfast. In addition to a plate, flatware, and napkin, he'd also placed on it a glass of grape juice, a glass of water, and a small vase of larkspur. He set it down beside the heating surface, dished the eggs from the pan onto the plate, then added three slices of toast when they'd done browning.

Before he went upstairs, he walked back out into the living room, where he opened an antique wooden box ornamented with metal fleurs-de-lis. From it, he removed a small, black velvet pouch that contained a gift he'd acquired for Antonia: a golden horseshoe, on the arch of which had been affixed a miniature red rose. *To soften the blow,* he thought as he returned to the kitchen and set the pouch down beside the breakfast he'd made.

Taking a deep breath, Kirk picked up the tray and carried it back through the living room and then up the stairs. When he reached the second floor, he balanced the tray against the jamb, took hold of the knob, and threw open the bedroom door. Across the room, Antonia looked up at him from where she still lay in the antique four-poster bed Kirk had obtained for the house. Her long dark hair spread on the pillow behind her head like a crown.

"At last," she said with a wide smile. She fluffed up the pillows behind her and sat up against them. Kirk caught a fleeting glimpse of her bare body before she pulled the sheet up across her chest. "I was wondering how long you were going to be rattling around in that kitchen," she said. "I'm starving."

"I'm not surprised," Kirk commented as he made

his way across the room. They had gone to bed before midnight last night, but had stayed up long past, exploring each other's bodies. "I wanted to get all of this just right," he said, settling the tray across her lap.

"Ktarian eggs," Antonia said excitedly, almost singing the words. She peered up at Kirk with an expression of surprise and delight. "When did you . . . ?"

"I brought them with me from Idaho," Kirk said. They'd come up here to Canada five days ago, wanting to spend some time in the Rockies before the big snows of the winter began.

Antonia picked up a fork and took a bite of the eggs, after which she hummed in appreciation. "Delicious," she said. "Thank you, thank you, thank you."

"My pleasure," Kirk said. He tried to smile, but felt only one side of his mouth rising. He dreaded what lay ahead.

After Antonia enjoyed another mouthful of the eggs, she looked back up at where he stood, one hand raised to the post at the foot of the bed. "Aren't you eating?" she asked.

"I'm—no," Kirk managed to say. "My stomach's a bit upset." As soon as he'd decided this morning to speak with Antonia about what had happened, his anxiety had physically unsettled him.

"I'm sorry," Antonia said. "Do you think you're getting sick? Can I make you some tea?" She reached as though to take the tray from her lap so that she could get out of bed, but Kirk stopped her.

"No, no, I'll be fine," he said. "Have your breakfast."

Antonia smiled at him, then looked back down at the tray. "What's this?" she asked, holding up the velvet pouch.

"How did that get there?" Kirk teased, trying to stay positive.

Antonia reached into the pouch and pulled out the horseshoe. "Jim, this is lovely," she said. She held it out before her, the ends up. "For good luck."

Again Kirk tried to smile, and again failed to do so convincingly.

"What's the matter?" Antonia asked. "Does your stomach feel that bad?"

"It's nothing," Kirk said.

"Jim, I've lived with you for two years now," she said. "I can tell when something's bothering you." She seemed to make an assessment while she looked at him. "It's not your stomach, though, is it?"

"It's not just that, no," Kirk said.

"What is it?" Antonia asked, clearly concerned now.

Kirk pushed off the bedpost and walked across the room to the far corner. When he turned back to face her, he knew that the time had come to tell her. "Antonia," he said, "Harry Morrow contacted me."

"Harry Morrow?" she asked, her brow creasing.

"An old friend," Kirk said. "He's also the commander in chief of Starfleet."

Antonia set the horseshoe down on the tray with a loud thump. "And what did Harry want?" she asked flatly.

Realizing that he'd unintentionally put distance between Antonia and him when he'd moved across the room, he walked back to the corner of the bed. "He wanted to tell me that he has a position open for me at Starfleet Headquarters."

Antonia gazed at him for a long moment without saying anything. Then she lifted the tray from her lap and set it gently down next to her on the mattress. As she reached for her silk robe at the foot of the bed, she said, "You told me that you would never go back to Starfleet."

"I didn't think I would," Kirk said. "But this is strictly a supervisory position, maybe with an opportunity to do some instruction at the academy."

Antonia stood from the bed and quickly pulled her robe on, as though she didn't want Kirk to see her naked form. After cinching the belt tightly about her waist, she looked up at him, her pain obvious. "You told me you weren't going back," she repeated.

"Antonia, this would be at Starfleet Headquarters, in San Francisco," he said. "I would wake up every morning in Idaho with you, and go to bed every night with you. Things wouldn't have to change that much."

Antonia's eyes widened. "You're actually considering taking this position?" she asked.

Kirk glanced down, not wanting to make this any more difficult for either one of them, but knowing that he had to tell her. Looking back up, he said, "I already accepted it."

"What!?" Antonia said.

Kirk stepped over to her, his arms out. "Antonia," he said, but she pushed his arms away and raced past him. "Antonia," Kirk said again, but she did not respond. Instead, she stood beside the upholstered bench in front of the bed, where she'd tossed her clothes last night. She quickly pulled on her socks and underwear, then her blue jeans. Kirk walked over to her and placed his hand on her back. "Antonia—"

"Leave me alone," she said, and she grabbed her sweater from the bench and marched to the other side of the room. Keeping her back to him, she took off her robe and let it fall to the floor. She tugged her sweater on over her head, then pulled at her long hair to get it through as well.

When finally she looked back over at him, he said, "We won't have to be apart. You spend a lot of your days with your practice anyway. We could still be together."

"Tell me," she said. "When did Harry contact you? When did you accept his offer?"

"Last week," Kirk admitted. "A few days before we left Idaho."

Antonia shook her head. "And you waited until we came up here to tell me." She walked over to the other side of the bed and bent over it toward the tray. "You made sure to make me Ktarian eggs before you decided to tell me," she said, lifting the plate up with two fingers and dropping it noisily back onto the tray. The grape juice splashed over the rim of its glass. "You made sure to give me a symbol of good luck before you told me." She picked up the horseshoe and then let it clatter onto the tray. Fixing him with a glare, her voice rising, she said, "You made love with me last night knowing that you would do this to me today." She shoved her hand beneath the tray and sent it flying across the bed and onto the floor.

"I didn't mean to hurt you," Kirk said, even though, on some level, he had always known that he would.

"Your intentions don't really mean much, do they?" Antonia said. "Because you think it's more important for you to go back to Starfleet than it is not to hurt me. You told me that you would never go back. You *promised* me."

"I promised that we wouldn't have a long-distance, part-time relationship," Kirk said, defensive despite knowing what he was doing to this woman that he loved—that he loved, but not enough.

"No," Antonia said. "You promised me that you wouldn't go back to Starfleet."

Kirk raised his arms and then let them fall back to his sides. "At the time, I meant that," he said. "I really didn't believe that I'd ever want to do something like this, but things change."

"That doesn't make your promise any less of a lie," Antonia told him.

"I didn't lie," Kirk bristled. "I believed what I told you at the time."

"A promise isn't something with a time limit on it," Antonia said. "What good does it do for somebody to promise one thing one minute that they believe and intend to live up to, if in the next minute they decide that they've changed and so now the promise no longer applies?" She strode over to where she'd dropped her robe and bent to pick it up. When she stood back up, she said, "You can rationalize this any way you want to, but you lied to me."

Though he knew it would do no good—he'd always known it—he said, "I can be back in Idaho every night."

"I know you mean that right now," she said, "but 'things change.'" She spat the last words back at him, a rebuke that told him she would never again trust him. "One day you'll come home from Starfleet to tell me that Harry's offered you the command of a starship."

"That's not going to happen," Kirk said.

"Sorry," Antonia said, "but your promises don't carry a lot of weight with me anymore."

"It doesn't have to be like this," Kirk said, walking toward her, wanting very much to find a way to ease Antonia's pain. "We can . . ." The notion of marriage had actually risen in his mind, though he refrained from saying so on the off chance that she might accept.

"We can what?" Antonia asked. "Get married? That's just a label if there's no promise to back it up." She looked down at the robe in her hand for a moment, then threw it back down on the floor and headed for the door.

"Where are you going?" Kirk asked.

"I'm leaving," she said from the doorway. "Don't come after me, don't try to see me, don't try to contact me." She thought for a second and then added, "I'll move my things out of the house when you're away during the day at Starfleet." She said nothing more, but she also didn't turn and walk away. She stared at him, and Kirk realized that, amidst her hurt and disappointment, some part of her wanted him to protest, to do something that would keep them together. At that instant, Kirk understood that there were things that he could say to Antonia that would begin to put this incident behind them, that would indeed save their relationship.

He said none of those things. Instead, he told her simply, "I'm sorry it has to be like this."

"You should be," Antonia said quietly, seeming to deflate before his eyes. Then she turned, took two steps, and started down the stairs. Kirk listened to her footfalls, then heard the front door open and close.

He felt terrible for what he had done, but there had been no choice in the matter. His mistake hadn't been in returning to Starfleet, but in getting involved so seriously with Antonia in the first place. He had lost sight of the fact that true love had already passed him by and that it would not come his way again. For that, Antonia had paid a hard price.

Kirk never saw her again.

THIRTEEN

2293

Even as the airpod skimmed evenly past fields that looked as though they had until recently been filled with wheat, Scotty sat at an auxiliary panel, checking engine performance. *Habits become nature,* Jim Kirk thought, recollecting the old Chinese proverb. As though he needed additional proof of the maxim, Chekov sat to his right at the forward console, working the navigational controls. "I thought you were waiting for an *exec* position to open up," Kirk said, looking at Pavel. Then he pointed over at Scotty and added, "And I thought you *retired* from engineering."

"Ach," Scotty scoffed in his Gaelic way. "I retired from Starfleet. I'll *always* be an engineer."

"What was I thinking?" Kirk said with a smile. It surprised him how good it felt to be with his two old friends. When he'd made the decision to leave the space service, he'd believed that the time had been right. The *Enterprise* had been decommissioned, many of his command crew had been ready to go their separate ways, and politics had more than ever insinuated itself into his job, but he'd also felt that he'd needed, in some regard, to get on with his life.

That hadn't been the first time that Kirk had reached such a point. He'd stepped away from Starfleet once before, retreated to his property in Idaho, and ended up becoming involved with Antonia for two years. He hadn't found whatever he'd needed at that time, but neither had he found it when he'd gone back to the service.

And so Kirk had decided to try again. After retiring this second time, he'd begun filling his days and nights with many of the activities that he hadn't had the opportunity to pursue over the years. Doing so had entailed journeying to various unique locations throughout the quadrant, and doing so as a civilian had proven different and interesting in and of itself.

Kirk had enjoyed all that he'd done during the past months, and he fully expected to feel the same about orbital skydiving today. After he'd learned that Scotty and Chekov would be joining him for the *Enterprise*-B launch tomorrow, he'd decided to invite them along today for his unusual exploit. They'd agreed to survey the landing site this morning, and they would greet him there later in the day for his touchdown.

Their presence in the airpod right now, and the satisfaction Kirk found in simply being with them, underscored how much time he'd spent alone since he'd begun his retirement. He had stayed by himself intentionally, believing that he needed to separate from his old life in order to determine how best to move on from here. But lost amid his frenetic schedule and the solitude he'd sought for self-reflection, he hadn't realized how much he missed his old friends.

He did now.

Kirk turned and peered out through the forward

viewport. In the early morning light, a dirt path passed below the airpod, with freshly reaped fields slipping by on either side of the small craft. Ahead, he saw a slight rise, and atop it, a pair of tall stone markers. "Is that it?" he asked Chekov.

"I think so," Pavel said, consulting a readout on his panel. "Yes, that should be the western perimeter of the landing zone."

"Excellent," Kirk said as the airpod began up the gentle slope. Chekov slowed the craft as they approached the markers, bringing it to a floating stop once they arrived there. "How large is it?" Kirk asked.

"Approximately two kilometers square," Chekov read from his instruments.

Kirk nodded. "Why don't you take us to the center of the area?" Chekov operated his controls, and a short time later, he once more brought the craft to a stop, this time setting it down in the panic grass. Kirk stood up, leaned on the console, and peered out left, center, and right. "Doesn't really look like much, does it?" he said.

"I don't suppose it has to," Chekov said, standing up beside him and gazing out.

"It wouldn't make a bit of difference if this field was made out of Kerlovian foam or cast rodinium," Scotty said, suddenly appearing between Kirk and Chekov. "If you don't execute reentry just right, either one would leave you a puddle of flesh."

"Thanks for the vote of confidence," Kirk said. "Now I know how you motivated your engineering teams all these years."

"Don't blame me," Scotty said. "You're the one running a bloody decathlon across the galaxy."

"'A ship in harbor is safe,'" Kirk quoted, "'but that is not what ships are built for.'" He paused, then dryly asked, "Are you sure you don't want to make a jump yourself?"

"The only jump I plan on making," Scotty said, "is into my boat once I reach the Norpin Colony."

"He says that now," Chekov cracked, "but I bet less than a week after he arrives there, he'll be working on the colony's generators or power grid or transporters."

Scotty looked at Pavel with an expression that seemed to indicate that he'd taken offense at the comment, but then he said, "Only if the equipment needs it." Without waiting for a response, he turned and opened the airpod's hatch. Kirk glanced over at Chekov, who smiled in obvious amusement at Scotty's remark.

After the engineer had exited, Chekov and then Kirk followed him outside. The clean, slightly sweet scent of wheat filled the air, the aroma at once calling to mind his childhood. He didn't fight to suppress the memories, as he so often did, but let them settle within him. "When I was a boy," he said, "the air in certain areas around town would smell like this." He breathed in deeply, and the three men stood quietly for a few seconds, taking in their surroundings. Finally, Chekov pointed off to one side.

"There," he said. He walked ten meters, then squatted and waved away some of the panic grass, uncovering a squat cylinder that rose about half a meter from the ground. "This is your homing beacon."

Kirk walked over and examined the device, which appeared well anchored in the ground. He strolled around it, then leaned down when he saw a small access panel on one side. He pushed it and it glided open, revealing a thumbprint scanner, a single control, and a small display. Kirk placed his thumb on the pad and a ray of light immediately shined across it. Almost at once, the words ORBITAL SKYDIVER—IDENTITY CONFIRMED appeared on the display, and the control came to life with a red glow. As he'd been instructed when he'd signed up for his jump, Kirk pressed the button. The readout blinked and read PERFORMING DIAGNOSTIC. He waited until the color of the control changed from red to green, indicating the functional status of the homing beacon. The display also confirmed the successful completion of the diagnostic.

"All set," he said, swinging the access plate closed and standing back up. Chekov rose as well.

"That's it?" Scotty blustered. "You really ought to let me have a look at that equipment."

"And how long would that take?" Kirk asked, playing along with the engineer.

"I could have it running at maximum efficiency in six hours," he said.

"It's a miracle that we could ever plan on the *Enterprise* making it from one planet to another in less than a year," Chekov gibed.

"Engineers," Kirk said with a shrug. "Just wait until you make captain and have a chief engineer of your own, Pavel."

"Do you think they'll let me do without one?" Chekov joked.

"Somebody's got to be aboard to keep you command types from blowing up the ship every five minutes," Scotty said in mock indignation.

"Well, that's true," Chekov said. "At least in your case, Captain."

"Now, now," Kirk said. "I only destroyed the *Enterprise* once."

"Not for want of trying to do it more often," Scotty said. "There was the time when the Kelvans hijacked the ship when you ordered me to rig the ship to explode on your order."

"There was also the time when Bele and Lokai came aboard," Chekov said.

"And then there was the time—" Scotty began, but Kirk interrupted him.

"All right, all right, I give," he said, holding up his hands before himself in a pose of surrender. "Well, I guess I should be on my way to Tunis." Together, they all started back to the airpod, and Chekov flew them back into Wichita.

When they'd returned to the public transporter at which they'd all arrived earlier, Kirk said, "So I'll see you gentlemen out at the landing zone this afternoon?"

"Four forty-nine," Chekov confirmed. "We'll be there."

"Good," Kirk said. "I'll see you then."

Chekov beamed away first, heading back to San Francisco, and then Scotty transported out to Aberdeen, Scotland, where he'd been living since beginning his own retirement. As Kirk stepped up onto the platform, he thought again about how much he'd enjoyed seeing his old friends. As much as he'd been anticipating his orbital skydive today, he now thought that he looked forward even more to the dinner that he and Scotty and Pavel had planned on having together this evening.

After I get back from the Enterprise *launch tomorrow,* Kirk thought, *I'm going to contact Spock and Bones.* McCoy had actually reached him last week, but Kirk hadn't really said much, other than to tell his friend about agreeing to participate in the *Enterprise*-B ceremony. *That's got to change,* Kirk thought. He realized that he really needed to reconnect with his friends.

At the console across the room, the transporter operator signaled his readiness, and Kirk nodded in reply. The operator worked his controls, and the hum of the transporter grew, bringing with it the blue-white light of dematerialization. Moments later, Kirk was not in Kansas anymore.

Kirk set down the carryall in the den of his counterpart's San Francisco apartment, then squatted down and hunted through it until he found the blue data card he'd brought back with him from his days in Idaho. He took it to the computer terminal, where he sat down and inserted it into an input/output receptacle. He wanted to review one last time the message he'd recorded, since once he left here today, he wouldn't have an opportunity to safely do so again.

On the display, his own face appeared. *"Jim,"* the message began, and as he implored the earlier version of himself to listen to the entire recording before taking any action, the strangeness of the situation struck Kirk. He had traveled in time before, but never had it resulted in such peculiar circumstances as these. *It did once for Spock, though,* he thought, remembering when his friend and first officer had leaped into his own childhood in order to save himself as a boy.

"I am you, but at a future date," his message continued. *"To make and leave you this recording, I arrived here through the Guardian of Forever. Because I am you, I know what the mere mention of the Guardian does to you, even after all these years."* Kirk knew that mentioning the time vortex in that way would have an impact on his alter ego.

When he'd finished watching the complete message and found himself satisfied with it, Kirk removed the data card and set it aside. He then accessed the Earth comnet and opened a transmission. After a few seconds, the Starfleet emblem faded in on the empty screen, replaced in the next moment by the face of Admiral Sinclair-Alexander's assistant. *"Captain Kirk,"* the young ensign said. *"May I help you with something?"*

"I'd like to speak with the admiral," he said.

"Admiral Sinclair-Alexander is in a meeting and therefore unavailable at the moment," the ensign said. Kirk could not recall her name. *"May I ask what this is in regard to?"*

"The launch of the *Enterprise* tomorrow," he said,

aware that when Sinclair-Alexander heard why he had contacted her, she would be concerned that he had changed his mind about attending the ceremony. Kirk remembered that when she had invited him in the first place, he had not particularly wanted to do as she'd asked.

"Is there anything that I can help you with?" the ensign wanted to know.

"No, thank you," Kirk said. "I really would like to discuss this with the admiral. The sooner, the better."

"Very well," the ensign said. *"I'll inform her as soon as she's out of her meeting."*

"Pardon me," Kirk said, "but do you have any idea when that will be?"

The ensign glanced away from the screen for a moment, doubtless consulting a chronometer. *"In just a few minutes,"* she said.

"Then if it's all right with you, Ensign," Kirk said, "I'd like to wait."

"Very well," she said. *"Is there anything else, Captain?"*

"No, that's it," Kirk said. "Thank you, Ensign."

"My pleasure, Captain," she said. *"I'll place you on standby then."* Kirk nodded, and the ensign reached forward to a control. The Starfleet emblem returned to the display. This time, beneath it, read the words:

OFFICE OF ADMIRAL MARGARET SINCLAIR-ALEXANDER, STARFLEET COMMAND

ENSIGN ELISA TEAGARDEN, ASSISTANT TO THE ADMIRAL

Teagarden, Kirk thought, remembering the name once he saw it. He waited for eleven minutes before the ensign's face reappeared on the monitor. *"Captain Kirk,"* she said, *"the admiral will speak with you now."*

"Thank you," Kirk said, and then Sinclair-Alexander's face replaced Teagarden's on the screen.

"Jim," she said at once, *"please don't tell me you're canceling for the* Enterprise *ceremony tomorrow."*

"No, against my better judgment, I'm still planning on being there," Kirk said, hopeful that the admiral's concern and her awareness of his reluctance would make her more receptive to granting the request he would now make of her. "Unless there's some reason that you think I shouldn't," he japed.

"No, no, not at all," Sinclair-Alexander said. *"Forget I even mentioned it. So what* can *I do for you, Jim? Ensign Teagarden said that you did want to talk about the launch."*

"Not precisely about the launch," Kirk allowed. "But you promised me a tour of the ship tomorrow."

"That's right," the admiral said. *"Is there a problem with that?"*

Kirk recalled the meeting he'd had with Sinclair-Alexander when she'd asked him to attend the launch and first voyage of the *Enterprise*-B, a meeting she'd had with his earlier self just a few days ago. "Actually, I'm looking forward to seeing the ship," he said. "I'm just not much interested in being rushed through it with the press at my heels or being ushered around like a plebe who's never seen the inside of a starship before."

"Jim, the whole point of having you on board the

Enterprise *is for the positive public relations,"* Sinclair-Alexander said. *"It really would be counterproductive to that end to bar the press from accompanying you on your tour."*

Kirk had not only anticipated such a response, he'd counted on it. "What about a separate tour?" he asked.

"The schedule is very tight tomorrow," said the admiral. *"I'm not sure that we could fit anything more in."*

"That's why I was thinking that I could do it today," Kirk said. "I mean, I'll still go with Scotty and Chekov through the ship tomorrow for the sake of the publicity, but if I went up today, I could take my time and really get a good look around."

"We've only got a handful of personnel on board right now," Sinclair-Alexander said, *"and most of them are engineers trying to get the ship ready for the launch. You'd really have to be on your own."*

"That'd be perfect," Kirk said. Although he could have accomplished what he needed to with an escort by his side, not having one would make his task easier.

"All right," the admiral said. *"Let me get you reactivated today then."* She looked away for a second, then asked, *"How does noon sound?"*

"That'll be fine," Kirk said.

"You can report to any of the transporters here at Starfleet; they'll send you up," Sinclair-Alexander said. *"I'll inform the officer of the deck that you'll be coming. Anything else?"*

"That's it, Admiral. Thank you," Kirk said. "It should be interesting."

"Enjoy yourself, Jim," Sinclair-Alexander said. She

touched a control and the Starfleet insignia showed once more, then disappeared in favor of the Earth comnet logo.

As Kirk reached to shut down the terminal, he suddenly saw a light flashing on the console, indicating that he—or rather, his counterpart—had received a message. He thought back to the day before the *Enterprise*-B ceremony, to when he'd gone orbital skydiving, and he tried to remember whom he'd heard from when he'd gotten home that night. Unable to recall a single message from that day, he quickly tapped a button to play it. When the sender's face appeared on the display, Kirk felt his mouth drop open.

"Hi, Jim," said Antonia.

To Kirk, she looked much the same as when last he'd seen her, which had been when she'd walked out of his vacation home up in Canada. The lines around her mouth had grown more defined and a few wrinkles had begun to show at the sides of her eyes, but she still wore her hair long and looked as attractive as ever. It stunned him to see her.

As though reading his thoughts, the recorded image of Antonia said, *"You're probably as surprised to hear from me as I am to be leaving this message."* She smiled with obvious nervousness. *"No, that's not the case. I do know why I'm contacting you. I read that Starfleet was sending out a new starship* Enterprise *tomorrow and that you would be coming out of your second retirement for a day to preside over the christening ceremony and then to go aboard for its first voyage."*

Antonia paused, a pensive looking coming over her.

"I didn't know that you'd retired again," she said. *"I did know that, not long after you went back to Starfleet the last time, you helped save my life and billions of others from that probe that wanted to communicate with humpback whales. I also knew that, after that, you went back to command the* Enterprise *again for quite a few years."*

Again she hesitated, for longer this time. Finally, she shrugged. *"Even if you're not in space regularly these days, it seems pretty clear that you belong up there. Anyway, I think I know how much the* Enterprise *meant to you, and I'm guessing that placing this new ship in the care of another captain might be difficult for you. I just wanted you to know . . . I just wanted to wish you well tomorrow. Take care, Jim."*

Kirk watched Antonia's face blink from the screen, and then he pushed back from the computer terminal, stood up, and paced across the room, driven by both shock and bewilderment. At the floor-to-ceiling windows, he peered out at the waters of San Francisco Bay. On one level, it delighted him to have heard from his former lover, who seemed to have forgiven him his transgressions against her, even if she hadn't said so outright. How else could he explain her contacting him for the first time in nearly nine years?

At the same time, Kirk knew that, in the course of his own life leading up to the launch of the *Enterprise*-B, he had never received a message from Antonia. Did that mean that he'd already somehow altered the timeline in his efforts to prevent the converging temporal loop? But how? He'd only been in this time a few days, almost all of which he'd spent alone up at his property in Idaho.

Deeply concerned, Kirk thought back to the first instance when he'd lived through this day. He'd left his apartment early in the morning to meet Scotty and Chekov in Wichita, Kansas, where they'd surveyed his landing site outside the city. After that, he'd traveled alone to Tunis, where he'd executed a simulated descent before transporting up to the orbital platform from which he would perform his actual dive. After checking and donning his equipment, he'd then made his jump, ultimately landing in Kansas in the late afternoon. After verifying his safe landing with the team aboard the orbital platform, he had eaten dinner with Scotty and Chekov in Wichita. They'd enjoyed one another's company, sharing stories of their shared experiences over the years. Afterward, they'd gone out for a drink and continued reminiscing.

Kirk recalled that he hadn't returned home until late, and when he had, he certainly hadn't found a message from Antonia waiting for him. But then, he hadn't watched any messages at all, had he? He remembered now that he hadn't even checked the terminal when he'd gotten home, but had simply fallen into bed after his long day. The next morning, he'd left the apartment as soon as he'd risen, headed for the *Enterprise*-B ceremony.

Antonia did leave me a message, Kirk thought. He simply hadn't seen it. The realization saddened him, even though he knew it wouldn't have made any difference in his life; just hours later, he would be lost in the nexus. *Except that I'm still alive now,* he thought, and although he could not respond to Antonia, he did take some solace in the notion that she seemed to have let go of her anger for the pain he'd caused her.

Kirk padded back across the den to the computer terminal. He called up a menu of options and selected the disabling of the system's monitor and alert functions. Although he knew that his counterpart would not check for any messages tonight or tomorrow morning, Kirk did not want to risk somebody contacting him during the time that his counterpart did spend in the apartment. In particular, he wanted to avoid any communication with Admiral Sinclair-Alexander, in which she might ask how he had enjoyed his tour of the *Enterprise*-B today. He thought that unlikely, but wished to take no chances.

Once he'd disabled the terminal, Kirk picked up the carryall and took it into the bedroom. There, he emptied the bag and then stripped, tossing all of the clothes into the recycler but for his uniform. After dressing in his official attire, he pulled out the jacket of one of the three uniforms hanging in the back of the closet. He also replaced the carryall where he had found it.

After retrieving the blue data card from the den, Kirk waited for the morning to pass. Just before noon, he left the apartment, headed for Starfleet Headquarters. From there, he would transport up to the *Enterprise*-B, from which, if all went according to plan, he would not return.

FOURTEEN

As he lay in what amounted to a launch bay, Jim Kirk could not help thinking of the many probes and photon torpedoes he'd ordered fired during his Starfleet career. Though he knew and understood the process that would begin his descent to Earth, it nevertheless felt strange to be configured like a projectile. It also reminded him of the few times he'd had to abandon ship in an escape pod.

Within Kirk's helmet, he heard the words of the dive controller, checking readiness. Kirk studied the readouts on the inside of his visor, then confirmed his status. The controller acknowledged, executed a scan of his own that he narrated, then initiated a countdown.

As Kirk listened to the numbers ticking down, he worked to keep his breathing and heart rate at acceptable levels. He felt more nervous than he'd expected to, particularly considering his long career in space and the several times that he'd had to perform extravehicular activities. Of course, his training had always essentially warned him away from circumstances similar to those upon which he was about to embark.

At last, the controller reached zero in his countdown. Kirk did not feel the acceleration, but he could at first measure his progress through the tube visually, though the surface of the metal around him soon became nothing more than a blur. His arms folded across his chest and held tightly against himself, he waited for the moment when he would leave the orbital platform.

When finally he shot out into space, the moment exhilarated him in a way even greater than he'd expected. He had launched into Earth's night above the Arabian Peninsula. To his right, he saw a spectacular array of stars, seeming so close that he felt as though he could simply reach out and touch them. To his left, the planet of his birth spun through the void, sprawls of light sparkling across its surface.

Launched opposite the direction of the platform's orbit, Kirk had actually been decelerated with respect to the planet's surface. As he arced above the northern coast of Africa, he knew that he began to fall toward the Earth, though he could not immediately perceive that motion. The dive controller made contact with him, and Kirk quickly checked his readouts to verify his optimal status. He noted the transporter recall on the inside of his helmet showed green, available to him with a flick of his chin or tongue. Another had been placed within his right glove, he knew, on the back of his hand. Should he encounter any problems, he could be back within the orbital platform in just seconds, either through his own action or that of the controller, who would monitor his entire descent.

For nearly an hour, Kirk seemed to float free above the Earth. As many light-years as he'd traveled, as many exotic locales as he'd visited, he didn't know if he'd ever seen a more breathtaking vista. He had been born on the great blue marble below him, and that fact counted for something on an instinctive level.

By degrees, he became aware of falling from space, the Earth growing larger below him. He examined his display and saw that indeed he'd begun to experience the effects of the atmosphere. He twisted his body around so that he would descend feet first.

As Kirk sailed across the coast of Morocco and out over the Atlantic Ocean, he saw the terminator ahead. The line separating day from night made it appear as though some great being had draped a curtain over the world there. Kirk soared in that direction, the atmospheric drag beginning to slow him more dramatically, his passage through the air growing noisy. He felt a slight increase in the heat within his dive suit, and a glance at his readings showed a sharp increase in its outer temperature. He peered down across his body and saw that the blue heat-resistant tiles lining the exterior of his suit had begun to glow red.

I've become a meteor, Kirk thought, imagining the view of his reentry from the ground.

It took nearly another hour for him to cross the ocean and the eastern coast of North America, finally approaching the heartland. His dive suit cooled as he slowed to terminal velocity. As he at last arrived in Kansas airspace, he changed his attitude once more, dropping facedown into a spread-eagle position. He felt the full resistance of the atmosphere now, and he used it to adjust his descent. He shifted his arms and legs based on the readings in his helmet, which now coordinated his location with respect to the homing beacon on the ground.

At four kilometers up, Kirk began paying strict attention to his altitude. Almost a minute later, one and a quarter kilometers above the ground, he deployed his parachute. His harness tugged slightly on his torso, but not nearly as much as he'd expected. He looked upward at his chute and saw that it hadn't fully unfolded, its lines tangled. Kirk quickly moved his legs in a cycling motion, and almost immediately, the lines straightened and the rectangular parachute unfurled completely. The rush of the air quieted and a strange sort of peace enveloped him.

As he neared the ground close to his target, he saw Scotty and Chekov gazing skyward and pointing in his direction. Kirk steered near them, proud to have navigated so well to his landing zone. He peered directly beneath him as he came down the final dozen or so meters, and the ground seemed to jump up toward him in stages, his eyes unable to make total sense of what they saw without a dimensional referent.

His feet struck the ground hard, but he bent his knees and dropped, taking the impact without incident. He quickly turned to pull in his lines and gather his parachute, but he saw that Scotty and Chekov had already taken hold of the canopy and had begun to fold it together. After signaling his safe landing to the dive controller, Kirk reached up and pulled off his helmet.

"Right on target!" he told his friends excitedly. "I jump out over the Arabian Peninsula and I end up here, a quarter of a world away, right on the mark."

"Actually, your precise target was thirty-five meters in that direction," Chekov said with a smirk, pointing. He and Scotty handed the condensed fabric of the parachute to Kirk, who hugged it to his chest.

"Thanks for mentioning that, Pavel," Kirk said. "I've come twelve thousand lateral kilometers, so I think I'll call this a bull's-eye anyway."

"Oh, well, twelve thousand kilometers," Chekov said. "That's even wider than Russia."

Kirk looked to Scotty, who rolled his eyes at Pavel's comment. "So how was it?" the engineer asked him.

"Amazing," Kirk said. "Absolutely amazing. Let's go get that dinner and I'll tell you all about it."

"Perfect," Scotty said.

A few minutes later, they had reached the airpod and Kirk had stowed his chute. By the time they reached Wichita, he'd slipped out of his dive suit and donned civilian clothes. The three men found a restaurant to their liking that overlooked the Arkansas River, and they sat and talked into the night.

On a day when Jim Kirk had jumped from orbit and traveled back down to Earth, it seemed appropriate that he felt as though he had suddenly reentered his own life.

Kirk stepped out of the turbolift and onto the bridge of the *Enterprise*-B. In the command chair, a young man—presumably Ensign Rousseau, the current officer of the deck—peered casually over his shoulder, but when he saw Kirk, he stood up and virtually snapped to attention. "Captain on the bridge," he said.

Glancing around, Kirk had to suppress a laugh, even given the gravity of the situation that had brought him aboard this new *Enterprise*. Other than the young officer and himself, he saw only one other person on the bridge, a technician lying on her back, partially hidden beneath the combined helm and navigation stations that stood forward of the command chair. As Kirk looked on, she rolled out from under the console and rose to her feet.

"As you were," Kirk told the two crewmembers.

"Yes, sir," said the officer beside the command chair, though he did not move. Slight of stature, he had cropped blond hair and light blue eyes. The technician, dark haired and with a serious expression that seemed to reflect concentration on her work, immediately lowered herself back to the floor and resumed what she'd been doing.

Kirk gazed around the command center of this new *Enterprise*. Larger than the bridge of any of the vessels he had captained, it now sat largely dark, as did much of the ship. He had asked Admiral Sinclair-Alexander to allow him to come aboard so that he could tour the *Enterprise*-B, and he had so far done just that, visiting main engineering, sickbay, one of the mess halls, one of the gymnasia, and various other areas. In several places, technicians had been working busily, but in others, Kirk had found himself alone. He'd been sure to be seen by those present, though he'd avoided engaging in conversation with any of them. Though he recalled having very little contact with the *Enterprise* crew during the brief tour of the ship he'd taken with Scotty, Chekov, and members of the press during the launch, he did not want to risk one of them feeling comfortable enough to approach him and say something like, "Nice to see you again, Captain."

Peering around the empty bridge, Kirk felt a sense of nostalgia for the command center of his first command, the *Constitution*-class *Enterprise.* In those days, nearly three decades ago, his bridge had physically been a brighter, more intimate place. Although he'd found a connection with each of the vessels he'd commanded and with each of his crews, he held a special fondness within him for that old *Enterprise* and the days of the five-year mission.

Kirk began slowly along the raised periphery of the bridge. He walked between the primary systems display—one of the few screens currently active here—and the tactical console, then past the communications station, past sciences. At a mission operations panel situated beside the dark main viewscreen, he turned and stepped down to the lower, central portion of the bridge. As he moved over to the helm and navigation stations, he noted that the young officer still stood beside the command chair.

"Ensign Rousseau, I assume," Kirk said. When he'd beamed aboard from Starfleet Headquarters, he had heard the transporter operator inform Rousseau, the officer of the deck, of his arrival. Traditionally stationed on the bridge while in port, the officer of the deck functioned as a representative of the captain and bore responsibility for the security of the ship. Aboard a

Starfleet vessel in Earth dry dock and that had yet to launch, the requirements for such a task would amount to little more than keeping track of who embarked and disembarked.

"Sir, yes, sir," the ensign said. His attentiveness and eager responses likely betrayed an anxiety born of inexperience, Kirk thought. He guessed that Rousseau hadn't been long out of the academy. The young officer seemed as though he might jump out of his own skin at any moment.

"At ease, Ensign," Kirk said.

"Yes, sir," Rousseau said. He relaxed his posture, but almost imperceptibly so. Kirk noticed the gray hue of the division bands circling the left wrist of the ensign's crimson uniform jacket and sitting atop its right shoulder. The color indicated the scientific nature of Rousseau's regular duties, meaning that he would be able to provide Kirk with the information he needed.

"Will this be your first deep space assignment?" Kirk asked.

"Yes, it will be, sir," Rousseau replied.

Kirk nodded. "I envy you, mister," he said, attempting to put the ensign truly at ease. "Your first time out exploring the universe, meeting the unknown head-on, making new discoveries. This will be an exciting time for you."

"Yes, I think so, sir," Rousseau said. "I'm looking forward to it."

"What's your position, Ensign?" Kirk asked.

"I'm an assistant science officer, sir," Rousseau said. "I have a specialty in geology."

"A science officer and a geologist," Kirk said appreciatively as he moved past the command chair and mounted the steps back up to the outer ring of the bridge. "Then you'll be getting a lot of landing party assignments," he said, looking back at Rousseau, who remained standing by the command chair.

"Yes, sir," the ensign said, a small smile stealing onto his face. "I hope so."

Kirk walked over to the main ship display at the rear of the bridge, which showed lateral and dorsal cutaway views of the *Enterprise* and detailed its primary systems. He studied it for a moment, then raised his hand and traced a finger along the underside of the saucer section to the phaser emitters. "Is phaser power no longer channeled through the warp engines?" he asked. He could actually see the redesign and the answer to his question, but he did not want the information he really needed to stand out when he inquired about it.

Rousseau climbed the steps and joined Kirk at the display. "The phasers are still augmented by being routed through the main engines," the ensign said, pointing to a location on the diagram, "but they can now also be fed through the impulse drive. That way, in the event of a warp power shutdown, there's still a means of increasing phaser strength."

"I see," Kirk said. He stared at the display for a few seconds, then asked another question, and another, and then several more. At some point while the ensign answered all of his queries, the technician who'd been working at the helm and navigation console reported to Rousseau that she'd completed her work and would be returning to main engineering. After acknowledging the captain, she left the bridge.

Once Kirk had finished at the main systems display, he turned his attention to the tactical console. He activated it, asked a few more questions of Rousseau, then shut it down again. He did the same thing at the communications station before finally arriving at the primary sciences panel. "Care to walk me through your neck of the woods, Ensign?" Kirk asked.

"I'd be delighted to, sir," Rousseau said. He sat down and switched the station on, its controls coming to life, illuminated from within, its monitors winking on. As with the main systems display, most of the readouts came tinted in blue and green. The ensign pointed out the primary computer interface and its associated controls, his manner shifting from nervous to confident. He talked about the ship's sensors, including one set of scanning nodes dedicated to astronomical objects and another to spacecraft. He detailed the nature and abilities of the large number of analytical laboratories aboard, the types of probes to be stocked on the ship, and the sizeable amount of scientific data available to the crew in a series of general and specialized databases. As before, Kirk asked numerous questions, including the most important one to which he had needed an answer: *At what frequency and intensity are the sensors operated?*

When Rousseau had finished his presentation of the sciences station, Kirk thanked him. "I appreciate your time, Ensign," he said.

"I enjoyed it, Captain," Rousseau said, obviously pleased by his exchange with Kirk.

"I'm going to continue taking a look at the rest of the ship," he said. "I thought I might go down to the hangar deck and take a look at the shuttlecraft. I understand the new class-Ks are capable of warp six and have nearly the range of a starship."

"That's true, sir," Rousseau said.

"I think I'd like to see that for myself," Kirk said. "Carry on, Ensign."

"Yes, sir," Rousseau said. "Thank you, sir."

Kirk headed over to the turbolift. As he turned around within the car, he saw the ensign descending back toward the command chair. Then the doors closed and Kirk ordered the lift to take him to the hangar deck.

Located at the aft end of the secondary hull, the shuttlebay reached upward through several decks. Before Kirk went into the hangar itself, he first visited the manual control room and the observation lounge, both of which overlooked it. He found the two compartments empty, and the control room, like many of the ship's systems, completely inactive. Through the viewports, he saw the shuttle *Archimedes* in launch position.

Kirk made his way down to the hangar deck itself. Inside, he walked to where the shuttlecraft sat at its center, his boot heels echoing through the large open space. He crossed one of three platforms that raised and lowered the *Enterprise*'s various auxiliary craft from and to their storage deck below. The *Archimedes* had been positioned forward of the second platform, seemingly prepared for launch.

Sleeker than most of the shuttles Kirk had ever seen, the class-K craft carried two pair of engine structures. The lower set appeared to house an impulse drive and also to serve as landing gear, while the upper nacelles composed a small warp system. The bow came to a point, and the lines of the hull swept aft in a streamlining effect. The shuttle's name had been rendered in cursive letters across its nose, while its registry—NCC-1701-B/1—marched in block characters near its aft end.

Toward the bow, Kirk reached up beside the hatch and tapped the hull within the outline of a small rectangle, which slid aside to reveal a control panel. He touched the entry switch and the hatch folded down across the landing gear, down to the deck. Kirk climbed aboard, sealing the shuttle behind him.

At the forward console, he took a seat and activated the internal power of the *Archimedes,* though not its engines. He accessed the craft's deflector systems, then worked to tune their frequency. It did not require much time. When he'd finished, he had configured the shuttle's defenses in such a way that the *Enterprise*'s sensors would not be able to penetrate them. He also set the shuttle's own sensors in such a way that their use would avoid detection. Kirk then moved into the rear compartment, which housed a refresher and a two-person transporter. It also provided storage for a number of items, including an emergency survival cache and environmental suits. In addition to powering up the transporter, he also found there the two last things he required: handheld phasers and individual transporter recalls. He took one of the latter, set it, and slipped it into his uniform beside the blue data card.

Having completed his preparations, he left the shuttlecraft and the hangar deck, heading for the transporter room. There, he told the operator, Ensign Odette, that he'd completed his tour of the ship and wanted to beam back down to Starfleet Headquarters. After Odette informed Rousseau, Kirk stepped up onto the platform and waited while she worked her console. The whine of the transporter rose around him, accompanied by the blue-white light of dematerialization.

Kirk reappeared back at Starfleet. He dismounted the platform and exited the building, then left the campus and started toward his old San Francisco apartment. Once he arrived there, he removed his uniform jacket and replaced it in his counterpart's closet. Then he pulled out the recall device he'd purloined from the *Archimedes*.

For just a few seconds, Kirk paused, pacing around the apartment in an attempt to make certain that he hadn't forgotten to do anything. Believing that he'd done all he needed to here, he activated the recall device. Once more, the high-pitched hum of the transporter surrounded him. This time, when the blue-white light released him, he stood in the rear compartment of the *Archimedes,* in the middle of the hangar deck of the new starship *Enterprise.*

Kirk deactivated the shuttle's transporter, but left the deflectors powered in order to mask his life signs, though he doubted anybody would be performing any internal scans of the ship before he'd be gone. He accessed the emergency survival cache, pulled out a ration pack, then took a seat to begin his wait. Later, he would program the shuttle's sensors, antigravs, and thrusters, as well as the communications panel. Beyond that, though, he would have nothing else to do until tomorrow morning, when he would take action to prevent the development of the converging temporal loop, while at the same time avoiding any disruption to history.

And after that? he asked himself. He had some ideas about that, but at this point, he didn't know. His own fate, as well at that of hundreds of millions—and possibly even many more than that—might depend on the Guardian of Forever.

That thought did not fill him with confidence.

FIFTEEN

2293

In all his years exploring the galaxy, Jim Kirk had never seen anything quite like it. The massive whipcord of energy twisted through the void like some spaceborne tornado. Jags of lightninglike bolts writhed around it, and dust and debris trailed from it in cloud-gray sheets. Already the strange phenomenon that filled the main viewscreen had claimed two Federation transport vessels, and with them three hundred sixty-eight lives. Scotty had managed to transport forty-seven survivors from the second vessel, the *S.S. Lakul,* before its hull had collapsed, the ship exploding violently.

Now, the *Enterprise*—the upgraded *Excelsior*-class NCC-1701-B—lurched to starboard, then back the other way. Kirk caught himself on the railing, then pulled himself up onto the outer, upper ring of the bridge. Behind him, he heard an explosion, and he looked in time to see a hail of spark's flying from the navigator's station. Smoke, shouts, and an alert claxon filled the bridge as the great ship trembled.

Kirk reached for the outer bulkhead and pulled himself forward, toward the sciences station. "Report!" he called as he passed behind the freestanding tactical console. He took hold of the bulkhead again beside the science officer.

"We're caught in a gravimetric field emanating from the trailing edge of the ribbon," she called over the chaotic sounds around them.

In the center of the bridge, the ship's captain, Harriman, cried, "All engines, full reverse!"

The right order, Kirk thought. The shaking of the ship eased as the power of its drive strained against the pull of the energy ribbon. He pushed away from the bulkhead and stepped down to the lower portion of the bridge, over to Harriman. Scotty, he saw, had already taken over at the forward station for the downed navigator.

"The *Enterprise*'s engines are far more powerful than those of the transport ships," Harriman told Kirk. "We might be able to pull free."

It sounded more like wishful thinking than a plan of action, but Kirk knew that it was the proper course to attempt. He'd never before met this new captain of this new *Enterprise,* but he'd known his father, the redoubtable—and difficult—Admiral "Blackjack" Harriman. This younger man seemed far different from his take-no-prisoners parent. Where the elder Harriman took bold, often rash, action, this younger man seemed more thoughtful, his approach more reasoned and cautious. Kirk understood the value of both approaches, though he knew that a truly successful starship command required a combination of the two.

"We're making some headway," Scotty said from the navigator's station. "I'm reading a fluctuation in the gravimetric field that's holding us." Kirk peered up at the main viewer, at the coruscating field of pink and orange light, brilliant white veins of energy pulsing through it. Despite the obvious danger it posed, he found it strikingly beautiful. He walked forward, around Demora Sulu at the helm, to stand in front of the viewscreen.

"You came out of retirement for this," a voice said quietly at his right shoulder. He looked at Harriman and was surprised to see a hint of a smile lifting one side of his mouth. The statement, the expression, both spoke volumes to Kirk, revealing a confidence in the young captain that he hadn't seen before now. Of course, Harriman had been hamstrung by some admiral in Starfleet Command eager to generate some positive media coverage. After the recent complicity of several Fleet officers in the conspiracy to disrupt the peace initiative between the Federation and the Klingon Empire—a conspiracy that had effected the assassination of the Klingon chancellor, Gorkon—Kirk couldn't argue that the image of the space service hadn't suffered. Still, even if nobody had anticipated the *Enterprise* having to mount an emergency rescue mission during this public relations jaunt, you didn't send a starship out of space dock without a tractor beam, without a medical staff; you didn't send a newly promoted captain out with a bridge filled with members of the media and a "group of living legends," as Harriman had earlier referred to Kirk, Scotty, and Chekov. The circumstances could have daunted even a seasoned captain.

"I'm still retired," Kirk said. "A one-day activation is not going to pull me back into Starfleet permanently."

"We could still use officers of your caliber and character, sir," Harriman said sincerely.

"Thank you, but it's gotten a little too political for me these days," Kirk said. He glanced around at the media reporters still on the bridge.

"Don't I know it," Harriman said under his breath, something of a faraway look crossing his visage. All at once, Kirk realized that Blackjack must've been the one who'd pushed for this publicity outing for the *Enterprise* and its new captain, as much a self-serving promotion for the admiral as for Starfleet or his son.

Kirk turned toward Harriman. "Don't let anybody else define you," he said quietly to him. "This ship is yours, and this crew needs you, the man, not some image you or anybody else wants you to live up to."

Harriman tilted his head slightly to the side, apparently considering Kirk's words. Before he could respond, though, the ship heaved once more. Kirk staggered to his right and started to go down, but righted himself beside the navigation console.

"There's just no way to disrupt a gravimetric field of this magnitude," Scotty said. Kirk knew that if the engineer could not figure out a means of freeing the *Enterprise,* then it likely couldn't be done.

"Hull integrity at eighty-two percent," reported the tactical officer from his station.

"But," Scotty said, "I do have a theory."

"I thought you might," Kirk said. Secure in his own abilities, he also knew that he'd succeeded as much as he had in his role as starship captain because of the senior staff that had for so long served with him. Certainly Scotty had been an instrumental element of that team.

"An antimatter discharge directly ahead might disrupt the field long enough for us to break away," Scotty theorized.

An antimatter discharge, Kirk thought. "Photon torpedoes," he said.

"Aye," Scotty agreed.

"We're losing main power," the science officer said as Kirk moved back around the navigation and helm consoles. As he passed Demora, he tapped the weapons readout at the corner of her display.

"Load torpedo bays," he ordered. "Prepare to fire at my command."

As he stopped in front of the command chair, Sulu said, "Captain, we don't have any torpedoes."

"Don't tell me," Kirk said, peering over at Harriman, who still stood in front of the viewscreen. "Tuesday." That's when the young captain had said that the tractor beam and medical staff would arrive on the *Enterprise,* so why not the torpedoes as well. Harriman opened his mouth as though to respond, but then he closed it and looked away. Kirk saw a flash of anger there and knew that it had been meant for Blackjack or whichever admiral had placed Harriman and his crew in such a predicament.

"Hull integrity at forty percent," said the tactical officer.

"Captain," Scotty said, "it may be possible to simulate a torpedo blast using a resonance burst from the main deflector dish."

A resonance burst, Kirk thought. Deflector systems were constituted in such a way as to avoid resonance, since sympathetic vibrations could disrupt both the deflector generators, other equipment, and even the hull itself. Right now, though, that seemed a small risk to take.

The ship pitched again, sending Kirk flying backward, toward the command chair. Grabbing onto the arm of the chair, he peered back at Sulu. "Where are the deflector relays?" he asked, knowing that they would have to be reconfigured.

"Deck fifteen," Sulu said, "section fifteen alpha." Kirk couldn't tell whether she'd brought up the systems chart that quickly or she'd pulled the information from her memory.

"I'll go," Harriman said at once. Looking up at Kirk, he said, "You have the bridge." He started immediately for the turbolift.

Kirk lowered himself into the command chair. How many years, how much of his life, how much of his soul, had he given to this position? He'd retired from Starfleet, but this . . . this felt right.

And wrong, he admitted to himself. Not wrong for him, but wrong for this ship and crew. "Wait," he said as he heard the turbolift doors whisper open. "Your place is on the bridge of your ship. I'll take care of it." He stood and wasted no time in changing places with Harriman. As he passed the younger captain, he saw a look of determination on his face. Kirk couldn't tell for sure, but he thought that, if they survived this situation, Harriman would be all right.

Turning back toward the bridge at the threshold of the lift, he said, "Scotty, keep things together till I get back."

"I always do," the engineer said.

Kirk stepped back and let the doors slide closed, a smile sneaking onto his face at Scotty's easy self-assurance. He specified his destination and the lift began to descend. As it did, Kirk regarded the schematic in the rear bulkhead of the car. He saw where the turbolift would stop and the route he would have to take from there to get to the deflector relays. He would have to open the main deflector control assembly, then access the override panel and reprogram it to allow the resonance burst. *The safety,* he remembered, thinking back both to his classes at the academy and to the many briefings he'd received over the years about starship systems design. He would have to remove the safety component from the deflector relays and plug it into the override housing in order to authenticate his intentions.

The lift eased to a stop, then began gliding horizontally through the ship, toward the port side. Kirk could sense the strain of the engines as they struggled against the gravimetric distortions caused by the energy vortex. The ship still shuddered in the clutches of the tremendous forces.

Kirk raised a hand to the ship's schematic and traced a finger along the unfamiliar lines of this *Enterprise. This doesn't feel right,* he told himself, just as he had on the bridge, but now he added, *Not even for me.* He supposed that if he took command of this vessel and ventured out into the galaxy, it would one day become his ship, but right now, it didn't feel like that. Not like the first day he had set foot aboard the *Constitution*-class *Enterprise* twenty-eight years ago, not like the times he had returned to that ship after its refits, and not even like when he'd initially reported to NCC-1701-A, the former *Yorktown* renamed as a reward to Kirk and his crew for their service after the destruction of their original *Enterprise*. He would be content to leave this ship to Captain Harriman. As much as he loved command, Kirk needed to explore more than space; he needed to explore his own life.

The lift eased to a halt and when the doors parted, Kirk shot from them like the beam from a phaser.

The *Enterprise* rocked, and with it, the *Archimedes*. Kirk sat at the shuttle's forward console, his feet spread wide to steady himself in his chair. As he studied the sensor readouts, he knew that the time for action had drawn near.

Turning to his right, he checked the placement of the data card on which he'd recorded his message. It sat in an I/O receptacle, and once he'd activated it, it would play after any control on the forward console or on the hatch had been pressed. He then peered into the rear compartment, where he saw half a dozen phasers sitting on the transporter pad. Finally, he checked the programming he'd executed that tied the shuttle's antigravs and thrusters into its sensors.

All his preparations complete and verified, Kirk waited. According to the chronometer, it had been three minutes since he'd detected the destruction of the second transport vessel, the *Lakul,* within the energy ribbon. It could not be more than a minute and a half or two minutes before his counterpart enabled the main deflector to emit a resonance burst and break the *En-terprise* free. When that happened, he would have only seconds to act.

While Kirk waited, he pressed a control that slid the protective shielding from the forward viewports, affording him a view of the hangar door. Thirty seconds passed. Sixty seconds. Ninety.

On the panel before him, an indicator detected a resonance burst emerging from the ship's main deflector. Kirk immediately touched a button, which would initiate thirty seconds later the condition for the playback of his recorded message. He then moved at once to the rear compartment, where he dropped to his knees and quickly triggered the maximum overload setting on each of the six phasers. Once he'd done that, he stood and performed a transport.

On the pad, the weapons disappeared in a nimbus of blue-white light. A glance through the forward viewports showed them materializing in the shuttlebay. Kirk then energized the transporter a second time.

As a halo of brilliant light formed in the air before him, he could only hope that he'd planned all of this well enough.

Jim Kirk found the ladder leading down into the maintenance corridor. He descended into the bowels of the ship and hurried forward, striving to keep his footing as the *Enterprise* continued to quake. Coolant leaks hissed in the enclosed space, intermittently sending up eruptions of vapor from rents in the bulkhead. Kirk raced through the clouds, feeling their cold touch.

Reaching the primary deflector control center, Kirk entered through its wide doors. Here too a fog of coolant blurred the air. Just a glance down into the compartment showed him where he needed to go. He climbed down a ladder to a walkway and removed the grating that covered the access to the main deflector relays. The ship reeled again, and the grate slipped from his hands and fell at least ten meters, rattling along the bulkheads as it did. Down another ladder, and at last he reached the main deflector control assembly. He opened the access plate and the relay emerged from behind it, automatically rising to situate itself beside the override panel. Kirk pulled himself back up the ladder and moved to the housing for the override. He opened the plate there to expose a series of optical chips utilized to program the main deflector. As quickly as he could, he chose the two that would allow him to do what he needed to do, and he started to reseat them in the circuit accordingly.

"Bridge to Captain Kirk," he suddenly heard Scotty's voice.

"Kirk here," he called as he slid the second chip into the appropriate slot. He jabbed at the override controls, reprogramming the relay to permit the resonance burst.

"I don't know how much longer I can hold her together," Scotty said, a familiar plaint. In other, less serious circumstances, Kirk would've laughed.

He finished working at the control panel, then hastily backed up and bent down to the deflector control assembly. With both hands, he grabbed the safety and pulled it free. Stepping back to the override panel, he bent and rammed the mechanism into place.

"That's it!" he called. "Let's go!"

"Activate main deflector," he heard Harriman order, his voice strong.

In the control center around Kirk, none of the equipment seemed to change, but he heard a loud whine that he knew must be the resonance burst. Even as the ship shook, he could feel it steadying by degrees, the feel of the drive becoming less labored.

"We're breakin' free," Scotty said.

The drone of the resonance burst ceased and the control center quieted dramatically. Kirk detected a change in the movement of the ship. He could never have described the sensation, but he had spent enough time aboard starships to recognize the change in attitude. He knew at that moment that this *Enterprise* and this crew would be safe.

Kirk started away from the deflector equipment, moving back along the walkway toward the ladder up. He reached it and began to climb, but then stopped. In the relative calm of the primary deflector control center, Kirk suddenly heard a familiar sound, its presence here and now making no sense to him.

Suddenly he saw bright blue-white light arising before his eyes, clouding his vision. He knew that he'd been caught in a transporter beam, but he had no idea why. Before him, the outer bulkhead vanished.

Then so did he.

SIXTEEN

2293

Jim Kirk materialized on a small transporter pad in a cramped space. He looked around, then stepped down and walked through the compartment's only exit. He found himself in what appeared to be the main cabin of a Starfleet shuttlecraft, though of a class he'd never before seen.

The deck moved beneath him, in the same relatively sedate manner that the *Enterprise* had as the resonance burst had broken the ship free of the energy ribbon. Kirk peered forward to the front of the craft, where through the viewports he saw a starship's hangar deck. He could understand why Harriman or Scotty or somebody else aboard the *Enterprise* would have transported him out of the deflector control room, since he'd seen the outer bulkhead breached just as he'd been beamed away. What he could not fathom is why he would be brought to a shuttle sitting in the ship's hangar. If he—

A bright flash of light suddenly flared through the viewports and a loud explosion filled the air. Kirk felt the concussion against the hull of the shuttle. It continued one second after another, and as he toppled to the deck, he couldn't tell whether the detonation was one long blast or several shorter ones. When finally the deafening noise quieted, he felt the shuttle shift beneath him, as though lifting off.

Kirk quickly scrambled to his feet and raced to the bow. Through the viewports he saw that half of the hangar door had been obliterated, exposing the shuttlebay to space. Intermittent blue sparks there indicated that an emergency force field had snapped into place. That should have prevented the shuttle from being blown out through the opening, but still it moved toward the missing half of the door.

Peering down at the console, Kirk searched the controls and readouts for the craft's status. Just as the shuttle hurtled from the *Enterprise*'s hangar, he saw what had happened: the antigravs had been charged and had carried the small vessel forward and into space. He looked up again and saw in the distance the whirling, thrashing form of the energy ribbon, but the shuttle, seemingly undirected, tumbled through the void, and he soon lost sight of the deadly phenomenon. Fortunately, the ribbon had appeared headed away from his location, but he would take no chances. Kirk sat down at the console and began working to take control of the shuttle.

"Jim," a voice suddenly said, and Kirk looked to the left to see his own image on a viewscreen. *"Please watch this entire message before taking any action— before engaging the shuttlecraft's engines or opening communications with the* Enterprise." Kirk stared at himself, knowing that he had never made such a recording. The man on it looked just like him, and even wore the white shirt and crimson vest of a Starfleet

uniform. *"I've locked down all of the controls in the shuttle, but I know that you're resourceful enough to free them if you try. I'm asking you to listen to me first. At the completion of this message, you'll find the shuttle released to your command."*

Kirk glanced down and reached across the panel to an engine control. When he touched it, it issued a short buzz, indicating its inactive state. *"I've programmed the thrusters and tied them into the sensors,"* the recording continued. *"Should the shuttle near the energy ribbon, the thrusters will engage to keep the craft safe."* Gazing again through the viewports, Kirk saw the energy ribbon return to view as the shuttle continued to spin through space, but the phenomenon seemed farther away now.

"I am you," the message went on, *"but from a future date. To make and leave you this recording, I arrived here through the Guardian of Forever."* Kirk felt a jolt at the mention of the time vortex. *"Because I am you, I know what the mere mention of the Guardian does to you, even after all these years."* The simple observation, the way it had been phrased, compelled Kirk to believe what he was being told. He continued to watch the recording.

"I also know that you think the Guardian was destroyed by the Klingons. I'll explain that. But first, know that I lived through the events that you just experienced: the christening and launch of the new Enterprise, *the unexpected distress call from the two transports, beaming aboard forty-seven of the* Lakul's *passengers, the destruction of the two ships within the*

energy ribbon, and then the Enterprise *becoming trapped herself."* Kirk noted the accurate rundown of the day's occurrences, sure that it too had been intended to convince him of the claims being made. *"Based on a theory advanced by Scotty,"* said his alleged future self, *"you went to the deflector control room and overrode the safeties to permit a resonance burst to be generated from the main deflector. That broke the hold of the ribbon's gravimetric field on the ship, but then a surge of energy ripped through the hull of the* Enterprise, *including punching a hole in the outer bulkhead of the deflector control room."*

"And that," proclaimed this other Kirk, *"was where the paths of our lives diverged. Unlike you, I was not transported to safety, but pulled into the energy ribbon, which it turns out is a gateway to a place called the nexus. I can best describe this place as a timeless dimension of the mind, though it must also have a physical component to it, since my body survived within it."* The other Kirk then described his experiences within the nexus, ending when he'd met another captain of another *Enterprise* from the year 2371. *"Picard reminded me how much I wanted to make a difference,"* he said. He told of how he had then left the nexus and come back to this universe in order to help that captain, Picard, prevent a madman named Soran from destroying the star Veridian and incinerating two hundred thirty million people. They had succeeded, stopping Soran on Veridian Three, but in returning to normal space, Kirk's presence had, by virtue of the significant buildup of chronometric particles in his body,

triggered something he called a converging temporal loop, which he then explained. He had been swept back into the nexus, but in this universe, vast tracts of time and space had been destroyed.

"And so I left the nexus again," the other Kirk said, "this time to the Guardian of Forever, five billion years in the past—before our sun burned hot in space." Kirk recognized the quote. "I came through the Guardian to this time by traveling backward through my own life. My intention was to find a way to prevent the converging loop without imperiling either the crew of the Enterprise-B or the population of Veridian Four, and without altering the timeline." Kirk understood well the necessity of avoiding changes to history.

"Now, if you're hearing this message, it means that I am no longer aboard the shuttle, but more important, it means that I have succeeded in preventing the destructive temporal loop. Because you did not enter the nexus, you did not leave it, and so you and your set of chronometric particles did not exist at two distinct points in time and space that were connected by the conduit of the nexus. Because I transported you to safety after you saved the Enterprise and her crew, that is no longer an issue either.

"But after the ship's encounter with the energy ribbon, you were presumed dead," the recording went on. "To avoid altering history, that must continue to be true. Using specific deflector frequencies, I hid your transport out of the deflector control room. I also simulated an explosion on the hangar deck as though it had been caused by the energy ribbon. The shuttle is *now tumbling through space. Because of the deflector frequency, the* Enterprise *crew will be unable to scan it for life signs, although they would not expect there to be any, since it appears to them as though the hangar deck had been breached and a shuttle blown out into space. As you know, the ship has no tractor beam to haul the shuttle back aboard. Should the crew attempt to beam it aboard, they'll find it impossible to fix a transporter lock on it because of the deflectors, though they will most likely attribute it to interference from the energy ribbon. They might intend to come back for the shuttle later, but for now they will leave it and head back to Earth so that the survivors of the* Lakul *can receive medical treatment."*

Well planned, Kirk thought.

"But there is still action to be taken," the message continued. *"Because you never entered the nexus, you will never meet Picard and never leave with him to stop the destruction of the Veridian star in the year twenty-three seventy-one. You must employ another means to do this, while at the same time averting any alteration to the timeline between now and then."* The other Kirk paused, then said, *"This is why I traveled to the Guardian. I know how you can do this."*

Kirk listened as his counterpart explained his plan. After that, the future Kirk listed a number of details about his life—about *their* life—in an attempt to further prove his identity. He talked about the first time he had ever traveled by transporter, on the occasion of his grandfather's funeral, and how it had seemed to him that the universe had dissolved around him, moved, and then re-formed. He mentioned what he had done in those solitary moments after learning of his father's death. He detailed how, in ancient caverns on the planet Vulcan, he had mourned his son David. And perhaps most convincing of all, he had spoken with difficulty about the private moments he had shared with Edith, moments that he had held close throughout the years.

After the recording had concluded, the forward console came to life. Kirk tapped at the gravity regulator and immediately felt a reduction in his apparent weight, confirming that the controls had, as promised, been unlocked. Before he did anything more, though, he sat quietly, attempting to process all that he had been told. Among other things, he wondered what had happened to his future self. According to the message, he had been aboard this shuttle when he'd transported Kirk out of the deflector control room, but he was not here now. Kirk imagined the sequence of events and their consequences. Because he had not been pulled from the *Enterprise* and into the nexus, he had also never exited the nexus, either to help Picard or to arrive on the world of the Guardian. He therefore had never leaped through the temporal vortex to the present, and so his future self no longer existed in this time period.

But then why didn't the recording cease to exist now too? Kirk asked himself, but he then gave the matter little thought. He knew well that the apparent paradoxes of time travel and the mysterious functioning of the Guardian of Forever often defied explanation. Instead, he really needed to concentrate on what he would do next. That, of course, depended on whether or not he believed the content of the message.

He decided that he did.

He looked down at the console and reached forward to work the passive sensors. He saw that the energy ribbon had now moved away from his location, and that the *Enterprise* had now departed the scene, no doubt heading back to Earth, just as the recording had suggested would happen.

Cautiously at first, Kirk operated the helm, steadying the shuttle and engaging its impulse drive. Once he had moved away from the site where the *Enterprise* had encountered the energy ribbon, he plotted a course and took the shuttle to warp. Behind him, he realized, lay a life of joy and pain, of success and failure, a life that Scotty and Chekov and the crew of the new *Enterprise*-B now believed had been lost.

Ahead of him lay the Guardian of Forever.

SEVENTEEN

2293

Kirk worked the helm controls of the shuttlecraft—the *Archimedes,* he had learned during his voyage—and brought it down through the cloud cover. Below extended the dull plain of this ancient, barren world. Fissures and rock formations appeared here and there, breaking up the otherwise-featureless surface.

The journey to this planet had taken weeks. Kirk had traveled well away from normal starship routes and shipping lanes, periodically setting down on some empty moon or asteroid. His goal had been to move through space unobserved, thus avoiding making any alterations to the timeline. He'd also throttled the shuttle back to impulse power a number of times in an attempt to mask his trail.

Up ahead, Kirk saw the horizon drop away. He checked the sensors and read the measurements of the crater. It descended to a depth of two hundred meters and stretched a kilometer in diameter. Here, twenty-three years earlier, while Kirk had lain comatose in a turbolift aboard the *Enterprise,* Korax had taken his own wounded starship and raced through the atmosphere, intent on laying waste to what he believed to be the site of a new Starfleet weapon. Instead, the Klingon commander had destroyed—or killed—the Guardian of Forever.

Or at least, so Kirk had thought. So everybody had thought. But on the recording that had brought him here now, Kirk's future self had revealed that when he'd left the nexus the second time and visited this place billions of years in the past, he had told the Guardian of its demise. More than that, he had asked both for its help and for it to save itself. It had seemed only reasonable to the future Kirk that a time portal would be able to move itself through time, and he had warned the Guardian to do just that before Korax's ship reached the surface of this world. He had also requested that when it did so, it moved itself to now, to the days after the *Enterprise* had encountered the energy ribbon. Kirk, his future self had hoped, would then be able to use the Guardian to complete his plan.

The shuttlecraft *Archimedes* flew past the raised rim of the crater and out over the wide hollow. Within, the depression seemed empty, devoid of any characteristics beyond the radial lines reaching out from its center. The place seemed as dead as the rest of this haunted world.

Kirk performed a sensor sweep. He found no life signs, but he also scanned in particular for waves of time displacement, a singular trait of the Guardian. He studied the area within the crater itself and then out beyond that, to the limits of the sensors.

He detected nothing.

Kirk brought the *Archimedes* down, following along the rounded slope. Near the center of the crater, he landed the shuttle. Before disembarking, he went to the rear compartment and retrieved a tricorder. He hesitated for a moment, then pulled out a phaser as well.

Outside, the ground crunched beneath his boots. The air seemed still and stale, the surroundings inert. Kirk corrected his earlier appraisal: this place did not feel haunted; it felt abandoned.

Activating the tricorder, Kirk scanned the immediate area. The readouts reflected the crash here of a Klingon starship: specific types and levels of radioactivity, certain metallic fragments atop and within the soil, the residue of materials unique to the construction techniques of the Klingon Imperial Fleet. He also detected, deep underground, rock strata of wildly varying ages: one hundred years, one thousand, one million. But while the latter readings indicated the presence at one time of the Guardian, they showed no sign of it being here now.

Maybe the Guardian was *destroyed,* Kirk thought. Or perhaps, prior to the impact, it had taken itself backward in time billions of years, spending its existence in an eternal loop. It had claimed to be its own beginning and its own ending, and perhaps that was what it had meant.

Kirk raised his eyes and peered along the rim of the crater above him. "Guardian!" he called. His voice seemed shallow in the empty place, and it generated no echo.

He waited for a few moments, then called again. He received no response, nor had he really expected any. Finally, he turned and headed back to the shuttle.

Seated at the front console, Kirk gazed out at the vacant crater. If the Guardian did not do what his future self had asked, if it did not save itself from being destroyed by Korax's ship by moving itself forward in time to now, then what would he do? *Or maybe I'm too late,* Kirk thought. Maybe the Guardian had already appeared during the weeks it had taken him to reach this planet, and then taken itself away again.

Whatever the case, if the Guardian did not appear, Kirk would have to choose another course. His future self had charged him with two responsibilities: work with Picard to stop Soran in 2371, and avoid changing history between now and then. If Kirk could not utilize the Guardian to reach Veridian Three at that time, then he would have to find another clandestine means of reaching the future.

Of course, you can always just live another seventy-eight years, he told himself. But he knew that he would need to live those decades in complete seclusion. In the years between 2293 and 2371, the universe had believed him dead, and in order to avoid altering the timeline, that would have to continue to be the case. Kirk did not relish the thought of living completely alone for all of that time, but even if he attempted to do so, and even if he managed to keep himself hidden away, he could not guarantee that he would even live to the year 2371. *And at one hundred thirty-eight, just how much help will I be in physically trying to stop a madman?*

No, much as he hated the idea, he needed the Guardian.

Kirk worked the sensor controls, programming to scan continuously for any indications of temporal displacement—and to be safe, for life signs. Then he stood up and moved to the rear compartment, where he opened the emergency survival cache. From it, he took a ration pack and a pouch of water.

Back in the front of the shuttle, he began to eat. It troubled him to have so little control of whatever would come next. The course his life would take from here, as well as the fate of the hundreds of millions on Veridian IV, might depend on the Guardian of Forever.

That thought did not fill him with confidence.

On his thirteenth day at the bottom of the crater, Kirk woke with the gray dawn, just as he had on the previous dozen days. He rose from his bedroll and immediately checked the sensors. They read clear, and the log confirmed what the lack of any alarms through the night had already told him: there had been no sign of the Guardian.

Kirk walked back into the rear compartment, into the refresher. Afterward, he ate his morning rations and drank the allotment of water he allowed himself. When he'd finished, he grabbed up his tricorder and phaser and went outside.

The days here had passed slowly and without variation. The overcast skies brightened and darkened, but other than that, they never changed. The impact crater caused by Korax's vessel stood as silent and unmoving testament to the destruction that could be wrought by distrust, but it too remained the same.

It seemed appropriate to Kirk that he had ended up here again. The sacrifice that this place had demanded of him had never left him. He had never expected to return here. After he and Spock had traveled back to Earth in 1930 to retrieve Bones and restore history, he had wanted nothing more than to put as much distance as he could between himself and the Guardian, between his life without Edith and his life with her.

But when the *Enterprise* had been scheduled a couple of years later to return, Kirk had relented. He and Spock and Bones had been ordered, by virtue of their previous experience with the Guardian, to directly support the efforts of a group of Federation historians, and he had not allowed his emotions to keep him away. He had instead focused on his duties as a Starfleet officer, suppressing as best he could the memories of his own shattered dreams. Still, the Guardian had demonstrated how easily the timeline could be altered, how effortlessly lives could be torn asunder.

The third time he'd come here, when the *Enterprise* had received a distress call from the Einstein research station that had once orbited here, he had not even made it down to the planet's surface. Rather, the temporal emanations had caused a Klingon squadron to assume the worst and launch an attack. Kirk and his crew had largely—and almost miraculously—survived that encounter, while many other Starfleet and Klingon officers had not. Kirk had not even seen the Guardian during that incident, and yet something—his proximity to it, he supposed—had left him with the uncomfortable feeling of being linked to it in some way. It made no sense, but—

The air suddenly shifted and cooled slightly, and

Kirk heard a sound he could not place, but that he vaguely recognized. He looked over to the center of the crater and saw a mist hovering above the land. His heart began to race, but whether out of anticipation or dread he could not tell.

A moment later, the mist cleared, and the irregular ring of the Guardian of Forever stood there, looking precisely as it had on the other occasions Kirk had seen it. He walked up to it at once, feeling a sense of urgency that he immediately recognized as foolhardy. Whether he traveled to Veridian Three now or a year from now, he would arrive at the same time, at the same place.

"Guardian," he said. "Do you know me?"

It did not respond, which did not surprise Kirk. Before his second visit here, he had read the reports of the researchers, who noted that the Guardian did not provide answers to every question put to it. Kirk decided to ask something he had asked before and which had netted a reply.

"Guardian," he said, "are you machine or being?"

Still nothing.

Kirk opted for a different approach. "Guardian, my future self helped to rescue you from destruction."

"I am my own beginning, my own ending," it said, sections of its asymmetrical loop glowing in time with its words. Its voice sounded loud and deep, even within the wide space of the crater.

"Have you come here, to this time, from twenty-three Earth years ago?" Kirk asked, wanting to verify what he had been told.

"I am the Guardian of Forever," the vortex declared. *"I am the union and the intersection of all moments and all places. I am what was and what will be. Through me is eternity kept."*

"Did you travel to this time to avoid your own end when a Klingon vessel crashed onto this world?" Kirk wanted to know.

Again, the Guardian answered only with silence.

There's no use waiting to see if this will work, Kirk thought. "I wish to see the past of Jean-Luc Picard, whose life once intersected with that of my future self," he said. He could have asked to see the life of the future Kirk, but since he had himself never entered the nexus, his future self had never left it, had never joined Picard's battle against Soran—at least, that's what he thought. Temporal mechanics frequently failed to make sense. Still, regardless of his own involvement or lack of involvement in fighting Soran, Picard definitely had, and so a replay of his life would reveal the time to which Kirk needed to travel.

"Behold," the Guardian said. *"A gateway to the past, if you wish."*

The white mist reappeared, falling from the top of the Guardian's ring and through the wide opening at its center. Then images began to form: a baby being born, being held by his mother, crying as he was fed. Sleeping, crawling, learning to walk. Going to school, walking between rows of plants, wrestling with a larger, older boy.

Kirk watched as the life of a man he had never met unfolded before him. The experience felt voyeuristic, like an invasion of this man's privacy. But he continued to look on, the lives of two hundred thirty million Veridians the overriding issue.

As the minutes passed, so too did the weeks and months and years, and eventually the decades too. Kirk saw Picard grow from an infant into a boy, from a teenager into a man, from a son into a student, from a cadet into a starship captain. He looked on in wonder as a Starfleet vessel with four warp nacelles became visible within the Guardian. Later, a larger ship appeared, and Kirk recognized its designation at once: NCC-1701-D.

Finally, he saw Picard materialize in a rocky wilderness. He looked just as Kirk's future self had described him, as did the man Picard subsequently fought: Soran. The *Enterprise* captain failed, though, and a missile launched from the planet's surface and traveled into the star it orbited. Above, the unmistakable form of the energy ribbon twisted through the air, and when the Veridian star collapsed, the ribbon shifted downward, skimming along close to the ground. Electric bolts shot from it across its length, and roiling clouds followed behind it as it advanced. It passed over Picard and Soran, surrounding them with jags of energy and a billowing haze.

And then the images within the Guardian ceased. The mist continued flowing through its opening, but where Kirk had been watching scenes from Picard's life, he now saw a shadowy emptiness. *The nexus,* he thought. Picard had been pulled into it and had continued to live, but he no longer did so within this universe. He asked the Guardian for confirmation of this, but it did not answer.

"Guardian, I wish you to stop," he said. The shadows within the time vortex faded and the mists receded. He would ask the Guardian to show Picard's past again. This time, Kirk would join him to fight Soran.

But not yet, Kirk thought. Before he stepped through the Guardian in an effort to save more than two hundred million Veridians, he decided to do something for himself. Alone on this world, and now alone in a life that all his friends believed had ended aboard the *Enterprise*-B, he would take one last look at the people he had loved.

"Guardian," he said, "I want to see the past of my father."

"Behold," the Guardian said. *"A gateway to the past, if you wish."* Again, mist drifted down through the time vortex. Within the white vapor, images appeared.

And then Jim Kirk watched his father being born.

The day had passed too quickly. In some sense, Kirk had spent it with the people who had meant the most to him in his life, seeing them from birth to death in a way that should have been impossible. He had watched scenes that had made him laugh aloud, a lonely sound quickly lost within the expanse of the crater. He had cried too, both from joy and from sadness at the images passing before him. Mostly, though, he had simply looked on quietly, stilly.

After seeing his father's past, he had asked to see his mother's. Then he'd watched the life of his older brother, Sam, and then that of Sam's wife, Aurelan. He'd watched his grandfather's life, his uncle's, his nephews', his son's. He'd watched Spock and Bones and Gary Mitchell, Miramanee and Antonia. Throughout each of them, he'd often seen himself moving through these lives not his own, affecting them. For those who'd survived him, he viewed scenes unknown to him: Spock holding an infant, Bones getting married, Antonia finding love again. It had been both easy and difficult, but in the end, something he'd been pleased that he'd done.

"Guardian," he said at last, almost ready to have the life of Jean-Luc Picard replayed so that he could step into it. But before he did that, he thought to ask to see the past of one other person. He didn't know whether or not he'd be able to watch, but he wanted to try. "Guardian," he said again. "I wish to see the life of Edith Keeler, whose life once intersected my own, through you."

"Behold," the Guardian said.

TERMINUS

Crucible

As Jim Kirk swept the floor of the 21st Street Mission, he stole glances across the room and into the kitchen. Along with one of the former vagrants who often worked at the mission, Edith washed the dishes from the night's last meal. Even now, after another long and tiring day laboring to help the downtrodden, she looked beautiful. Kirk had never met anybody with her spirit. A woman of vision and compassion, she saw a future she could not possibly know and that should have been impossible for her even to imagine, a future in which all of humanity would work together for the common good. Far removed from those distant hopes, though, Edith did what she could in her own present to move society in that direction, helping the less fortunate because she felt a responsibility to the civilization of which she was a part. Kirk could not have loved her more.

Ahead of him, Spock lifted the last of the chairs from the floor and placed them upside down on the end of the table. He then walked over to the raised platform at the side of the room, to where Kirk had left the dustpan and wastebasket. As the Vulcan did so—the points of his ears as always covered by the black knit cap he wore—Kirk saw him look over at Edith.

Kirk knew that his friend did not approve of his relationship with the social worker. They had traveled to Earth in 1930 to find McCoy, the victim of an accidental cordrazine overdose and an equally accidental trip back through time. The doctor had changed history in a way that had allowed Nazi Germany and its fascist allies to win World War II, completely altering the future. Kirk and Spock had come back after McCoy, to a time before he'd arrived in the past, and though they had yet to find him, they had learned just how he had impacted the timeline: he had prevented Edith from dying in a traffic accident. Now they had to stop him from doing so.

That knowledge wounded Kirk deeply. He had fallen in love with Edith weeks ago—almost as soon as he'd met her—but he knew what he must do. He could not follow his heart, for then, as Spock had told him, millions would die who had not died before.

I should just stay away from Edith, Kirk told himself as Spock walked over to him with the cleaning implements. He'd had the same thought over and over again, even before he'd found out that Edith would soon die—that she *had* to die. For no matter what McCoy had done to alter the past, once Kirk and Spock had prevented him from doing so, they would presumably return to their own time in the twenty-third century. Whether Edith survived or not, Kirk would be forced to leave her. Falling in love and continuing to spend time with her therefore made little sense. But then, love often carried its own meaning, its own reason for being. *Better to have loved and lost,* Kirk thought, quoting Tennyson.

He reached the corner of the mission's main room and finished sweeping. When Spock came over with the dustpan and wastebasket, they worked together silently to gather up and discard the dirt and refuse Kirk had collected. They finished in short order and Spock went to put away all of the cleaning tools. As he did so, Kirk gathered up their coats, as well as Edith's cloak. When Spock returned and reached for his, Kirk said, "I'm going to wait for Edith." Because of her importance to the timeline, Kirk and Spock had agreed that at least one of them should keep her under surveillance at all times. Apart from all of that, though, Kirk recognized the simple truth that he *wanted* to be with Edith.

"Of course," Spock said. It seemed obvious to Kirk that Spock also saw his desire to spend time with her.

"Has McKenna gotten those components you needed yet?" Kirk asked, seeking to change the subject, but also curious about Spock's efforts to restore the mnemonic memory circuit he had created, a computer aid that had helped him determine McCoy's role in modifying the past. A watchmaker, Mr. McKenna had at one time also done radio repair work, and in addition to allowing Spock to use some of his fine tools, he'd been able to help him secure various pieces of equipment. Recently, after a particularly demanding search via the mnemonic memory circuit had over-loaded it, Spock had ordered vacuum tubes and a transformer from the watchmaker.

"He has," Spock said. "He told me that I could stop by his apartment tonight to pick them up, which is what I intended to do."

"Very good," Kirk said. "The more information we have, the better." Though Kirk believed that, he also didn't know whether it would help him to know precisely when Edith would die. Bad enough that he knew she would not live much longer, but to be able to count down the time he had left with her might be too much for him to bear.

Thinking of Edith, Kirk looked over to where she continued working in the kitchen. She saw him and smiled, then said, "We'll be done in just a few minutes."

"Oh, that's okay, Miss Keeler," said the man washing dishes with her. "I can finish up here. You can go."

"Are you certain?" Edith asked.

"Sure, I don't mind," the man said. "You go on."

"Thank you," Edith said. As she patted the man on the arm in an obvious gesture of appreciation, Kirk felt a smile bloom on his face, grateful for any extra time he could have with her. He watched her dry her hands on a rag, then bend down behind the counter. A moment later, she came through the kitchen's swinging doors holding her pale blue hat and her handbag. She wore a simple outfit of a black skirt and a white blouse, modestly covering the lovely body that Kirk had come to know so well.

Edith put on her hat, and then Kirk held open her cloak, helping her on with the navy blue garment. After he and Spock had donned their own coats, they headed for the double doors at the front of the mission. There, Spock held open one of the doors, and Kirk followed Edith out into the cool night. The lights of street lamps and automobiles reflected from the damp surfaces of the sidewalks and roads, wet from an earlier rain shower.

"Good night, Mister Spock," Edith said, glancing behind her as Spock exited the mission.

"I'll see you back at the apartment," Kirk told him with a quick wave.

"Good night," Spock said, returning Kirk's wave with his own clumsy gesture. Given their circumstances, Spock had done what he could to blend in to their ancient setting, his efforts essentially succeeding, though to varying degrees.

As Spock moved off down the sidewalk to the right, Kirk put his arm around Edith's back and started into the street. They stepped down from the sidewalk, but then two quick beeps sounded to their left. At the same time that Kirk saw an automobile bearing down on them, he hauled Edith backward. Tires squealed on the pavement as the automobile stopped right before them. The driver honked his horn again, and then once more for a longer burst.

Kirk's heart raced. Not only had Edith just been endangered, but he realized that he might at that moment have changed history, relegating Earth to a Nazi victory in World War II. *But McCoy's not here yet,* Kirk told himself. *This can't be the time.*

Edith's hand had gone up around his back, and now she urged him forward. As they passed in front of the stopped automobile, Kirk made an effort to cover his anxiety, offering a wave of apology to the driver. He dropped his arm from around Edith and took her hand as they hurried to the far sidewalk.

"Oh," he began, remembering that he and Edith had earlier talked about taking a romantic walk down by the waterfront. Before he could continue, though, Edith excitedly suggested that, if they hurried, they could see a movie over at the Orpheum. As she mentioned how she'd love to see the film, Kirk said, "What?" He knew that he'd much prefer spending time with Edith in a setting where he could interact with her, rather than in a place where they would have to remain silent.

As they stepped up onto the sidewalk, Edith said, "You know, Doctor McCoy said the same—"

The name struck Kirk as effectively as a blow to the face. He whirled around to Edith, letting go of her hand and grabbing her by her upper arms. "McCoy?!" he said. "*Leonard* McCoy?"

Edith gazed up at him in evident confusion. "Yes," she said. "He's in the mission, he's—"

"Stay right here," Kirk told her forcefully. He looked past her then, down the street in the direction that Spock had walked. He shouted his friend's name, then let go of Edith and started back across the street, back toward the mission. "Stay right there," he called back to her. As he saw Spock hurrying back along the sidewalk, Kirk could only think one thing: *McCoy!* If they had found him, then maybe they could determine some means of repairing the damage to the timeline without having to let Edith die. Maybe they could even find a way of bringing her back with them to the future.

Kirk ran in front of another automobile, earning him another beep of a horn, but he paid it little attention. He leaped the curb in front of the mission just as Spock arrived there. "What is it?" the first officer asked.

"McCoy," Kirk said, pointing to the front doors. "He's in—" He stopped in midsentence as he looked toward the mission and saw the doctor emerging from within. "Bones!" he yelled, and he rushed toward his old friend.

"Jim!" McCoy called. Kirk embraced Bones, saying his nickname again, almost as though trying to confirm his presence here. Beside them, Spock had reached for McCoy's hand, and now the two shook enthusiastically, a rare show of emotion for the Vulcan.

"I'm so happy to see you two," Bones said. As he spoke, Kirk peered back toward Edith. He saw that she had started walking back across the street, her eyes focused on the trio in front of the mission. Without looking, Kirk heard the sound of an approaching vehicle, and in an instant, he knew that the time had come. "I didn't know where I was, or how I got here," McCoy began, but he stopped as Kirk stepped away from him and back across the sidewalk.

Kirk staggered forward even as both of his friends yelled to him. "No, Jim!"

Kirk stopped at the curb. "Edith—" he said, the single, desperate word not much more than a whisper. Edith continued walking toward him, seemingly unaware of the danger. Kirk wanted to go to her, wanted to throw himself into her path and save her from her fate, no matter the consequences.

Instead, he stood there.

And then somebody bumped him from behind, attempting to push past him. Kirk knew it had to be McCoy. He raised his arm to block the doctor's progress, then turned and threw his arms around his friend. Unable to watch, Kirk buried his head atop McCoy's shoulder, his eyes slammed shut. He heard the whine of tires on the street, and then he heard Edith scream. He did not even recognize her voice, but then a terrible sound reached him as her head struck the pavement.

That quickly, Kirk had lost everything in his life that could have been.

The beat of footsteps went up as people rushed to the scene of the accident. Kirk couldn't move, couldn't even open his eyes. The pain of his loss pressed in on him, filled him, and he wanted nothing more in that moment than to let go, to crumple lifeless to the ground beside his beloved.

"You deliberately stopped me, Jim," McCoy accused him, and Kirk realized that he still held on tightly to the doctor. He opened his eyes as McCoy continued his indictment. "I could have saved her," he said. "Do you know what you just did?"

Kirk pushed away from McCoy then, lurching over

to the front doors of the mission. There, he leaned heavily against the jamb. *What have I done?* he thought, and even though he knew the answer, it didn't matter; he knew that the question would remain with him always.

"He knows, Doctor," he heard Spock say. "He knows."

Kirk felt empty and weak. He clenched his fist, fighting just to maintain his equilibrium. In his mind's eye, though, all he could see was Edith's face.

EIGHTEEN

Within the mysterious mists of the Guardian, the events of Captain Jean-Luc Picard's life played out once more. Jim Kirk had completed his preparations for the journey to come, taking the shuttlecraft out of the crater and hiding it in the base of a deep crevice. He then fixed its engines to explode in a way that would leave behind as little evidence as possible, then beamed back to the Guardian of Forever. There, he watched closely, waiting for the right moment. When it came, he jumped through the time vortex.

As he landed softly on a rocky surface, he saw a sandstone wall rising before him. A hot, dry wind blew past, bringing with it the scent of dust and the grit of the air. He turned and peered out across the rocky terrain, recognizing the surface of Veridian Three from the images he'd seen within the Guardian. He looked for any sign of Picard or Soran, but then an explosion ripped apart a stone ridge twenty or twenty-five meters away. Rubble rained down on the landscape as a cloud of dust rose into the air. Through it, Kirk thought he saw movement, a dash of color, red and black, but then it vanished behind other rocks.

He stepped forward, believing that he'd just seen Picard. Suddenly, two bright green pulses screamed through the air, obviously shots from an energy weapon. Kirk backed up against the sandstone wall, taking cover as best he could as the ridge where he thought he'd seen Picard exploded again. Above it, the orange spark of a massive force field blinked on and off. On the ridge, a rock slab fell from its place and tumbled heavily to the ground.

More debris showered down around Kirk. He waited, not wanting to reveal himself to whoever had fired the weapon—Soran, no doubt. As the seconds ticked away, he watched the surrounding area, which offered numerous places to conceal oneself: fissures cut the ground and boulders stood tall all around.

Finally, unwilling to wait any longer for fear of failing in his mission, he started forward. But then he saw a hand appear at the edge of a crevice just in front of him. Cautiously, he stepped over to it and looked down. There, he saw Picard attempting to pull himself upward. The future captain of the *Enterprise* saw him and froze, clearly unsure what to make of another person here on Veridian Three.

"I'm here to help you stop Soran," Kirk said. He bent down and reached for Picard's hand. For a moment, the captain didn't move, but then he seemed to make a decision and he allowed Kirk to take his hand and pull him out of the crevice. When Picard stood before him, Kirk said, "I'm—"

"Kirk," Picard said, obviously bewildered by his realization. "James T. Kirk."

"Yes," he confirmed, and then he told an abbreviated version of the tale that his future self had offered.

"When I was lost aboard the *Enterprise*-B," he said, "I didn't die. I was pulled into the nexus." An expression of at least partial understanding seemed to dawn on Picard's face. "I was able to leave it now, to come here and help you stop Soran from destroying the Veridian star and the two hundred thirty million on Veridian Four."

"How is that possible?" Picard asked.

"I don't know, but does it matter?" Kirk asked. "That was Soran firing at you just now, wasn't it?"

"It was," Picard said. He paused, and Kirk knew that he weighed the current circumstances as best he could. Kirk felt no need to try to convince Picard of his identity or his intentions, knowing that the captain would reach his own conclusions. One fact, he knew, would stand out for Picard: no matter who Kirk actually was, he could easily have subdued the captain when he'd stood over him a moment ago; instead, Kirk had helped him.

"Soran's got a handheld energy weapon," Picard said at last, "but he's alone here. If we attack him from opposite sides, one of us should be able to stop him. The missile he wants to launch into the star is in that direction—" He pointed. "—but he's also got ladders and bridges and platforms scattered all over the mountainside."

"How much time is there before he launches the missile?" Kirk asked.

"Soon," Picard said. "Perhaps only a matter of minutes."

"Then we'd better get going," Kirk said.

* * *

Kirk leaped.

He felt the hanging section of bridge beneath him shake as he sprang forward across open space, and then he landed hard on the other side. He took hold of a chain there with one hand, pushing the fingers of his other hand through the grated surface and grabbing on there. That section of the bridge shifted and swayed, its metal components whining and cracking beneath the force of his landing and his continued weight on it. It dropped suddenly to an even steeper angle, and he quickly let go of the chain and clutched that hand through the grating as well.

He heard a clatter above him, and he glanced upward just in time to see Soran's control pad sliding down the surface of the bridge toward him. Letting go with one hand, he reached up and somehow caught the device. He studied its marking and controls for a moment, then pointed the pad toward where Soran's trilithium missile sat cloaked. With the bridge trembling beneath him, Kirk pushed a button—fortunately, the right button. Atop its platform, Soran's deadly weapon faded into view. Below it, Picard climbed the ladder leading up to it, rushing to stop the missile from launching.

Kirk tucked the control pad into his waistband, then reached again for the chain. He intended to pull himself up as quickly as he could, but then he heard the snap of metal fracturing above him. He knew that he didn't have much time.

That was when the bridge fell.

* * *

Kirk had no idea whether he'd retained consciousness or how much time had passed, but he heard what he gradually recognized as the scrape of footsteps in the dirt. He tried to move, but found it impossible even to keep up the effort for more than a second or two. He'd fallen to the ground on his back, and the great mass of the wrecked bridge pinned him there. Though he felt no pain, he knew that he'd been crushed, his organs damaged to a fatal degree. His eyes and ears still functioned, and he tasted blood in his mouth, but he could do nothing now but wait for death to take him.

Somebody or something moved about him, in the rocky surroundings and the metal ruins that would form his tomb. He saw a metal bar slide away, and a chain, and he heard the heavy pieces clanking to the ground. Then, above him, Picard gazed at him through the ruins of the bridge.

Kirk blinked, searching for the strength to speak. "Did we do it?" he asked softly, remembering how his future self had told him the way in which Picard had urged him to leave the nexus. "Did . . . we make a difference?"

"Oh, yes. We made a difference," Picard said seriously. "Thank you."

"Least I could do," Kirk struggled to say, "for the captain of the *Enterprise*." He peered away from Picard, thinking of the odd course the last moments of his life had taken. On the brink of being swept into the nexus, only to leave it to come here in an attempt to save the lives of two hundred thirty million people he had never met, he had instead taken a final trek through space and one last trip through the Guardian. In the end, he had come here after all, had done what he had apparently done once before, namely stopping Soran and preventing the destruction of the civilization on Veridian IV. "It was . . . fun," he told Picard. Kirk smiled as best he could.

Time seemed to slow down. He peered past Picard and into the sky over his right shoulder. Amid the high clouds scattered across the field of blue, Kirk saw something. At first impossible to make out, the faint image gradually resolved itself into hazel eyes, a slender nose, lips that curled upward in an inviting smile. *Edith,* Kirk thought, and in that moment, he felt fulfilled all of the desperate hopes he had never even dared to have. He knew that, impossibly, she waited for him on the other side.

"Oh, my," Kirk said. Though he did not close his eyes, his vision faded, dimming from the outside until he could see nothing. But in his mind, the image of Edith's face remained.

More ready than he'd ever been to rejoin his true love, Jim Kirk let go of life.

EPILOGUE

The Edge of Forever

James T. Kirk stood in the middle of the great, empty plain, watching as first the images and then the mists within the Guardian of Forever faded. He had just viewed the life of his counterpart, whom he had transported out of the *Enterprise*-B's main deflector control room and into the shuttlecraft *Archimedes*— where before that earlier Jim Kirk had materialized, Kirk had been pulled back here by the Guardian. Although he hadn't known whether the time vortex would accede to his request, Kirk had actually asked to be returned here if he managed to prevent the converging temporal loop. Once he had beamed his alter ego out of the path of the energy ribbon, that had been the case.

Now, he stood before the mysterious portal, having just watched the last moments in the life of that other Kirk, confirming that he had aided Picard and had thereby saved the population of Veridian IV. Remarkably, everything had transpired more or less as he had planned just before he had left the nexus the second time. He had no idea whether any echo or other version of himself remained within that timeless other-space or not, since he had stopped himself from entering it in the first place. And he didn't quite understand how he had essentially managed to replicate himself, since five billion years from now he would die on Veridian Three beneath the mass of a metal bridge.

He did know this: he stood here on a world before Earth's sun had formed, all of his responsibilities satisfied. The converging temporal loop had been averted, the crew of the *Enterprise*-B had been rescued from the clutches of the energy ribbon, the people of Veridian IV had been saved, and he had avoided altering the timeline between 2293 and 2371. The universe believed him dead. Now, alone here with the Guardian, his thoughts turned to Edith.

When Kirk and Spock had traveled back in time to 1930, the only option they'd had in restoring history had been to stop McCoy from damaging it. In the years since, though, when he'd been unable to keep his memory from returning to Edith, Kirk had occasionally imagined taking some action not only to save the life of his beloved, but to allow him to then spend his life with her. He'd considered going back to the Guardian and somehow finding a way of bringing Edith safely forward, or of remaining in the past with her, without altering the timeline. Although he'd had a number of ideas on the subject, he'd never seriously considered attempting any of them.

But now, standing here with the Guardian of Forever before human beings had ever even evolved on Earth, before there had even been an Earth, he reconsidered. In many ways, he had all the time in the world. All the time in the *universe,* really.

"Guardian," he said.

AFTERWORD

Here There Be Dragons

And by dragons, I mean to say spoilers. If you haven't yet read the novel that you are holding in your hands, or if you intend to read either of the other volumes in the *Crucible* trilogy for the first time, then turn back now. You can always return here and read this afterword at a later point.

In the forewords to this and the other two books, I wrote in nonspecific terms about the process involved in penning the three tales. There, in those introductory pieces, I didn't want to reveal too much about the stories, preferring to allow them to speak for themselves. Now, though, with the trilogy completely written—and, I hope, completely read—I thought that some readers might find interest in my revisiting in a more explicit way some of the details involved in the development and creation of *Crucible*.

After editor Marco Palmieri offered me the opportunity to write a *Star Trek* trilogy and I accepted the invitation, I began to consider just how I should go about crafting it. I decided almost at once that I didn't want to plot out a single, large story that would spread across the three books. Rather, I preferred to tell a trio of individual tales, all self-contained, but also inter-weaving with and informing one another. With that viewpoint in mind, it soon became clear to me that one way to approach the trilogy would be to center each volume around one of the three main characters of McCoy, Spock, and Kirk. After all, the episodes of the Original Series had primarily been rendered in such a fashion, and since these novels would help celebrate the fortieth anniversary of *Star Trek*, why not have them reflect that aspect of the show?

At the same time, I also had a vague notion in the back of my mind that I would like to somehow follow up my own favorite TOS episode, one of those often found at the tops of various fan polls regarding *Trek*'s finest hours. For a long time now, I've held aloft Har-lan Ellison's "The City on the Edge of Forever" as a high-water mark of the Original Series. So I asked my-self if I could find some compelling means of em-ploying the elements of that episode in the trilogy.

While allowing that idea to percolate, I took the time to view the entire series from beginning to end, from the first episode to the last, and then through the seven feature films. Although I had already seen each installment on many occasions over the years, this time I watched them from a different perspective, with an eye toward finding some facet of the characters that ei-ther hadn't yet been explored or that would at least permit me to say something about them in a unique manner. As I saw and enjoyed one hour after another,

I also realized that since the novels would be a part of the show's anniversary celebration, I should attempt to deeply ground them in those original episodes. I did not wish to limit the tales to the five-year mission necessarily, but I thought that period should in some way play a significant role in the books. Of course, if I managed to tie in "The City on the Edge of Forever," that likely would be the case anyway.

In watching the complete run of the series, I began to notice something about Dr. McCoy that I previously hadn't. While I had at first imagined that fashioning a story to tell about the *Enterprise*'s chief medical officer would be more difficult than doing so for the ship's captain and first officer, I suddenly saw that might not be true. McCoy, I realized, had lived as something of a loner, at least in terms of romance. Such a circumstance might not be considered that unusual during a long space voyage in the service of Starfleet, perhaps, but I also spied hints that this might be true of the good doctor even apart from his time aboard the *Enterprise*.

In "The Man Trap," the very first *Star Trek* episode ever aired, back on Thursday, 8 September 1966, McCoy briefly mentions his involvement a decade earlier with a woman named Nancy, now married to Professor Robert Crater. In his captain's log, Kirk refers to her as "that one woman in Doctor McCoy's past." McCoy himself seems alternately anxious and reluctant to see her, but little else is revealed about the erstwhile relationship, other than that they "walked out of each other's lives ten years ago."

Later in the first season, in the episode "Shore Leave," McCoy appears to enjoy a dalliance with crew member Tonia Barrows, but the red-tressed yeoman never appears in the series after that, nor do any of the characters ever even speak of her again. McCoy then traverses the entire second season without even a hint of romance. In *Star Trek*'s third year, he finally finds love again, this time with Natira in the episode "For the World Is Hollow and I Have Touched the Sky." But McCoy's entanglement with the high priestess of Yonada seems as much a consequence of the unexpected discovery that he has xenopolycythemia and only a year left to live as of a real depth of romantic emotion.

And that's it. Through the seventy-nine aired hours of *Trek,* and then through the seven films, those are the only instances in which McCoy's love life is at all revealed. Still, throughout the three seasons and the movies, there is ample evidence that the doctor has an appreciation for the opposite sex. In "Mudd's Women," he is bewitched by Ruth; in "Wolf in the Fold," he is anxious to visit a place that Kirk knows "where the women are so . . ."—so something left to the imagination; in "Is There in Truth No Beauty?" he appears enamored of Dr. Miranda Jones; and in *The Wrath of Khan,* he notes Saavik's good looks. In even more episodes than that, McCoy demonstrates an obvious fondness for women.

Despite all of that, though, he is almost never seen to be involved with anybody. Even in "This Side of Paradise," when he falls under the uplifting influence of the spores on Omicron Ceti III, he remains alone, sipping mint juleps by himself. Now, I'm sure that the numerous writers of the Original Series did not intend to convey anything in particular about McCoy by this dearth of romantic relationships, that my observations about the character are merely the result of an accidental artifact of episodic television in the 1960s. Still, all of that led me to a question for which I wanted to find an answer: Why did Dr. McCoy have so little love in his life?

At that juncture, I recalled a piece of non-canon information about the doctor long accepted by many *Trek* fans, namely that he had a failed marriage in his past, a difficult, broken relationship that ultimately had driven him out into space with Starfleet. This backstory originated, I knew, in early drafts of the episode that would ultimately become "The Way to Eden." Instead of Chekov's former girlfriend, Irina Galliulin, McCoy's daughter Joanna came aboard the *Enterprise*. Further supporting the existence of Joanna, McCoy makes reference to his daughter in one of the twenty-two animated *Star Trek* adventures, "The Survivor." It then occurred to me that an unsuccessful marriage spun McCoy's character in a slightly different direction. Coupled with the loss of his relationships with Nancy, Tonia, and Natira, his failed attempt at matrimony made the question not why he'd had so few romances, but why they had never worked out for him.

I speculated that perhaps something in McCoy's personality prevented him from remaining in long-term relationships. He might have developed a fear of intimacy or a fear of abandonment. There are reasons that such characteristics arise in a person, oftentimes tracing all the way back to their childhood. I already knew from the fifth *Trek* film, *The Final Frontier,* that McCoy had with great difficulty assisted in his father's suicide when the elder McCoy lay dying and in pain. But what of McCoy's mother? I wondered.

While I attempted to work out such details, I thought again about "The City on the Edge of Forever," and suddenly I realized something. In that episode, when McCoy leaps through the Guardian of Forever and changes Earth's history from the twentieth century onward, he causes the alteration to the timeline by preventing the death of Edith Keeler. Miss Keeler subsequently founds a peace movement that delays the United States's entry into World War II, which in turn allows Nazi Germany and its allies to capture the world. As a result, the remainder of the *Enterprise* landing party find themselves totally alone on the Guardian's planet, with no ship circling in orbit above them and, as Spock notes, "with no past, no future." But in the modified past, I asked myself, what had become of McCoy?

All at once, I saw that an entire period of the doctor's life had been hiding in plain sight. Yes, his time in Earth's altered past had occurred in an alternate reality that ultimately gets reset, erased by Kirk and Spock chasing him back to 1930 and foiling him from stopping Keeler's death, but still, it *had* happened. If I wanted to investigate that time, I knew that I would need to do two things in order to make the story work for readers. First, I would have to find some means of having the events of McCoy's "other" life inform his "real" life, and second, I would need to utilize that other life to help explain and then deal with his pattern of unsuccessful relationships.

From there, the details of the story at last came together. I would produce parallel narratives, one taking place in McCoy's "present," during the *Enterprise*'s five-year mission and afterward, and one in his alternate past, beginning with his arrival in New York City in 1930. A title even suggested itself fairly quickly: *Provenance of Shadows*—making reference to the origin of the dark side of McCoy's life that had prevented him from finding happiness with a romantic partner.

Once I had finished beating out the plots and themes for the McCoy novel, I turned my attention to Spock. I at once found a starting point for his story late in McCoy's life, at a time when I knew that the two characters would come together in *Provenance*. I immediately liked that, seeing how I could tie the books together. From the two-part *Next Generation* episode "Unification," I knew that Spock's last canonical appearance had him on Romulus, where he sought to further the cause of reintegrating the Vulcan and Romulan peoples, who had common forebears. I actually wrote a complete outline in relatively short order, putting together a highly complex political tale that employed elements of the first *Crucible* novel, the TNG episode in which Spock appeared, and the tenth *Trek* film, *Nemesis*. From a character point of view, it explored how and why reunification had become so important to Spock.

After sitting on the outline and mulling it over for a few days, though, I decided that I had made a mistake. Too much of the story took place in a time frame far beyond that of the TOS series and movies, and the study of Spock relied on his hopes for uniting the Vulcans and Romulans, an examination far less personal than would satisfy me. Consequently, I scrapped my ideas without ever even submitting the outline to my editor.

And so I began again, this time concentrating once more on the episodes of the Original Series and asking some of the same questions about Spock that I had posed to myself about McCoy. What didn't I know about the character, and what would be worth discovering? I reviewed Spock's arc, beginning with the earliest canonical experiences of his life—his birth, as depicted in *The Final Frontier,* and his near-death ordeal at the age of seven, as seen in the animated episode "Yesteryear"—through to his experiences as a Federation special envoy in the sixth film, *The Undiscovered Country*. To my satisfaction, I found something that didn't quite scan for me, though I had never before thought about it. In *Star Trek*: *The Motion Picture,* it is revealed that, after the *Enterprise*'s five-year mission under Captain Kirk, Spock returned to Vulcan and sought to achieve the *Kolinahr*—the shedding of all emotion. I wanted to know why he had chosen to do that.

Now, I understood as well as any *Trek* fan that

Spock has always considered himself Vulcan, not human, and that he subscribes to the lifestyle of the former and not the latter. He purports to control his emotions—a claim observably true in most cases—but it also seemed clear to me that he *felt* friendship for Kirk and McCoy, even if he rarely expressed himself in quite that way. Spock also appeared satisfied with his life. Why then had he elected to leave Starfleet, to leave his friends, and to endeavor to fully purge himself of emotion?

I thought about this for some time. *The Motion Picture* also revealed that Captain Kirk had been promoted after the end of the five-year mission to admiral, and posted to the position of chief of Starfleet Operations. Could that have motivated Spock to do what he'd done? That seemed unconvincing and not quite right to me. I couldn't justify Spock's resigning his commission and wanting to totally rid himself of emotion simply because his friend had moved on in his career.

Perhaps a traumatic event had befallen the first officer, I speculated. Because of their appearances in later films, I knew that both of his parents, Amanda and Sarek, were alive during the time frame in question, though *The Next Generation* would reveal their later demises. Surely Spock's own death and then his rebirth in *The Wrath of Khan* and *The Search for Spock,* respectively, could be considered disturbing, but again, both had occurred *after* his decision to undergo the *Kolinahr.*

Since I could see nothing that would have reasonably impelled Spock to go back to Vulcan and try to completely eliminate his emotion, I wondered if I could develop that drive myself. But what form would that drive take? Once more, I looked to "The City on the Edge of Forever," and again, that episode revealed something to me that I had never before realized.

When Kirk and Spock travel back in time through the Guardian of Forever in an attempt to avert the change McCoy made—or will make—to history, the first officer counsels his captain and friend that it is of paramount importance to restore—or maintain—the timeline. This appears quite clearly to be a core principle to Spock, one that he espoused quite plainly in an earlier first-season episode, "Tomorrow Is Yesterday." It also seems reasonable: time and events have taken place, people have lived and died, and it would be unethical, perhaps even immoral, to alter those occurrences.

But then I considered the other occasions when Spock had traveled in time, and to my surprise, I saw that he had not always acted in concert with his professed convictions. In the animated episode "Yesteryear," he intentionally alters the flow of history for the purpose of saving both his mother's life and his own. And in *The Voyage Home,* he actually suggests plucking humpback whales from the past and bringing them into the future in order to attempt to save the population of Earth from an attacking alien probe. In both instances, though Spock possessed positive intentions which ultimately bore the fruits of his labors, he nevertheless violated the principle of striving to keep the timeline intact. He never appeared to consider doing so through the course of events in "The City on the Edge of Forever," nor did he search for any means of sparing Captain Kirk the terrible loss of Edith Keeler. Perhaps he wouldn't have been able to find a method of preserving the past without the death of Keeler, but he never even seemed to try.

This amounted to a subtle distinction in behavior, I knew, but one that I thought Spock and his acute, logical mind would discern. I also believed that Spock's understanding of what he had done—acting in opposition to principle when it suited him, but having failed to do so when it would have most benefited his best friend—could prey on him, particularly when provoked to think about it during extreme circumstances. Such circumstances, I thought, might include Jim Kirk's death.

It occurred to me then that, though Captain Kirk had passed away—at least as far as the people of the Federation knew—aboard the *Enterprise*-B, as seen in the film *Generations,* Spock's reaction to that loss had never been seen. Faced with his friend's death, perhaps the recollection of Spock's failure to even try to save the love of Kirk's life might resurface and push him to emotional distraction, perhaps even to the point where he would decide that he could no longer live with such intense feelings. And maybe a similar event had taken place at the end of the five-year mission as well, with Kirk believed dead and Spock having to face his guilt for having failed his friend in his time of need with Edith Keeler.

But if I chose to employ such a motivation for Spock at the end of the five-year mission, might that not also hold true when Kirk apparently died aboard the *Enterprise*-B? I saw then that I could explore Spock's *Kolinahr* not by going backward to the time between the Original Series and *The Motion Picture,* but by sending Spock to Vulcan to attempt a purging of his emotions a second time. In so doing, I could then also explain his first such experience, while at the same time moving the character forward from the continuity of the films.

By choosing this course for my storytelling, I understood that I would have to address Spock's emotional side, as well as his consistent decision to practice stoicism. I knew that the tale would be difficult to tell; investigating the feelings of a Vulcan, as well as the delicate nature of his guilt with Kirk, would not be easy. Still, I thought it a risk worth taking, in part because I recalled lines from the poem "Little Gidding," by T. S. Eliot:

> And all shall be well and
> All manner of thing shall be well
> When the tongues of flame are in-folded
> Into the crowned knot of fire
> And the fire and the rose are one.

In my mind, the fire represented Spock's emotional life, his hidden, controlled passions, while the rose signified the perfect form of his logic. I also knew T. S. Eliot's first lines in that stanza:

We shall not cease from exploration
And the end of all our exploring
Will be to arrive where we started
And know the place for the first time.

That seemed perfect to me. I could explore Spock's internal battle between emotion and logic, attempt to deliver a richer, deeper understanding of the character, and yet not conclude with a Spock vastly different than the one everybody already knows, and who would later appear in *The Next Generation*. I knew that it would be a complex task, dealing with the feelings of a mostly impassive personality, an individual in whom intellect often won out over heart, but I thought it would be worth shining a light on Spock in this way. So I decided to give it a shot.

Finally, then, I came to the tale of Captain Kirk. All along, I had believed that this would be the easiest of the three novels to develop. As with the other two stories, I would root the tale within the series and tie it into "The City on the Edge of Forever." As dramatic as Kirk's sacrifice of the woman of his dreams had been in that episode, there had never been any follow-up to it. Since "City" had taken place near the very end of the first season, and since Kirk's brother and sister-in-law had also died in the very next installment, I thought that I could go back to the ensuing period, before the next year of episodes, and examine the captain's reaction to such terrible losses in his life. What could be easier?

Except that I don't really enjoy doing things that are

easy. And I certainly do not like doing the expected. I reasoned that since the first two novels of the trilogy would be such heavy character pieces, perhaps I should consider a more action-oriented story for Kirk. I would still want to tie it in to the other two books through the crucible of the events in "The City on the Edge of Forever," but I wanted to find an unpredictable means of doing so. I looked at Kirk's life again, searching for the proper place to set my story, or at least to begin it.

Because of the impact his death would have on Spock in *The Fire and the Rose,* I found myself focusing on that incident. In *Generations,* Kirk acted nobly, agreeing to essentially eschew paradise and assist Picard in trying to stop Soran from causing the deaths of millions on Veridian IV. He and Picard succeeded, but Kirk perished in the attempt. A fitting end for the captain—selflessly saving lives—but I decided that I wanted him to save the universe just one more time.

But how could I do that? And how could I tie that in with Edith Keeler? Thinking about the events of *Generations,* and in particular about Kirk's time within the nexus, I considered the existence of Antonia, a woman with whom the captain had shared a serious relationship for two years, and whom he apparently regretted not having married. I remembered that when I'd seen the film for the first time, I'd felt disappointed that Kirk had not conjured up Edith Keeler within the nexus. I had always felt that Edith had been his one true love, and I so wanted that to be the case.

Maybe it was, though, I told myself. Maybe he had cared for Edith so much that even all those years later, even within the wonderfully illusory realm of the nexus, he could not face having lost her. And maybe he had loved Antonia, but ultimately hadn't married her because the memory of the love of his life remained too strong.

As I considered all of this, I saw a means of addressing it all, first employing the nexus as a narrative device, and then returning to the Guardian of Forever. Flashbacks suggested by the nexus would allow me to shine a light on Kirk's relationship with Antonia, and in so doing, reveal the deep impact that Edith's death had continued to have on him throughout the course of his life. I would leave the character as I had found him, dying essentially alone on a barren, alien world, the result of a final heroic act.

Once I had completed the outline and submitted it to my editor, Marco expressed some reservations about ending the fortieth-anniversary trilogy with a main character's death. I saw his point, even though I had envisioned writing that death in a stirring and positive way. It occurred to me then, though, that another avenue existed for Captain Kirk at the end of the book, a road he could take that would be, I thought, completely unexpected. I reframed the denouement of *The Star to Every Wandering*—a title I appropriated from a Shakespearean sonnet and that referred to true love—and then I set about writing the actual novels.

As I made my way through the first pages of the first book, I strived to keep all of the tales in mind so that I could tie them together at various points. I didn't really think much about the nature of the outlines initially, simply hoping that I had put together solid stories that would entertain and surprise readers. But as I continued along, I realized that I had actually crafted three unusual *Trek* stories. Marco felt the same way, and at a convention would later remark that I had told the stories within the trilogy in a way that had never before been tried in *Star Trek* novels.

As I've mentioned, I like to defy expectations, but I also felt a responsibility then to do something more explicit in terms of celebrating the anniversary of the Original Series. Early on in penning the first of the novels, I knew that I had made a number of references to TOS episodes, even going so far as to novelize and expand some scenes from the series itself. In thinking about how I could commemorate the show, the idea rose in my mind that I could attempt, through the course of the trilogy, to make a unique reference to *every* episode. Personally, I feel that continuity references can easily be overdone, and I don't usually like to make them in too obvious or too frequent a manner. But I thought that this special case merited a different perspective on my part.

And so I went back over the pages I'd already written and took notice of those references that I'd already made. The number already exceeded my expectations, and so I decided to go for it. I listed every single TOS episode—from the three seasons of the Original Series, to the two years of animated adventures, and through the seven feature films—and I began noting my exclusive references to each. In the end, I found a way to bring up every single episode, animated adventure, and film in a unique way. That is, a reference to, say, Lieutenant Kevin Riley would not be an example of such a reference because that character appeared in two episodes, "The Naked Time" and "The Conscience of the King." On the other hand, an allusion to Governor Kodos of Tarsus IV would constitute such a reference, since that character (and planet) occurred only in the latter of those two episodes.

After I finished writing the three novels, I wondered—as I always do—how they would be received by the readers. I felt that I had once again defied expectations, but perhaps even more so than usual with my unorthodox stories. Would they work? Would readers be able to accept and enjoy what I had written?

I didn't know at that point, and as I sit putting these words down, I still don't. But I like challenging myself, and I hope that readers will enjoy the challenge I've set them as well, asking them to put aside any preconceived notions they might have about this trilogy and simply going along for the ride with an open mind. The *Star Trek* characters you all know and love are here, though perhaps in different settings and situations than you might have imagined. I've tried to take Kirk and Spock and McCoy on personal journeys, and I sincerely hope that you've enjoyed taking those journeys with them—and with me. For opening the pages of these books—as well as those of my other works—I thank you. A writer is nothing without readers. My whole purpose in putting pen to paper or pixels to screen is to reach people I don't even know, to offer brief moments of enjoyment in their lives, perhaps even occasionally to enrich them or to make them think, to *connect* with them on some level. I hope I've done that, and I am grateful to all of you for allowing me that opportunity.

Until next time . . .

ACKNOWLEDGMENTS

In each of my last five novels, including the other two in the *Crucible* trilogy, I have commenced my acknowledgments by thanking my editor, Marco Palmieri. Well, nothing's changed. As a writer, I could not be more fortunate than I have been in working with Marco. He is so very good at his craft, and it is always a pleasure to have him toiling by my side. I consider him both an ally and an asset in my professional life, and a friend in my personal life. In so many ways, for so many reasons, Marco is simply the best.

I would also like to thank John Picacio, the talented artist who produced the beautiful triptych comprising the three covers for the *Crucible* books, *Provenance of Shadows, The Fire and the Rose,* and *The Star to Every Wandering*. His art speaks for itself, and if you'd like to see more, check out John's website, johnpicacio.com, or his new book, *Cover Story: The Art of John Picacio*. I had the good fortune of meeting John and spending some time with him at and after a recent convention, and he could not have been nicer or more friendly.

I would be remiss if I did not acknowledge the contributions of two men without whom this trilogy would not have been possible. During the tumultuous 1960s, Gene Roddenberry created *Star Trek,* and with it, a stage on which to tell stories of alien civilizations in the future, stories that actually addressed important societal issues on present-day Earth. On that stage, Harlan Ellison crafted his serious and poignant "The City on the Edge of Forever," an episode that, even when I watch it today, causes me to experience chills during its heartrending climax. I am privileged to be allowed to write within Mr. Roddenberry's now-vast universe, and doubly so to coax my own tales out of Mr. Ellison's masterful story. At the same time, I wish to acknowledge all of the people who have contributed to the considerable creation that is *Star Trek*— from the production assistants, to the costumers, to the camera operators, to the writers and producers and directors, to each and every behind-the-scenes or onscreen individual who added to this wonderful mythos. I salute you.

Thanks also to Alex Rosenzweig, who once more came through for me with some critical *Star Trek* research. In this case, I am particularly grateful to him because he did so on such short notice. While some might think that details of the *Trek* universe are easy to find, that's not always the case, and especially not with respect to the subtle or complex pieces of information that I often seek. For *The Star to Every Wandering,* Alex graciously saved me a great deal of time and effort when I faced an impending deadline.

On a very personal note, I want to thank Mary and Bill Dunlap for their love and support through the years. We've shared many adventures together—from taking a tour of the National Baseball Hall of Fame in Cooperstown, New York, to attending Jeanette and Rich Thomas's blowouts on their vineyard in Lodi,

California, from embarking on a manic cab ride through London, England, to experiencing a wild game on a soccer field that had been converted into a base-ball diamond on a military base in the middle of the woods in Balashikha, Russia—and I certainly hope that we have many more. Mary and Bill are among my very favorite people in the world, and I always look forward to our time together.

Thanks too to Victoria and John Ratnaswamy for their friendship. John and I have also had our fair share of escapades over the years—from meeting a ship's captain somewhere in the Caribbean Sea, to making astronaut Jim Lovell's acquaintance at his son's restau-rant in Lake Forest, Illinois, from visiting a mock-up of space station *Freedom* in Southern California, to participating in a pair of space shuttle mission simula-tions at the U.S. Space and Rocket Center in Huntsville, Alabama—and I trust that we have more to come. I adore Victoria and John, and I feel privileged to have them and their three wonderful children, Alec, Julia, and Lily, in my life.

I also wish to thank Kathy Golec for her long com-radeship. We did time in the trenches together, and I managed to make it through relatively unscathed, at least in part due to her presence there with me. Kathy is a bright, vibrant woman whom I am lucky to count as a friend.

I also want to thank the United States Submarine Veterans, and in particular the men of Tang Base. Only a small percentage of the U.S. Navy serve as sub-mariners, and they are indeed a unique breed. I am honored to be an associate member of Tang Base, and I have Walter Ragan to thank for inviting me aboard. Walter himself "rode the vents," and I love listening to his stories about that time. He is a man of honor and integrity whom I treasure.

Thanks to Anita Smith for her constant love and support. Quick to smile and laugh, always willing to lend her assistance with anything, she is a pleasure to be around. Anita is a very special woman, somebody who improves my life simply by being in it.

I want to express my appreciation to Jennifer George as well. Her love and support never waver, and she makes my life not only easier and better in so many ways, but more fun too. I think the world of Jen, and I respect and admire her more than words can say.

Thank you to Patricia Walenista too. A touchstone for me, she is a woman of great character—not to mention being something of a character as well. Energetic and fun, supportive and loving, she is one of the most important people in my life.

Finally, I want to thank the universe at large for Karen Ragan-George. As many times as I have sung Karen's praises, both in the pages of my books and in my personal life, there are simply not enough melodies, not enough refrains, to do so sufficiently. Still, I can say that since Karen and I met, everything is different. All she asks of me is that wherever she goes, I go too, and I know that she'll always stand by me, come what may. Oh, and hers are the sweetest eyes I've ever seen.

ABOUT THE AUTHOR

The three volumes of the *Crucible* trilogy—*Provenance of Shadows*, *The Fire and the Rose*, and *The Star to Every Wandering*—mark the first ventures by David R. George III into *Star Trek*'s Original Series. He has previously contributed a television story, four novels, and a novella to the *Trek* universe. He cowrote the story for the first-season *Voyager* episode "Prime Factors," which deals with the consequences of the crew having to face the noninterference directive of an alien race, and which was nominated for a *Sci-Fi Universe* Award in the category "Best Writing in a Genre Television Show or Telefilm." With Armin Shimerman, he wrote the *Deep Space Nine* novel *The 34th Rule,* a serious tale of Ferengi machinations, racism, and war between the Alliance and Bajor. He also penned two other *DSN* novels, *Twilight* and *Olympus Descending,* both set after the final episode of the series (the latter work appears in the book *Worlds of Deep Space Nine, Volume Three*). Additionally, he wrote a *Lost Era* novel, *Serpents Among the Ruins,* featuring Captain John Harriman and First Officer Demora Sulu of the *Enterprise*-B, which tells the story of the Tomed Incident. Finally, he authored the novella *Iron and Sacrifice,* another Demora Sulu yarn, this one contained in the *Tales from the Captain's Table* anthology. David's books have appeared on both the *USA Today* and *New York Times* bestseller lists.

A native of New York City, David presently makes his home in Southern California, where he lives with his delectable wife Karen. They are both aficionados of the arts—books, theater, museums, film, music, dance—and they can often be found partaking in one or another of them. They also love to travel, and are particularly fond of Paris, Venezia, Roma, Hawai'i, New York City, and the Pacific Northwest. They also enjoy sailing on cruises.

David has not yet been approved for nonprescription use by the FDA.

AVAILABLE NOW

STAR TREK®
MIRROR UNIVERSE

An unprecedented two-volume exploration
of the OTHER *Star Trek* universe.

GLASS EMPIRES

Michael Sussman with Dayton Ward &
Kevin Dilmore (*Star Trek: Enterprise®*)
David Mack (*Star Trek*)
Greg Cox (*Star Trek: The Next Generation®*)

OBSIDIAN ALLIANCES

Keith R. A. DeCandido (*Star Trek: Voyager®*)
Peter David (*Star Trek: New Frontier®*)
Sarah Shaw (*Star Trek: Deep Space Nine®*)

From Pocket Books
Also available as eBooks
www.startrekbooks.com

Turn the page for a sneak peek at
The Sorrows of Empire by David Mack

Crushing Captain Kirk's windpipe was proving far easier than Spock had ever dared to imagine.

The captain of the *I.S.S. Enterprise* struggled futilely in the merciless grip of his half-Vulcan first officer. Kirk's fists struck at Spock's torso, ribs, groin. His fingers pried at Spock's grip, clawed at the backs of the hands that were strangling him. Spock's hands only closed tighter, condemning Kirk to a swift death by suffocation.

Killing such an accomplished officer as Kirk seemed a waste to Spock. And waste, as Kirk's alternate-universe counterpart had reminded Spock only a few days earlier, was illogical. Unfortunately, as Spock now realized, it was sometimes necessary.

Kirk's strength was fading, but his eyes were still bright with cunning. He twisted, reached forward to pluck Spock's agonizer from his belt—only to find the device absent. Removing it had been a grave breach of protocol, but Spock had decided that willfully surrendering to another the means to let himself be tortured was also fundamentally illogical. He would no longer accede to the Terrans' obsessive culture of self-inflicted suffering. It was a time for change.

Marlena Moreau stood in the entryway of Kirk's sleep alcove, sharp and silent while she watched Spock throttle Kirk to death in the middle of the captain's quarters. There was no bloodlust in her gaze, a crude affectation that Spock had witnessed in many humans. Instead, she wore a dark expression, one of determination tinged with regret. Her sleepwear was delicate and diaphanous, but her countenance was hard and unyielding; she was like a steely blade in a silken sheath.

Still Kirk struggled. Again it struck Spock how great a waste this was, and the words of the other universe's Captain Kirk returned to his thoughts, the argument that had forced Spock to confront the futility of the imperial mission to which his civilization had been enthralled. The other Kirk had summed up the intrinsic flaw of the Empire with brevity and clarity.

The illogic of waste, Mr. Spock, he had said. *Of lives, potential, resources . . .* time. *I submit to you that your empire is illogical, because it cannot endure. I submit that* you *are illogical, for being a willing part of it.*

And he had been unequivocally right.

Red stains swam languidly across the eyes of this universe's Captain Kirk. Capillaries in the whites of his eyes had ruptured, hemorrhaging blood inside the eye sockets. Seconds more, and it would be over.

There had been no choice. No hope of altering this

Kirk's philosophy of command or of politics. His doppelganger had urged Spock to seize command of the *I.S.S. Enterprise,* find a logical reason to spare the resistant Halkans, and convince the Empire itself that it was the correct course.

Spock had hoped he could achieve such an aim without resorting to mutiny; he had never desired command, nor had he been interested in politics. Science, reason, research . . . these had always been Spock's core interests. They remained so now, but the circumstances had changed. Despite all of Spock's best-formulated arguments, Kirk had refused to consider mercy for the Halkans. Even when Spock had proved through logical argument that laying waste to the Halkans' cities would, in fact, only impede the Empire's efforts to mine the planet's dilithium, Kirk had not been dissuaded. And so had come Kirk's order to obliterate the planet's surface, to exterminate the Halkans and erase their civilization from the universe.

To speak out then would have been suicide, so Spock had stood mutely by while Kirk grinned and chuckled with malicious self-satisfaction, and watched a planet die.

Now it was Spock's turn to watch Kirk expire in the grip of his fingers, but Spock took no pleasure in it. He felt no sense of satisfaction, nor did he permit himself the luxuries of guilt or regret. This was simply what needed to be done.

Kirk's pulse slowed and weakened. A dull film glazed the captain's eyes, which rolled slowly back into his skull. He went limp in Spock's grasp and his clutching, clawing hands fell to his sides. Dead weight now, he sagged halfway to his knees. Not wanting to fall victim to a ruse, Spock took the precaution of inflicting a final twist on Kirk's neck, snapping it with a quick turn. Then he let the body fall heavily to the deck, where it landed with a dull thud.

Marlena inched cautiously forward, taking Spock's measure. "We should get rid of his body," she said. Stepping gingerly in bare feet, she walked over Kirk's corpse. "And his loyalists—"

"Have been dealt with," Spock interjected. "Show me the device." He did not need to elaborate; she had been beside him in the transporter room when the other universe's Kirk had divulged to him the existence of a unique weapon, one that Kirk had promised could make him "invincible." The device, which Marlena called the Tantalus field, had, apparently, been the key to the swift rise of this universe's Kirk through the ranks of the imperial Starfleet. Marlena led Spock to a nearby wall, on which was mounted a trapezoidal panel. She touched it softly at its lower right corner, then its upper right corner, and it slid soundlessly upward, revealing a small display screen flanked by a handful of buttons and dials.

"This is how you turn it on." With a single, delicate touch, Marlena activated the device. "These are the controls."

"Demonstrate it," Spock said. "On the captain's body."

He observed her actions carefully, memorizing patterns and deducing functions. With a few pushed buttons, she conjured an image of the room in which they stood. Some minor adjustments on the dials narrowed the image's focus to the body on the floor. Then she pressed a single button that was segregated from the others inside a teardrop-shaped mounting, and a blink of light filled the room behind them.

Marlena lifted her arm to shield her eyes, but Spock let his inner eyelids spare him from the flash. It was over in a fraction of a second, leaving him with a palpable tingle of electric potential and the lingering scent of ozone mingling with Marlena's delicately floral Deltan perfume. On the floor there was no trace of Kirk—no hair, no scorch marks, no blood . . . not a single bit of evidence that a murder had occurred. Satisfied, he nodded to Marlena, who shut down the device. "Most impressive," he remarked.

"Yes," she replied. "He let me use it a few times. I only know how to target one person at a time, but he told me once that it could do much more, in the right hands."

"Indubitably," Spock said. The communicator on his belt beeped twice. He lifted it from its half-pocket and flipped it open. "Spock here."

"This is Lieutenant D'Amato. The ship is secured, sir."

One detail loomed paramount in Spock's thoughts. "Have you dealt with Mister Sulu?"

"Aye, sir," D'Amato replied. *"He's been neutralized."*

"Well done, Mister D'Amato. Spock out."

Spock closed his communicator and put it back on his belt. He crossed the room to a wall-mounted comm panel, and opened an intraship PA channel. "Attention, all decks. This is Captain Spock. As of fourteen twenty-six hours, I have relieved Captain Kirk and assumed command of this vessel. Continue on course for Gamma Hydra IV. That is all. Spock out." He thumbed the channel closed and turned to face Marlena. "It would seem, for now, that circumstances favor us."

"Not entirely," she said. "Last night, Kirk filed a report with Starfleet Command about the alternate universe. He called its people anarchistic and dangerous . . . and he told Starfleet that he suspected you of helping breach the barrier between the universes."

Her news was not entirely unexpected, but it was still unfortunate. "Did the captain speculate why I might have done such a thing?"

"No," Marlena said. "But he made a point of mentioning your attempts to convince him to spare the Halkans."

He nodded once. "It would have been preferable for there to be no official record of the other universe's existence," he said. "But what has been done cannot be undone. We must proceed without concern for details beyond our control." Looking into her eyes, he knew that, for now, she was the only person on the ship—perhaps even in the universe—whom he could really trust, but even her motives were not entirely beyond suspicion . . . at least, not yet. But if the Terran Empire and its galactic neighbors were to be spared the ravages of a brutal social implosion followed by a devastating dark age unlike any in recorded history, he would have to learn to trust someone beyond himself—and teach others to do the same.

Picturing the shifting possibilities of the future, he knew that he had already committed himself, that there was no turning back from the epic task he had just set for himself.

The great work begins.